Meet Me at Sunrise

Michele Brouder

Editing by Jessica Peirce
Book Cover Design by Rebecca Ruger

Meet Me at Sunrise

Chapter One

Alice

It was hard for Alice Monroe to believe that only a few days had passed since she'd been in Hideaway Bay for Gram's funeral. Memories of the service were still fresh and raw, and her late grandmother, Junie Reynolds, was never far from her mind, but images of the time spent with her sisters—sitting on the front porch with a glass of wine or collecting beach glass as they walked along the shore early in the morning—were already beginning to fade.

But now, back in Chicago, it was time to get back to work and forget about her hometown. When she walked into the office at seven in the morning, it felt as if she'd never left. The familiar coil of tension in her neck and shoulders reappeared as soon as she stepped off the elevators and onto the twenty-eighth floor of the law offices of Jones, Steadman, and Billings, where'd she'd been an associate for the last six years, since she passed the bar exam.

With her briefcase in one hand and her cardigan over her other arm in case the air conditioning was running at full blast, she walked along the hallway that led toward the law firm offices, her stilettos clicking on the marble floor. To an outsider, Alice Monroe would appear polished and put together. Her wild curly hair had been straightened that morning to within an inch of its life and now appeared sleek and shiny. She sported one of her many expensive tailored suits and her favorite accessory: a pair of red-soled Christian Louboutin shoes. The suit was in deference to her position. The shoes indulged her passion for footwear and were a nod to her femininity.

The lights were dimmed in the reception area, and the front desk was empty as the receptionist didn't start until nine. Like most associates, Alice arrived early to get a head start on the day. And there'd be a lot of catching up. She'd been gone for three weeks, and she dreaded the workload that awaited her. Her normally twelve-to-fourteen-hour workdays were guaranteed now to be along the lines of fourteen to sixteen hours until she cleared her backlog.

She unlocked her office door, flipped on the lights, and hung her coat on the back of the door. She set down her briefcase, and she pulled out her chair and sat, kicking off her shoes beneath her desk as she picked up her desk phone to listen to her voicemails. When the automated voice reported *You have sixty-eight new messages*, her heart sank. While she was in Hideaway Bay, she'd checked her voicemails occasionally but clearly not enough. She had wanted to totally step away from work and deal with Gram's death. Couldn't she just have that? When she'd approached the human resources manager about taking bereavement days and found out she was only allotted three, Alice was appalled. She'd ignored the disapproving look on the woman's face when she informed her that in addition to her bereavement days, she'd take her three weeks' vacation. She hadn't taken time off in years, and she wanted time to process Gram's death. Surely, they wouldn't begrudge her that.

She had only listened to two messages when one of the senior partners, Dan Billings, popped his head in the doorway. One of the founding members of the firm, he still put in sixty hours a week despite being in his seventies. Known to be a stickler for details and rules, he didn't suffer fools.

"Welcome back, Alice," he said. The senior partner had a long, narrow face that suited his tall, lean frame.

His eyes were gray and maybe a little too close to his patrician nose. His cologne was spicy but subtle.

"Thank you, Mr. Billings," she said, reaching with her feet beneath her desk for her shoes. She managed to slip one on. The other remained out of reach.

"Did you get the firm's flowers?" he asked, referring to the large floral arrangement that had been sent on behalf of the firm for Gram's wake.

Alice nodded. "I did, thank you. They were lovely, and my sisters and I really appreciate it."

He nodded. "Can you give the partners an update on your caseload at nine?"

It was a rhetorical question, not requiring a yes-or-no answer. It was also a demand to be accountable to the partners later that morning.

"Of course," she said. She should have anticipated that. The partners had their eyes on her as she was being considered for junior partner.

He gave her a tight smile, tapped on the doorframe, and disappeared.

Once he was out of her sightline and out of earshot, she leaned back and sighed. Two hours to see how far her associates had gotten with her caseload. Hopefully, she wasn't too far behind. She'd be buying their lunches for a while as a thank-you.

The previous year, she'd been passed over for one of the junior partner positions and it had been a huge disappointment. She'd worked her bum off for this firm but instead, the position had been given to Anthony Meskowitz, an associate who'd started a year after she did. That had been a bitter blow. But Anthony was a go-getter and had had a year where he'd been on fire. Begrudgingly, she respected that and knew it was the right choice.

She knew she should listen to the rest of those voicemails. She should also reach out to the associates who'd handled her workload and have them bring her up to speed, but she couldn't seem to get motivated. Mr. Billings would no doubt use the meeting as an opportunity to chastise her in front of the other partners for taking so much time off when they were busy. But the firm was always busy, and Mr. Billings wasn't the type of person to prioritize family commitments. Twice divorced, he was on his third wife, who was the same age as Alice.

Instead of getting down to work, Alice spun her chair around to stare out the window. Just five minutes, she told herself. She didn't see the skyscrapers of downtown Chicago or even the lake beyond them. Her thoughts had drifted to her hometown, Hideaway Bay, on the shores of Lake Erie in New York State. So much of her family was gone: her mother, Gram, Granddad. Alice felt as if she'd been unmoored from the anchors in her life and set adrift. There was no one left now except Alice and her two older sisters, Isabelle and Lily. The reunion with her siblings had not been as bad as she'd anticipated, their united grief tempering any longstanding bitterness. Overall, they had some nice sisterly moments. Granted, there were moments of spikiness too, but nothing that had furthered their estrangement.

After Gram's death, the three of them learned that they had inherited her house on Star Shine Drive, and all Alice could think about was turning the place into an inn or a bed-and-breakfast. The house was perfect: an old Victorian with an unobstructed view of Lake Erie across the street. But Isabelle had left town immediately after Gram's funeral, and Lily hadn't seemed keen on the idea. Alice had never worked in the hospitality sector, but how hard could it be? Images of pulling trays of homemade blueberry muffins out of the oven, the sound of the surf outside the window and colorful beach towels drying across the porch railing, filled her mind. She wished she could convince her sisters of the possibilities the idea presented.

Lily, the middle sister, might be the more amenable of the two. But being recently widowed and having just lost Gram, she was in a fragile state and couldn't be expected to make any big decisions right away. People needed time and space to grieve and heal. Isabelle would be difficult to convince. Her oldest sister was unlike any other she'd ever encountered. The friends she had growing up in Hideaway Bay had older sisters who fit the stereotype: bossy, organized, take-charge. Even Alice's assistant here at the firm, Donna, had an older sister who'd stepped in when their mother died and made sure everyone got together on a regular basis. Isabelle was none of those things. She was a free spirit loaded with wanderlust. There'd be no way she'd want to tie herself down to Hideaway Bay. She went wherever the wind blew her.

Alice couldn't explain why the three of them had drifted apart. She thought of Gram's lifelong connection with her childhood friends Thelma and Barb. Through ups and downs, no matter what life had thrown them, they'd always stuck together and looked out for one another. Alice wished she had that kind of relationship with her sisters. But there was such an age difference between them—Isabelle was older by eight years and Lily by six—that by the time they'd left home, she was barely coming into her teenage years.

She'd been disappointed when Isabelle took off as soon as the funeral was over, but at least they got to spend some time together and had parted on good terms. It warmed her heart to know that Lily had chosen to remain in Hideaway Bay for the time being.

Gram's will had stated that the house was not to be sold until twelve months had passed, and maybe it was nostalgia or sentiment, but Alice already knew she did not want to let the place go. It represented the last link to her mother and her grandparents and her hometown. Once that house was sold, all ties to Hideaway Bay would be completely severed, and the already fragile ties binding her to her sisters would be weakened further.

Clearly, her five minutes and then some were up, and Alice swiveled her chair around and faced her desk and all the obligations. With a sigh, she pulled her chair closer to the desk and got to work.

Two weeks later, Alice sat in a bar in downtown Chicago, waiting for her blind date to arrive. It was an old pub that had recently been renovated. Reclaimed brick walls, wide-planked hardwood floors, copper lighting, and plants had turned a dive into a trendy spot.

Alice had met her blind date on an online dating app. It was her second time giving it a try. The first date had been a non-starter. It was dead in the water when he kept referring to himself in the third person. And he'd seemed so promising, an investment banker who worked in downtown Chicago. She had fantasies of meeting him for lunch, going for happy hour, and spending the weekends going antique shopping and to museums and football games. But it hadn't worked out.

With her work schedule, it was hard to meet people. And there was no way she was going to date anyone at work. That would only open up a can of worms. She twisted her watch on her wrist and glanced at it. She'd arrived fifteen minutes early. His photo on the app had been very appealing, with his sunny good looks and blond hair.

Her eyes were on the door, and she didn't have to wait long for him to appear. Jonathon was tall and looked trendy in his jeans and T-shirt. So far so good, she thought.

When he approached the table, he broke into a wide smile and asked, "Alice?"

She nodded, straightening her posture.

As he sat, he said, "You're even prettier in person than in your photo."

She blushed and thanked him.

Dinner flew. They'd ordered appetizers, mains, desserts, and a bottle of wine. When she pushed back her dessert plate, she thought the whole thing was promising. He was a great conversationalist and had a lot of hobbies. His job sounded normal: he went home at five and didn't have to put in any overtime at the electrical engineering company where he worked. She thought he was lucky.

As he paid the bill, he looked up and asked, "Shall we see each other again?"

Alice didn't want to appear too eager, but she smiled and said, "I'd like that."

"What about Saturday night?" he asked. "I can get us tickets to the Cubs game."

"I love baseball!"

"Great, I'll call you," he said.

"Perfect," she said.

And it was.

They parted at their cars, and he gave her a chaste kiss on the cheek. He watched her drive away with a wave.

It was going to be a long week until Saturday, she thought. The next morning, she looked up the game time, and was pleased to see it was an afternoon game. Perfect for a second date. If they went out to eat afterward, she'd buy. It was only fair.

Alice didn't panic when she didn't hear anything from him right away. After all, they'd only gone out on Monday; she didn't really expect him to call her the next day. It would have been nice, but not necessary. When she still hadn't heard from him by Thursday, she debated on whether she should call him or not. Would it make her look desperate? He had asked her to the game, hadn't he? Or had she imagined it?

After five, when the support staff had left and the lights in the hallways had dimmed, Alice pulled out her cell phone and dialed the number Jonathon had given her. She leaned back in her chair, thinking about what she would say.

It rang twice and an automated voice came on, announcing that the number was no longer in service.

Alice redialed, assuming she'd made a mistake, but was greeted with the same message.

Oh.

Determined not to take the rejection personally, Alice shoved any thoughts of Jonathon out of her mind, reminding herself that it had only been one date. Nothing invested.

Turning her attention to her desktop, she buried herself in work. Grateful for the distraction, she soon became lost in going over contracts for their client's merger.

Chapter Two

1955

Thelma

Thelma Kempf sat on the sofa next to two of her brothers, Frank and Del. The younger ones, Mikey and Johnny, had been put to bed earlier by Aunt Linda. The house was full of people, but their voices were hushed.

Dressed in her Sunday best, she sat squished in the corner of the sofa with Del leaning on her. Yesterday had been her twelfth birthday. Usually, her mother made her a chocolate cake using Hershey's cocoa powder, and there would have been a small gift, often an item of clothing, which beat the hand-me-downs from her cousins that made up most of her wardrobe. But then her mother would slip her some coins and tell her to walk up to the corner store, the Chesterfield Deli, and get herself some penny candy. But Mama was upstairs in her bedroom; she couldn't get out of bed anymore. Her birthday forgotten, Thelma sat there, her arms folded across her chest, tugging at the scab on her bottom lip until it bled.

The lights were dim in the house. They lived in a single-family home on Lockwood Avenue on the south side of Buffalo. The Christmas tree stood in the front living room window, its lights on. She stared at it, thinking how weeks earlier her mother had been in a hurry to decorate it, how she kept pushing her hair off her forehead and muttering, "We have to get the tree up for the children." She'd said that over and over again. At the time, Thelma didn't know what she was going on about, so she'd ignored her.

Deep voices floated out from the kitchen. From where she sat, she had a straight view of her father sitting at the kitchen table. He scratched at the damp label of the beer bottle in front of him. He wasn't alone. Uncle Johnny, her mother's favorite brother, sat with him, along with the next-door neighbor, Mr. Pike. They'd been there since early morning. Occasionally, her father would stand and quietly go up the staircase to the bedroom he shared with her mother. Thelma watched him as he went up and then came back down. It was as if his body weighed a ton, for all the difficulty he had getting it up the stairs.

Mrs. Pike from next door had brought over a black enamel roasting pan of pork chops and scalloped potatoes and a bowl of applesauce, and Aunt Linda had sat Thelma and her brothers around the dining room table so as not to disturb the men sitting in the kitchen drinking their beer.

Thelma had been hungry, and the food was good. Aunt Linda let her have two slices of bread with butter spread all over it. Mrs. Pike's applesauce had been heated, and Thelma had never had it that way; her mother always served it cold, straight out of the refrigerator. She felt guilty for preferring the way Mrs. Pike served it.

Mrs. Richards, who was the mother of Thelma's best friend, Junie, came down from upstairs. She was Mama's best friend. She dabbed her eyes with a handkerchief and stuffed it into the pocket of her shirtdress. Just as her foot landed on the bottom step, the doorbell rang. Thelma didn't know why, but she thought of her friend Barb Walsh's doorbell. Barb was the daughter of a doctor, and their doorbell chimed gently. The doorbell in Thelma's house buzzed, obnoxious and angry.

Mrs. Richards answered the door, and Thelma couldn't see who it was.

"Father Harmon, come in," said Mrs. Richards in a near-whisper.

Aunt Linda joined them and said, "Let me get Teddy and Johnny."

Father Harmon said something, but Thelma couldn't hear. That was followed by Mrs. Richards muttering, "No, it won't be long now," her voice cracking on the last word.

Father Harmon marched up the staircase without a glance in the direction of the parlor. His back was ramrod straight, and his black cassock moved fluidly with him. In his hands was a small wooden box. He disappeared from sight at the top of the staircase, and then there was the sound of a door opening and closing upstairs.

Thelma's father appeared, his red hair going in all directions. Thelma and her four brothers had inherited their father's hopeless red hair. Their mother used to say there was nothing that could be done about it. He stood at the bottom of the stairs, looking up toward the top as if it was a mountain he couldn't climb. Uncle Johnny nudged him and said, "Come on, Teddy, the priest is waiting for us."

Her father nodded but the gesture seemed to fatigue him, and he closed his eyes for a moment. He walked slowly up the stairs, pausing halfway to grab hold of the banister and sighing like a man condemned to his fate.

Frank elbowed Thelma. "Why is Father Harmon here?"

Thelma shrugged. "How would I know? I'm not a fortune-teller." Irritated, she swung her legs. She wanted all these people out of her house. She wanted her mother to come downstairs and tell them they needed to get ready for bed. But no one came.

Half an hour later, the priest made his way down the stairs, the little wooden box still in his hands. Aunt Linda followed him, her rosary hanging from her hands.

"Thank you, Father Harmon, for coming out so late at night," she said as she ushered him to the door. She removed his coat and hat from the coat stand and held them for him to put on.

Father Harmon said something to Aunt Linda, and she nodded her head in return and said, "I will."

Thelma wished the priest would speak up. She wondered why he didn't use that voice he used during his homilies at Sunday morning Mass. The front door closed behind him and from Thelma's position on the sofa, she turned to look out the window. She could barely see past the Christmas tree in the front window as the priest made his way along the sidewalk and back toward the rectory, which was only two blocks over.

Aunt Linda stepped into the parlor, hands on her hips, and said, "Come on, you three, time for bed."

Thelma waited until Frank and Del were on their way upstairs, fiddling with the hem of her dress as she lingered.

"Come on, Thelma, upstairs. You've got school in the morning."

Thelma looked down at the floor. It was covered in an old rug, an ambitious floral pattern in black, purple, and white. It was threadbare in many spots. "Can I say goodnight to Mama?"

Aunt Linda hesitated. "Not tonight, dear, she's resting."

Thelma had a bad feeling. It was something inside her stomach that felt queasy, like she might throw up. "Just for a minute. I'll be quiet."

Aunt Linda shook her head. "No, Thelma, be a good girl and go to bed."

"Please," Thelma asked.

Aunt Linda put her hand on Thelma's shoulder and attempted a reassuring smile, but it wavered. "You can see her tomorrow. Now go on up like I've told you."

Thelma made her way up the stairs but hung back a bit to see what Aunt Linda would do. When she heard the water running in the sink and the clatter of dishes being put into the dishpan, she ran up the stairs and headed down the hallway to her parents' bedroom.

Quietly, so as not to disturb her mother, she turned the doorknob and opened the door a few inches. In that small, narrow strip of an opening, she spotted her mother in the bed, sleeping. Or she looked like she was sleeping. She was on her back with her arms outside of the blanket, extended at her sides. Her hair had been brushed back, and her face leaned toward the wall. On the bedside table stood a small porcelain lamp whose amber glow barely spread past the edges of the table. On the dresser were two lit candles. Her father sat in a chair at the side of the bed, hanging his head in his hands. Thelma couldn't see his face, but his shoulders shook.

She pushed the door open further but Mrs. Richards appeared, blocking the view of her mother. Her face softened at the sight of Thelma.

"Go on, Thelma, go to bed," Mrs. Richards said softly.

"I want to say goodnight to Mama," Thelma protested, leaning over to try and see around Mrs. Richards.

Mrs. Richards stepped out of the room and closed the door behind her. "Your mother can't be disturbed, and those are the doctor's orders."

"I only want to say goodnight," Thelma tried again.

Mrs. Richards shook her head. "Not tonight, Thelma. Go on, be a good girl. It's getting late and you have school in the morning."

Not caring, Thelma stomped off to her bedroom at the other end of the hallway at the front of the house. She slipped into her room, mindful of her youngest brother, who slept in a small trundle bed by the closet door.

In the dark, Thelma tugged off her clothes, not caring if she ripped anything. Reaching beneath her pillow, she pulled out her flannel nightgown and pulled it over her head, slipping her arms through the sleeves and tugging it down and straightening it out.

Barefoot, she walked over to the front window, moved aside the lace curtain, and pressed her hand against the cold pane of glass. Snow fell gently, adding to the blanket of white that already covered everything. Snow piled up in the nooks where the branches met the trunk of the tree. Under the streetlights, it glittered like shards of broken glass. Along the street were lined familiar cars: theirs—an old clunker as her father called it—and Mrs. Richards's, and the Pikes' car was parked in front of their house next door. Aunt Linda and Uncle Johnny's car was parked across the street in front of old Mr. Tamarack's house. Thelma was surprised that the old man hadn't come storming over, banging on the door and asking the offending party to remove it. Mr. Tamarack didn't have a car of his own, but he wanted the spot free and clear in front of his house.

The floorboards were cold, and Thelma hopped back over to her bed, flipping her quilt back and jumping in. She hated the way her nightgown twisted around her body, and she tugged it down. As she rolled over to her left side, she pulled the quilt up around her shoulders. Her mother always teased her about how she kept a leg outside the covers, even on the coldest, darkest night of the winter. Sticking out and looking like a boat oar, she'd say with a laugh, adding that she was half tempted to try and row with it before sticking it back beneath the blankets. Thelma wondered if her mother would ever put her feet back beneath the covers in the middle of the night again and somehow doubted it. Then she scolded herself for such thoughts, thinking she'd jinx her mother. She stared out the front window of her bedroom for a long time, mesmerized by the falling snow. Finally, she decided that she didn't care what the adults said; come morning, she was going in to see her mother. Feeling better that a decision had been made, Thelma drifted off to sleep.

The morning dawned bright but cold, and Thelma wondered what time it was as she had to get ready for school. Her brother was still sound asleep in his bed. It had stopped snowing, and Thelma looked up and down the street. The same cars were there that had been there the previous night, except Mrs. Richards's. She must have gone home. Of course, she had to, she had to get Junie up for school.

Shivering, Thelma sat on the edge of her bed and pulled on yesterday's socks because her feet were cold. Slowly, she opened her door and saw no one. She stepped out of her room and took a few tiptoe steps until she reached the top of the staircase, and she leaned over the banister and listened. She could hear voices in the kitchen, but she couldn't hear what was being said because they were hushed. She wanted to see her mother.

She was ready. She was going to go into that room and push any adult out of the way who refused to let her see her mother. No one was going to stop her. She was twelve now.

But she pulled up short. The door to her parents' bedroom was wide open. The bed was made, the salmon-colored chenille bedspread spread smooth, and the curtains pulled open to let in the bright winter light. But there was no sign of her mother.

Relief swept through Thelma. Her mother was all right. She was most likely downstairs getting their breakfast ready before they went to school. She flew down the stairs and Del ran past her, shouting, "We don't have to go to school today!"

Thelma came to a halt in the kitchen.

Aunt Linda stood at the stove, wearing her mother's apron and stirring a pot of oatmeal. Uncle Johnny leaned against the kitchen sink, smoking a cigarette, the ash dangling precariously. He seemed not to notice it. His eyes were watery, and his nose was swollen and red. Thelma's father sat at the kitchen table, looking dazed, a piece of uneaten toast and a full cup of tea in front of him. All three looked up when she entered the room.

"Where's Mama?"

Chapter Three

Alice

Alice was not to be deterred in the world of online dating. It was in her life plan to get married and have children, and she didn't want to wait until she was forty to start looking. Brushing off the setback with Jonathon, she soldiered on and met up with a man named Leon Feltz. She was excited about this prospect. They'd been on two dates so far and things had gone well. Exceptionally well, Alice thought.

Her phone beeped, interrupting her as she worked at her desk and she picked it up. Immediately, a smile spread across her face when she saw Leon's name on her screen.

Can you meet up for a drink later?

A smile formed on her lips. He mentioned some bar she was familiar with. It was within walking distance of her office. A frown contorted her features. She couldn't meet up with him. There wasn't a hope. There was the contract signing. She'd even be coming in early in the morning. Disappointment filled her.

I'd love to but I can't. Working.

No problem. Dinner tomorrow night?

Alice's shoulders slumped as she sat in her chair, and a huge sigh of frustration escaped her lips.

Ugh. Can't. Working late tomorrow night. Looking forward to Sunday. Not working then, lol.

After she had to turn down the second date, she wondered if she'd ever hear from him again. But Leon was not to be denied and he texted her Friday afternoon.

Any chance you could meet me for happy hour after work?

Alice had no business leaving work early to go on a date. But damn, she was going to have a personal life. That much she had decided in the weeks since she'd returned from Hideaway Bay. She wanted marriage, kids, a career. She wanted it all. Did that make her selfish? She didn't think so.

Finally, Alice sent a reply. *Six at McMurphy's?*

Perfect

They'd agreed to meet at six at a little Irish pub around the corner from where she worked. Alice decided she had two options regarding the pile of work on her desk. Either option didn't thrill her, but her choices were limited. Her personal life was trying to elbow its way into her work life. And her work life didn't seem to be budging. She pictured Mr. Billings using a magnifying glass to go over her work on the contracts and her billable hours.

As she closed her office door behind her, she said to her assistant, "I'm going on a quick date."

Donna said with a grin, "A quick date? How does that work?"

Alice sighed. "You know what I mean."

"You need to have a personal life," her assistant said, arching an eyebrow.

"I know, I know, but there are only so many hours in the week," Alice replied.

Donna nodded and looked around the place, which was emptying out as ancillary staff left for the day. Donna needed extra hours as she was saving for a down payment on a house, and Alice was only too happy to give them to her.

"What do I say if anyone asks for you?"

"Tell them I had to run an errand," Alice said, lifting her purse over her shoulder.

"Will you be back tonight?"

"I might," she said. "Or I'll have to come in early in the morning."

"All right. Have fun." Donna waved and smiled.

"That's the plan," Alice said hopefully. She glanced at the clock. "I better get going, I don't want to be late."

On her way out, she stopped by the restroom to freshen up her makeup and to take down her hair. Leon didn't need to see austere Alice.

It always surprised her when she stepped outside into the blazing heat. Acclimated to air conditioning all day long, the humidity made the air feel thick, like she was wrapped in a wet wool blanket.

The sidewalks were thronged with people leaving work. She picked up her pace, which was no small feat in her high heels. Because she'd had to decline the previous two engagements, she was picking up the tab for tonight, she told herself. She liked this guy and he had lots of potential.

McMurphy's was packed with the after-work crowd. Alice adjusted her eyes from the brightness outside to the dim interior of the bar. She scanned the sea of faces, looking for the familiar countenance of Leon. At the back of the bar, she spotted an arm go up and wave toward her. With a nod of acknowledgment, she made her way toward Leon.

"You made it!" he enthused. He slid an arm around her waist, pulled her close, and kissed her on the cheek. He smelled nice.

Alice smiled. "It's good to see you."

"I was hoping you wouldn't cancel," he said.

Alice grimaced, trying not to feel guilty. "I'm here now, so let's enjoy ourselves."

"What are you drinking?" he asked, raising his hand to get the bartender's attention.

"A Chardonnay," she said, deciding immediately that she wasn't going back to work later.

Leon leaned over the bar and ordered wine for Alice and a bottle of beer for himself. Alice laid a couple of twenties on the bar. Leon went to protest but Alice put her hand up.

"No, this night is on me," she said. "Consider it an apology for turning down your first two suggestions."

Leon smiled, flashing white teeth. "Apology accepted. Thank you."

As the bar was noisy, Leon edged closer to her and a warmth spread through her. He touched her elbow with two fingers, leaned in, and spoke close to her ear. His breath was warm on her neck, and the vibration of his voice caused all sorts of little fires to be set off inside her.

After an hour, Alice made her way to the ladies' room. She walked as if she were on a cloud. Leon was perfect. So funny. They'd gotten into a spirited debate about whether the Chicago Bears would ever win another Superbowl. She dug through her purse for her lipstick, thinking she might make going out for the evening a frequent event. Out of habit, she checked her phone, and her heart sank when she spotted two missed calls from Donna. Her gut twisted. Could she not just have a couple of hours without interruption? But her assistant knew her well enough not to bother her with anything trivial.

Reluctantly, she dialed Donna, who picked up on the first ring. "Alice, I'm sorry to bother you—"

"What's going on?" Alice asked, cutting her off, anxious to deal with whatever problem Donna was going to throw in her lap so she could get back to the bar and more importantly, to Leon.

"It's Mr. Billings. He wants to see you."

"Now?" Alice asked. She looked up to the ceiling and groaned.

"He stopped by right after you left and said to tell you to come to his office," Donna said.

Alice rolled her eyes. This was the kind of luck she had. She couldn't remember the last time one of the partners had summoned her to their office after six o'clock. It felt as if the whole world were conspiring against her.

"What did you tell him?"

"I told him you had an errand," Donna said.

Alice chewed her lip, thinking, but her assistant continued to speak.

"When he came back a second time wondering when you'd be back, I lied and told him that you had female problems and were at a doctor's appointment."

Alice cringed. She hated using the female problem card but, in this instance, it had bought her time.

"If he comes back, let him know I'm on my way," Alice said, and she hung up. She pulled her brush out of her purse and pulled her hair back into the sleek updo she always wore at work, muttering angrily to herself. God forbid she should try to enjoy herself.

With dread, she made her way back to the bar and back to Leon, noting he'd just ordered another round for them. When he took in her hairstyle change, his eyes widened, and confusion clouded his face. He handed her a glass of wine, which she set down on the bar. She was tempted to take a sip, but Mr. Billings would frown if he smelled alcohol on her breath. Luckily, she'd only had two glasses, and the walk back would freshen her clothes up a bit.

"Leon, I hate to do this, but I've been called back into work," she said.

There was a flicker of a shadow across his face as if he didn't believe her, as if she were bailing on the date when nothing could be further from the truth.

But his faltering expression recovered, and he asked, "Now?"

She nodded, slinging her purse over her shoulder. "My assistant has been trying to get a hold of me. Apparently one of the partners wants to see me."

"Now?" he repeated, taking a gulp of his beer.

Alice was half tempted to knock back the entire glass of wine in front of her.

"Can't it wait until morning?"

She shook her head and scoffed. "At my office? No. When the powers that be summon you, you go." She realized how sad this sounded as she said it, but there was nothing she could do about it.

Echoing her thoughts, Leon said, "That doesn't sound right."

"I know it doesn't, but it is what it is."

"Well, it was good to see you, Alice," he said. He leaned forward and brushed a kiss on her cheek.

Emboldened, Alice turned her head until her lips were against his. She slid her hand around his neck and pulled him closer so she could kiss him properly. His lips were warm and yielding, and the look of surprise in his eyes gave her some satisfaction. Before she pulled away, she smiled against his lips and whispered, "I'm not blowing you off, I really do have to go back to work."

He nodded and traced his finger along her lip. "When will I see you again?"

"Sunday for sure," she said with a laugh.

"I'll look forward to it. Is it okay if I text you?"

"Yes, definitely!" she said with enthusiasm, and she leaned in and kissed him again.

She smiled as she made her way back to work. This one felt right. This one felt good. For the first time in a long time, she felt excited about something.

Mr. Billings was behind his desk in one of the partner offices on the top floor. The floor-to-ceiling windows offered a commanding view of downtown Chicago with glimpses of the lake beyond that.

"There you are. I thought you'd deserted us," Mr. Billings said with a laugh. It was meant to sound like a joke, but Alice knew he wanted to get his point across.

"No, I had an appointment," she said with a tight smile. She was not going to elaborate.

"Have a seat, Alice," he said with an expansive wave of his hand.

As she settled herself into her chair, he leaned forward and said, "You've done some great work here at the firm, Alice."

"Thank you, Mr. Billings," she said, smoothing out her skirt.

"It has not gone unnoticed by George, Allan, and me that you've kicked yourself into high gear since your return," he said, referring to the two other partners.

Alice nodded, unsure if she was supposed to comment. She figured this was his preamble before he got to what he really wanted.

"We've got an interesting case before us," he said. He looked at the paperwork in front of him. But Alice knew

Mr. Billings well; even before summoning her to his office, he'd have known this case inside and out and how they were going to play it.

She gave a slight nod, indicating to him that he could go on. She wondered why this couldn't have waited until the morning. Why did it have to be tonight? She pushed down her annoyance and opted for a neutral but interested expression.

"You might have heard of Dennis Ballantine?" he asked. His gaze remained fixed on her expression while he twiddled his fountain pen between his long, bony fingers.

You would have had to be living in a cave not to have heard about Dennis Ballantine. Seventy-ish, he was one of Chicago's movers and shakers. He'd bought his first piece of property when he was twenty-five and had continued from there, building up an impressive real estate portfolio. His latest venture had been a string of trendy nightclubs.

"Although I've never met him, I know of him," she said.

He nodded, satisfied. Probably figured as much.

"He's a good friend of mine. We go way back. Graduated from Harvard together, and then he went on for his master's in business and I went to law school. We've been good friends for a long time. I was his best man, and he was mine at my first and second weddings."

Mr. Billings had had a quiet ceremony when he'd married his third wife, obviously no wedding party then. Alice knew that Dennis Ballantine was still married to his first wife and had five children. They were always in the paper.

"Anyway, he's in a bit of a bind," Mr. Billings said slowly, looking off to the side as if considering how he was going to say what needed to be said.

Alice thought this might be interesting. What business law might Mr. Ballantine have broken to need to hire their law firm? Was he being sued by someone? There was that incident years ago when a chef at one of his restaurants had set the kitchen on fire and got caught in it, resulting in some serious third-degree burns. She wondered if he'd finally been served a lawsuit over this. As much as she disliked the thought of defending a claimant against an injured person, she'd do her best.

"What kind of a bind is he in, exactly?" Alice asked.

"He's been accused of sexual harassment by a couple of his employees," Mr. Billings said. He watched her reaction.

Although this was not what she had expected, she kept her expression impassive.

"How many employees are we talking about?" she asked. One employee and it was her word against his. More than two and there might be an established pattern.

"Three, to be exact," he said.

Alice was puzzled. "Mr. Billings, this is not my area of expertise, as you know. I'm corporate law. Wouldn't Mel Bronson be more suited for this?"

"Oh, Mel will be the lead, but I want you on the team," he said.

She hesitated. Based on her own experience, she'd bet that every woman had been harassed at least once in their lives. It had nothing to do with looks or sex but with power. And the fact that three employees had come forward indicated that there might be an actual problem. Although Alice loved a challenge, she'd prefer not to take this case. She wondered if she had any choice.

"It would look good on your resume here," Mr. Billings said, "especially when we're deciding on junior partners at the end of the year. There'd be a lot of billable hours with this one, and it would be a high-profile case."

There it was. In order to get that coveted position, she had to jump through a few flaming hoops. Even if it was a case she had no interest in. What if the man was guilty? Didn't she owe an allegiance to the universal sisterhood?

"Again, I don't know what I can bring to this case that would serve it," she said.

"Oh, come on, Alice, don't be modest about your skills. You're sharp, and we need you on board for this particular case."

It was the way he said "particular" that left Alice wondering if she was simply being asked to be a window dressing. In other words, how could Dennis Ballantine possibly be guilty of these crimes when he had a young female attorney on his team. It left a bitter taste in her mouth.

"Do you play tennis, Alice?" Mr. Billings asked.

"Poorly," she responded, which was the truth. Isabelle had been the athletic one in their family, and that gene had totally bypassed Alice. She wondered what this had to do with anything.

"That's all right, I'm an excellent player," he said.

She frowned, not sure what he was getting at.

"Sunday, we'll meet at eleven at the country club for doubles tennis with Dennis and his wife. Audrey. Then afterward, we'll have lunch at the club."

Alice paled. "This Sunday?" She'd told Leon she'd spend the day with him.

"Yes, that's all right, isn't it? You don't have plans, do you?" The tone of his question indicated that she shouldn't have plans. And if she did, she should cancel them.

"No, I'll be there at eleven."

"Great. Now in the meantime, get up to speed with Mel over the particulars of the case," he instructed. He picked up his phone, indicating the meeting was over.

Alice stood and headed toward the door.

"And Alice, I'm expecting your best work on this case," he said with a wink.

Walking out of his office, Alice wondered if Mr. Billings winked at the male staff of the office. Somehow, she didn't think so.

Chapter Four

January 1956

Thelma

Christmas holidays were over, and it was time for Thelma and her brothers to go back to school. It had been an odd few weeks. Thelma felt as if she were in a dream, a bad one, and she kept praying she'd wake up. Her father didn't say much, rarely mentioned the fact that their mother had died, as if not mentioning it meant it wasn't real. He spent most of his time after work sitting at the kitchen table and drinking beer. Despite five children living there, the house was quiet, unusually so. There was no fighting between Frank and Del, and Mikey had stopped sliding down the banisters. Christmas Day had also been different. There was an unusually high number of presents from relatives, and they'd gone to Uncle Johnny and Aunt Linda's for turkey and ham, where no one seemed to know what to say as they sat at the table. Thelma was relieved when her father and Uncle Johnny began to speculate about what the upcoming season would look like for the Brooklyn Dodgers. They clung to the high the team's recent World Series win had produced. There was nothing Thelma loved more than baseball.

She was due to meet Junie and Barb up at the corner to walk the three blocks to school together, but when she dragged herself downstairs, she found Mikey and Johnny sitting at the table, still in their pajamas.

Her eyes widened. "What are you doing? Mikey, you have to go to school. Johnny, you have to go to Mrs. Van Houten's. Why aren't the two of you dressed?"

"Where's Mama?" Johnny asked like he did every morning. It was hopeless to try and explain that Mama was never coming back. At three, he was too young to understand.

She ignored his question, thinking that she couldn't bear to have to answer it again. It occurred to her that she'd have to get their breakfast. How could she expect them to do it?

"It's going to be cornflakes this morning, boys," she said as she dashed around the kitchen and pulled bowls from the cabinet and spoons from the drawers. Cereal spilled out of their bowls as she hurriedly poured it. Milk splashed over the sides. She grabbed the sugar bowl and dusted the top of their cereal with a spoonful each, then she slid the bowls toward them. Both boys picked up their spoons and dug in, hungry.

As she headed back to the front of the house, she glanced at the clock. She couldn't expect her friends to wait for her. Sister Bernadette would give them holy hell.

Thelma stood at the foot of the stairs and shouted, "Frank! Del! Come on, you're going to be late."

"All right, Thelma," Del called back. There was no response from Frank, and Thelma didn't know whether he was still sleeping or had already left. She charged up the stairs and opened the door to their bedroom.

Del was putting on his coat, and Frank was dressed but sat on the edge of his bed, staring out the window.

"I told you about barging in here and not knocking," Frank said without turning around.

"Well, then answer me when I call your name," she barked. She wasn't in the mood to get into a fight with Frank. Besides, there wasn't any time.

"Come on, get a move on or you'll be late," she said.

"You're not my mother," he spat.

An ache pierced Thelma's heart as she thought *I'm not trying to be,* but she recovered and said, "And I'm not

Sister Bernadette either!" She banged her hand against the doorframe. "Come on, let's go."

Before Frank could give any backtalk, Thelma grabbed Mikey's uniform and flew down the stairs with Del following her.

"Don't forget your lunch, Del," she said. Their dad had lined up their brown paper bags with their lunches inside on the hallway table.

Del grabbed his and headed out the front door. "Bye, Thelma."

"Bye, Del!"

Del left the front door open, and Thelma spotted Junie and Barb walking up the driveway. There was still a lot of snow outside and they were all bundled up in wool coats, mittens, scarves, and knitted hats.

Thelma let them in, a blast of cold air hitting her in the face.

"We waited at the corner for you," Barb said.

"I know, I know, I'm trying to get my brothers out of the house," Thelma said. She didn't wait for their response as she headed back to the kitchen to see how Johnny and Mikey were getting on. "Go on without me, I'm not going to be on time."

"Maybe we can help you with something," Junie said, slipping out of her boots and pulling off her mittens.

"You don't have to," Thelma said, but three pairs of hands were certainly better than one.

Johnny and Mikey were just about finished, and Thelma took their bowls from them and piled them in the white enamel sink with the rest of the morning dishes. There was no time for a washup. It would have to wait until she got home.

Junie and Barb removed their coats and laid them on the backs of the kitchen chairs.

"What do you want us to do?" Barb asked.

With a nod toward her younger brothers, Thelma said, "If you could help them get dressed, I'll run up and get ready."

Junie took Johnny, the youngest, and Barb stared at Mikey for a minute, unsure. Thelma rolled her eyes. In Barb's house, her mother had a maid, and the maid probably dressed Barb.

"Mikey, get your pajamas off, and Barb will help you with your uniform," Thelma instructed.

"But I need to brush my teeth," he cried.

Thelma shook her head. "Nope. No time. We'll brush them twice tonight before we go to bed."

This seemed to satisfy Mikey, and he struggled to undo the buttons on his pyjama top.

As she ran toward the staircase, she said over her shoulder to Barb, "He can't do buttons, I don't know why. You'll have to help him."

She dashed up the stairs and took one last look in the bathroom mirror. Why couldn't she have beautiful hair like Barb? Her vibrant red hair stood up on end. Her mother used to braid it for her, but that was in the past. Haphazardly, she pulled the brush through it and swept it back into a ponytail, securing it with a rubber band.

Within ten minutes, the five of them were exiting the house. Thelma looked at the clock on her way out and sighed. There was no way they'd make it on time, and she didn't want to get her friends in trouble. At the corner, she said to Junie and Barb, "Go on ahead without me. Take Mikey with you. I've got to run Johnny over to Mrs. Van Houten."

Mrs. Van Houten lived one block over in the opposite direction. It couldn't be easy, could it, Thelma thought. She couldn't have lived in a house on the way to school.

Junie hesitated. "Are you sure? We could walk with you."

That didn't make sense to Thelma, and she said as much. "There's no sense in all of us being late. We'll get in trouble. Go on, go on. I'll be there in a few minutes."

When Junie and Barb exchanged looks, Thelma shooed them on with her hands. "Go on. I'll be right there."

She took Johnny by the hand and started in the opposite direction.

"I like going to Mrs. V's house," Johnny said. "She gives me candy."

"I know," Thelma said. Her father said that Johnny wouldn't have a tooth in his head by the time he started school, thanks to Mrs. Van Houten.

After she dropped Johnny off, she ran all the way to school. Her heart sank as she arrived, as there were no kids milling around outside. The bell had already rung. She was hot and sweaty from her run, and errant strands of thick red hair had escaped her ponytail. As she walked in, she removed her mittens and hat and shoved them into her pockets. She unbuttoned her coat and shrugged it off.

Bright lights shone in the corridor, the industrial tile floors gleaming. The honeyed wood trim glowed. There was the faint smell of furniture polish. All the way down the hallway, students' work was tacked up along the walls next to their classrooms. Outside Sister Ann's second-grade class, it was all their cursive work. Next to the first-grade class, there were the children's Christmas-themed paintings. There was also a crucifix and religious pictures of Jesus, Mary, and St. Joseph. It was an odd mix.

She slowed down, not anxious to meet Sister Bernadette and her ruler. She'd been the victim once of the ruler across the knuckles, and it was an experience she didn't care to repeat.

She could hear her thudding heart in her ears. Outside the sixth-grade classroom, she paused and drew in a deep breath. Slowly, she opened the door and as quietly as she could, she slipped in. She hoped they wouldn't notice her so she could sneak into her seat. But all eyes of the thirty-plus students in her grade turned toward her, as well as the eyes of Sister Bernadette. Thelma steeled herself and lifted her chin.

"Miss Kempf, you're late!" Sister Bernadette said.

All eyes swung back to the nun, with a half-written math problem on the blackboard behind her.

"Sorry, sister," Thelma mumbled.

She hoped that would be the end of it, but the nun picked up her wooden ruler from the desk and pointed to the door. "Outside in the hall, please, Miss Kempf."

Thelma exhaled and stepped back out into the hall, grumbling, her posture sagging, resigning herself to her fate. Best to just get it over with.

Sister Bernadette was a large woman, and the skirts of her black habit swished around her as she walked. In her meaty right hand, she gripped that dreaded wooden ruler. The nun closed the door behind her and stepped away from the window of the door and the prying eyes of Thelma's classmates.

"Why were you late this morning?" Sister Bernadette demanded.

Thelma shrugged. She didn't know what to say. That her mother wasn't there? That her father hadn't told her what to do? That none of them knew what to do?

"Barbara Walsh informed me that you had to get your brothers ready for school," Sister Bernadette said.

Thelma quickly picked her head up and looked at the nun. There might have been kindness in the nun's eyes, but Sister Bernadette was noted for many things and not one of them was compassion. It could have been a glare from the bright hallway lights.

The nun lowered her voice. "You've been given a cross, Thelma, and there's nothing that can be done about it. It's best to accept it with resignation like our Lord did."

"Yes, sister," Thelma said with a nod.

"Now, you're an intelligent girl, Thelma Kempf. And I think you'll be able to get yourself and your brothers organized in the morning starting tomorrow."

"Yes, sister."

"If you're late again, it will be the ruler. Do you understand?"

Thelma nodded, relief flooding her that her knuckles were to be spared.

"All right, now hang up your coat and take your seat, please," Sister Bernadette said, taking her by the shoulder and shoving her in the direction of the classroom.

"Yes, sister."

Thelma ignored the looks of her classmates and didn't even make eye contact with Junie or Barb. She'd see them at recess.

In the cloakroom, she breathed a huge sigh of relief, and it was then that she realized she was shaking. The cloakroom was dark, narrow, and warm. It smelled of damp wool. All the hooks and cubbies were taken. She spotted Junie's wool coat and forced her coat over the top of it. She shoved her brown bag into the cubby next to her friend's.

"Um, Thelma?" asked a voice in the darkness.

Thelma startled and looked up to see her classmate, Stanley Schumacher, standing there. She was half a head taller than him.

"Yes?"

"I'm sorry about your mother," he said. He handed her a Hershey bar.

The wrapper on the bar was creased, and she could feel that it was broken. He must have bought it the day her mother died. Still, her eyes felt hot, and her throat began to close up. He was the only person to offer her words of sympathy.

"Stanley Schumacher, where are you?" bellowed Sister Bernadette.

With an impish grin, Stanley pointed over his shoulder. "I gotta go."

Thelma managed to get out, "Thank you, Stanley."

With a nod, he turned and headed out. "Sorry, sister, had to get another pencil."

"Take your seat, Mr. Schumacher, or you'll have a meeting with my ruler," the nun said.

"Yes, sister."

Thelma smiled as she slipped the chocolate bar into her lunch bag and made her way to her seat.

CHAPTER FIVE

Alice

Alice had prayed for rain for Sunday's tennis match. Her prayers were answered with bright sunshine, blue skies, and above-average temperatures. She pulled on what she hoped was a suitable outfit for tennis. It was something Donna had found online, for which Alice had paid extra to have shipped in one day. By the time she arrived at the country club for doubles' tennis, she had a pretty good idea about the case.

The three plaintiffs were of varying ages and had met Dennis Ballantine in various settings: one had been an office worker, another used to be a cocktail waitress in one of his nightclubs, and the third had been a worker at the charity foundation he'd founded, and which his wife, Audrey, chaired. Mel had gone over the brief with her and what their plan was for defense. Settlement was out of the question, Mel had said. Mr. Ballantine did not want his reputation tarnished, and he wanted to clear his name no matter the cost. In this day and age, when sexual harassment had come to the forefront with the #metoo movement, it was hard to defend and even harder to escape the consequences. The first line of defense for Mr. Ballantine was going to be to discredit the plaintiffs. The fact that there were three made it more difficult but certainly not undoable.

Mel had informed her that the office investigator was already digging into the background of the three plaintiffs. Alice knew this would include their sexual history, and the whole affair left her feeling as if she needed to take a bath. But still, it was only fair to give their client the benefit of the doubt. She would reserve judgment.

Alice had never been to the country club. She knew the partners all had memberships as a lot of business was conducted on the tennis courts, the golf course, and poolside at the club. It was about what she expected with courteous, polished staff, manicured lawns, magnificent rose bushes, and state-of-the-art everything.

She met Mr. Billings outside, and he informed her that it was to be a couple of sets and then showers, and then they'd meet for lunch.

As Dennis and Audrey Ballantine approached, Mr. Billings lowered his voice and said, "Don't forget, today counts as billable hours."

Dennis Ballantine was more or less what Alice expected. He'd aged well, and she suspected he had had some work done. Tan and slim, he had a thick head of hair and teeth that were unnaturally white for someone his age. His wife, on the other hand, appeared to have no need for surgical enhancement. Her hair had been dyed a beautiful auburn shade and her makeup was minimal. She wore a white tennis outfit, and the way she looked so completely at ease in her surroundings suggested to Alice that she was a regular member and a longtime tennis player.

After brief introductions had been made, Dennis reached out and shook Alice's hand, holding onto it a second longer than was necessary.

"I've heard only the highest praise from Dan about you," Dennis said with a smile. "I'm confident of my legal team's success."

Alice cast a sideways glance at her boss, but he was deep in conversation with Audrey.

Audrey Ballantine, she liked. Audrey told it like it was and seemed cordial.

Dennis looked at his wife with adoration.

His wife smiled a smile that seemed only for him. Alice couldn't decide if their behavior toward each other was natural or a concerted effort to deceive others. Granted, they'd been married a long time, over forty years was what Mel had told her, but that didn't mean anything either. Maybe he was guilty as sin, but Audrey had decided to stick by her man no matter what. She wouldn't have been the first woman to do so.

But maybe there were men out there who were devoted to their wives, who did treat them respectfully but had another side that felt that all other women were for the taking and to be used at their disposal.

For Alice, the sets proved disastrous. But she had warned Mr. Billings that she played poorly, so her lack of skill and their defeat was on him.

At the end of the three sets, when the Ballantines had beat them handily all three times, Audrey met Alice at the net. Mrs. Ballantine appeared to have barely broken a sweat, and all Alice wanted was a nice cold drink. Leon came to mind. He hadn't been happy when she had to cancel, and she wondered if she could wrap this up early and meet him somewhere. Maybe drinks and dinner later.

"Why don't you come to the club during the week, and I can help you improve your tennis game," Audrey suggested.

"I couldn't impose on you like that," Alice said diplomatically.

"That would be a great idea," Dan Billings said. "Maybe make it a weekly thing."

"By the time this case goes to court—if it goes to court—she'll be a pro," Dennis said with a smile. When he smiled like that, Alice was reminded of a shark.

She tried to put her foot down. "That's really not necessary. I'd prefer to spend my time researching your case."

Something flashed behind Dan Billings's eyes. Something that suggested he wasn't happy with her answer. Firmly, he said, "I'm sure you'll find time in your schedule to accommodate Audrey." His voice was tight, and Alice found herself making plans with Audrey to meet early Tuesday mornings before Alice went into work.

How had she got roped into that? Why did she have to play along? She said nothing, just retreated to the changing rooms and changed into casual wear after a quick shower.

Over a lunch of poached salmon in a white wine sauce and drinks to accompany it, the case was spoken of in generic terms. Audrey jumped in to defend her husband.

"They see Dennis as a way to make a quick buck," she said as they waited for their main dishes to arrive.

Beside her, Dennis nodded.

"It's no secret that he has a lot of wealth—money that has been hard-earned, I'll add—and these girls are looking for a way to cash in."

Alice didn't interrupt to say that one of the "girls" was fifty-three. It was apparent that Audrey Ballantine believed in her husband's innocence. But Alice figured she didn't know the particulars as she did. She hadn't been privy to the accusations—in explicit detail—that she herself had. They were scurrilous and stomach-turning. Alice had to remind herself that no matter how charming Dennis was, he'd been accused of some very depraved things. She reminded herself not to get caught up in the charm that both Dennis and his wife seemed to have in copious amounts.

When she finally got back to her loft apartment late that afternoon, she texted Leon, asking him to meet her for drinks and dinner. He quickly texted back that he was up in Wisconsin visiting his family and wouldn't be back until later that night. She envied him for two reasons. First, he had family to visit on the weekends and second, he had the time to do it.

Alice pushed through the crowd the following Saturday to meet Leon for dinner. She was ten minutes late. She'd been about to leave the office when one of the partners, Mr. Steadman, pulled her aside to ask for a quick debriefing on a merger she'd worked on. Quickly, she'd given him a summary, hoping he wouldn't ask any follow-up questions. He did, of course. There were three questions, none of which were urgent, and all of which could have waited until Monday. When he wished her a good weekend, Alice had to bite her tongue to keep from saying "It would be a good weekend if I could get out of here."

When she spotted Leon, he was glancing at his watch. He was not smiling when he looked up at her. Alice didn't blame him. She pasted on a bright and cheery smile and focused on him. He had a beautiful mop of naturally golden hair streaked with the summer sun. The way it lay was a hairdresser's dream. Alice often dreamed of running her fingers through it. But they couldn't seem to get out of the starting gate.

By the time she landed at the table, she was breathless.

"I'm sorry I'm late, Leon," she said, setting her purse on a vacant chair.

Leon stood, but said nothing as he held out her chair for her.

"Thank you," she said, smoothing her dress beneath her as she pulled the chair in closer to the table. She leaned her elbows on the table and nervously twisted the diamond stud in her ear.

Before she could say anything, the server appeared and handed them two menus. She rattled off the specials, and Alice was leaning toward the beef tenderloin. She ordered a glass of Cabernet Sauvignon when asked, but Leon put his hand up and said quietly, "Nothing for me, thanks."

Alice regarded Leon. It dawned on her that he hadn't greeted her with his usual hand on her elbow and a kiss. "I am sorry for being late—"

"I know, work," he said. He looked at everything but her.

"I . . ." she started, but then she realized she had nothing to say.

Leon picked up his fork and absentmindedly tapped it against his water goblet. It was oddly familiar, reminiscent of what was done at wedding receptions by guests when they wanted the bride and groom to kiss. Somehow, Alice didn't think Leon would be leaning over the table to kiss her. He still hadn't made eye contact, and a sense of panic rose within her.

"Look, Alice, I've been thinking," he started. He set the fork down, put his elbows on the table, and leaned forward on his crossed arms.

With that preamble, Alice leaned back and tilted her head slightly, her posture sagging. His tone, his air of disappointed resignation, made her certain that what was coming was not going to be positive. He was not about to invite her for a weekend away to meet his family.

"I really like you," he said. Finally, he looked up at her, his gaze locking on hers. "A lot."

She drew in a deep breath, pressing her lips together and rolling them inward.

"But I don't think you're in a position to start a relationship with anyone," he said quietly.

"Leon, I know it's been a little crazy at work lately, but I assure you, I am interested in seeing you again," she said. She didn't want to use the word relationship yet. They'd only had a handful of dates.

Leon looked at her with an expression she couldn't figure out. He was closed off.

"Alice, do you realize that you've canceled or been late for most of our dates? Except one," he said. "No, excuse me, you were on time for two dates, but one of them you had to leave to go back to the office."

"I can make more of an effort," Alice started. She sat up and leaned forward.

He shook his head. "But that's just it. It's a new relationship, it shouldn't take any effort on either of our parts. We should *want* to be with each other."

She couldn't argue with that. He had a valid point. But she liked him, and she wanted to make it work. She did want to be with him.

"Your job does not allow you to have a personal life," he said.

Even though what he said was the truth, it still stung. She loved being a lawyer, but the cost was high: it came at the cost of her personal life.

As much as she wanted to prove to him that she could be invested one hundred percent, she knew that he'd already made up his mind, and no matter how much she wanted to promise to do better, to be more available, she knew it would be an empty promise. Eventually, they'd circle back to this point, probably sooner rather than later. And as much as she hated to do it, she had to let him go.

They were interrupted by the server arriving with her glass of wine.

"Are you ready to order?" she asked.

Leon smiled and said, "We need a few more minutes."

After the server disappeared, he said, "I'm sorry, Alice. But I know what I want in life. I've got my career where I want it. Now, to be blunt, I want marriage and a family. But I want that with someone who wants it as much as I do. Someone who is able to be there. As much as I like you and I really thought we had a good connection, I think we're not on the same page."

Alice nodded. Leon stood and stepped next to her, leaning down and kissing her on the forehead. As he walked away, she thought sadly, *I want those things too.*

Chapter Six

1956

Thelma

"Your mother's gone now, and you'll be in charge of the house," Thelma's father barked. His shirt was unbuttoned and the suspenders on his trousers hung loose.

She frowned, not comprehending. "In charge of the house?" She had been sprawled in one of the armchairs, her legs hanging over the side, tossing a baseball back and forth between her hands.

"It'll be up to you to keep everything clean, look after your brothers, and have the dinner on the table when I get home from work," her father said evenly, as if he were telling her to clean her room and pick up her clothes off the floor.

"Cook dinner? I don't know how," she said. The ball remained static in one hand. Thousands of thoughts raced through her mind, the first being that she was only twelve. The second being that she hadn't a clue as to what went on in the kitchen. That was something her mother had always done. Meals had appeared as if by magic every night at five.

"You'll learn. Your mother must have some cookbooks around here somewhere," he said.

"I don't even know how the oven works," she stammered.

Her father sighed, his displeasure evident. With him, there was never any room for argument or rebuttals; he liked to be obeyed and obeyed right away.

"You have to do the cooking, Thelma," he said. "I can't come home from work and then get a dinner together for all of us."

Thelma kept her mouth shut, deciding it wasn't worth the argument.

"We can't expect Junie's mom to keep sending dinner over to us."

Why not?

The first night Thelma made dinner, her face was red from exhaustion and the heat of the oven in the small kitchen. Her brothers ran wild around the place and at one point, she heard the coffee table tip over, but she was too busy in the kitchen to do anything about that. If they were stupid enough to incur their father's wrath by throwing furniture around then that was on them. She had enough to do.

She heard her father before she saw him.

"Hey! Hey! Pick this furniture up, you bunch of hooligans! Frank, Del, Mikey. Now!" She heard Frank start to say something, but her father must have shot him a look, because everything went quiet. Next, she heard her brothers grunting as they put the furniture back into place.

Her father came into the kitchen and walked over to the stove. He lifted the lid on the frying pan. Thelma stepped back, waiting, swallowing hard. She blew out a deep breath and it lifted her bangs off her forehead. He lifted the lid off the other pot and inspected the mashed potatoes. She'd overcooked them, the result being they were soggy. Thank God for canned vegetables. You couldn't go wrong there. Heat them up and serve them.

"Get it all on the table and we'll eat in five minutes," he said. He parked his lunchbox on the counter.

When her father disappeared from the room, she removed his thermos from his lunchbox and rinsed it out in the sink. At least she didn't have to make all the lunches. That job had been assigned to Frank.

When they all sat down, her father cut into his chop and speared a piece with his fork. Thelma had overloaded his plate with canned green beans and peas, hoping he wouldn't notice the disaster that was the pork chops and mashed potatoes.

"This meat is as tough as shoe leather," he pronounced, but he continued to cut it up.

Thelma bit her lip. Mikey burst out laughing to the point where he was almost hysterical. She shot him a warning look.

Her father pointed his fork at her younger brother. "Keep laughing and you'll be crying in a minute."

"The potatoes are supposed to be mashed, not mushed."

Thelma was upstairs when Aunt Linda and Uncle Johnny arrived one evening after dinner. Immediately, she wondered if something was wrong, although they popped in from time to time, usually to drop off groceries or clothes for her and her brothers. The best was Sundays. They had a standing invitation to Aunt Linda and Uncle Johnny's for Sunday dinner, and it meant that Thelma had a break from the cooking. She looked forward to that more than anything. Plus, Aunt Linda was a good cook, and they didn't eat the same thing all the time. Last weekend, she'd asked Aunt Linda if she could show her how to make a roast chicken, as hers always turned out dry and she had to listen to her father complain about it. Aunt Linda had looked at her funny and then had said, "Of course."

Thelma ran down the stairs, glad to see them. She was always glad to see Aunt Linda and Uncle Johnny, but her uncle always seemed so sad when he came over. She knew he missed her mother. They all missed her mother. Her father had turned into a grump since her mother died. There was no pleasing him.

"There's a bag of sweets for you and your brothers," Linda said, handing her a large brown paper bag.

Oh, the weight of it! Thelma thought. She'd take it to her room first and pick out her favorites, and then she'd dole the rest out to her brothers.

"Why don't you take it upstairs and keep the boys busy. We want to talk to your father."

"Sure, Aunt Linda," Thelma said. Something was up. Aunt Linda had never told her to stay upstairs before.

When she made it to her room, she threw the bag of candy on her bed, momentarily forgetting about it. She parked herself on the hardwood floor near the Victorian heating grate. It was connected directly to the front parlor below, and she used to listen to her parents' conversations all the time.

"Teddy, we want to talk to you about the kids," Uncle Johnny started.

"What about my kids?" her father demanded.

Thelma should have warned Uncle Johnny and Aunt Linda to come back another day. Her father had arrived home from work in a foul mood. He'd slammed down his metal lunchbox on the counter, chipping the edge of the porcelain sink.

Aunt Linda either was oblivious or ignored it, because she soldiered on.

"I know you're broken up over Theresa's death, as we all are, and we thought the kids could come and stay with us for a while. You know, just until you get your bearings."

Although Thelma didn't want to leave her home, the thought of moving into Uncle Johnny and Aunt Linda's house appealed to her simply for the fact that she'd have help with the housework, and she wouldn't have to cook anymore. It was a proposition she liked. She was ready to throw all her belongings into a bag and meet them at the front door. Plus, they were always so nice. And she had grown tired of looking after her brothers. Regularly, she wondered why she had to; after all, they weren't her kids. Frank was strange, always sitting on the edge of the bed, staring at the wall or off into space. Del was okay—he tried to help but he needed a lot of direction and sometimes, Thelma didn't have the patience and it was just easier to do it herself rather than try and explain it all. And the younger boys, Mikey and Johnny, were a handful. She had no idea where they got their energy, but they went from the time their eyes opened in the morning to the time they fell asleep, hardly coming up for air. No, she'd be perfectly okay with someone else raising her brothers. All her father did was yell and scream at them. That could hardly be called raising them.

"What are you saying?" her father demanded.

Thelma gulped. She could tell by his tone that this was not going to go down well with him. That somewhere in their generous offer, he'd find fault or worse, take offense. For the moment, she'd hold off on packing up her belongings.

"It's a lot of work raising kids on your own," Uncle Johnny said. His voice betrayed no emotion.

"Haven't I got Thelma?"

"Thelma's only a kid herself," Aunt Linda cried.

"But that's her job. She'll have to do the things Theresa did."

"But she has to go to school. It's not fair to expect her to manage the boys and the household," Linda pressed.

Thelma didn't miss the exasperation in her voice. But the more Aunt Linda pushed him, the more her father would dig in his heels. Thelma was tempted to run down and advise her to back off a bit.

Her father lowered his voice and asked, "What brought this on? Has Thelma complained?"

Thelma reared back. If her father got that idea in his head, she'd be in big trouble as soon as her aunt and uncle left.

"She's never said one word to us," Linda said. "She didn't have to. We're not blind."

Uncle Johnny spoke up. "Listen, Teddy, don't you think it would be better for the kids to be in a house where there were two parents instead of one?"

Thelma closed her eyes and groaned. That wasn't the way to go about it either.

"They have two parents. But Theresa's gone. And the last time I checked, I was still their father."

"We'd like to give all the kids a home with us," Linda said.

"You know they'd be loved and well looked after," Uncle Johnny said.

"No, no, no," Thelma's father said. "They're my kids and they stay with me. I made a promise to Theresa that I wouldn't break up the family no matter what."

"You could see them every day if you wanted," Aunt Linda pleaded.

But Thelma knew that her father would not change his mind and for the foreseeable future, she'd still be doing the cooking, the washing and ironing, and taking care of her brothers. She sat back on her heels and sighed as a wave of depression rolled over her.

"Look, I appreciate your offer, but my answer is no and it's final," her father said.

"Just think about it," Linda pushed. "Don't say no yet."

"And we won't be able to make dinner on Sunday," her father said with finality.

Oh no, Thelma thought. *Don't do that to me,* she wanted to scream.

"It's getting late, I appreciate you stopping," her father said.

There were no more words from her aunt and uncle, and she heard their footsteps in the hallway and the door close behind them. She flung herself on the bed and sobbed into her pillow.

When she felt she could cry no more, she opened the bag of candy and pulled out a rope of red licorice and bit into it, chewing thoughtfully. Maybe they wouldn't go to Aunt Linda's this Sunday for dinner, but if her father thought she was giving up the weekly Sunday dinner at her aunt and uncle's house, he had another thing coming.

Chapter Seven

Alice

It had been almost six weeks since Leon broke up with her and three months since she returned from Hideaway Bay after Gram's funeral. If she'd hoped to make it back for a long weekend, she'd been sadly mistaken. Every couple of weeks, she spoke to Lily on the phone. Her sister liked her new job as an assistant to Simon Bishop, the writer; and Charlie, her goofball dog, was doing fine. Alice envied her. She hadn't heard from Isabelle in over a month. She was in Alaska at some remote camp accessible only by seaplane for an article she had to write. She'd warned Alice that she'd be out of reach for a few weeks as there was no cell service where she was staying, but cell service or not, Alice wouldn't want to bother her too much in case she was hanging off a cliff or hang gliding down the side of a mountain.

As for Alice, the work continued to pile up, and now that summer was almost over, she realized she'd missed the most of it, spending the majority of her time in an air-conditioned office building. She'd begged off the last two tennis sessions with Audrey Ballantine, using her husband's case as an excuse, saying she was knee deep in research. As for Dennis Ballantine, the longer she worked on the case and the more contact she had with him, the less inclined she was to believe in his innocence. It was the way he looked at women. More than once, his gaze lingered a little too long on certain parts of the female anatomy. And it left her creeped out having to defend him.

It was almost ten by the time she arrived home from work. Her loft apartment was dark, but the floor-to-ceiling windows showed a glittering downtown. As she walked through, kicking off her shoes and laying her briefcase on the kitchen island, she flipped on a few lights. Absentmindedly, she picked up the remote and turned the TV to her favorite women's-channel network, coming in halfway through a movie. She'd gotten used to this pattern and by this time, was able to figure out the plot and at least see how it ended up.

She opened her refrigerator, hoping a hot meal would jump out, but the shelves were almost bare save for a few takeout containers. Pulling one out, she inspected it, decided it wasn't worth the risk of food poisoning, and tossed it in the garbage. There was always the option of toast. But she didn't even have the energy for that.

Walking over to the sofa, she loosened the zipper on the side of her skirt and sank down against the luxurious cushions. Immediately, exhaustion washed over her. Her head lolled on the back of the couch.

What am I doing? Is this really how I want to live my life?

Here she was in this magnificent apartment with a shoe collection to die for, and she was seriously unhappy. When she'd first moved in to this place, she'd been so excited she couldn't sleep. It had felt like a major accomplishment. And it was. But what good was it if she was never here to enjoy it? It was more like a place she spent the weekends in. Even then, she was so busy between work and getting together with friends that she was in and out. Despite her love of baking, her gourmet kitchen sat mainly unused. Shiny, brand-new appliances lined the countertops, but she'd yet to get her money's worth out of them.

Hot tears pricked her eyes and she blinked to prevent a torrent of tears. As much as she loved what she did, she didn't treasure the pace or what was required to get that high salary anymore.

Forcing herself to sit up, she picked up her phone off the coffee table. Noting the time, she wondered if Lily was still up. After pressing her contact list, she hit the button to call Lily. Before Gram's funeral, she would never have dreamed of calling either of her sisters.

Lily picked up on the third ring.

"Alice?"

"Were you in bed?" Alice asked, immediately feeling guilty.

"Nope, just sitting out on the porch with Charlie," Lily said.

When Alice didn't say anything, Lily prompted, "Is everything all right?"

"Yes. No," Alice said. "I'm thinking of quitting my job and moving back to Hideaway Bay."

"Why? What happened?" Lily asked.

"I'm not happy with my life," Alice admitted. There, she'd said it out loud.

"Okay," Lily said slowly.

"You probably think I'm ungrateful," Alice said.

"No, no, I don't think that at all," Lily said. "I know you work God-awful hours, and I suppose that doesn't leave much time for anything else."

"No, it doesn't," Alice agreed. "I'm thirty-one years old, and I'm thinking there has to be more to life than this time-consuming career."

"Okay."

"When I go into work in the morning, I am full of dread. When I first started the job, I loved it. Couldn't wait to get to work and roll up my sleeves. But now, when I get there all I can think of is all the work I need to do and how it never ends, and I feel like I don't accomplish anything." She paused and caught her breath. "I'm irritable and I've been having crying jags. I mean, I know I'm the sensitive type but even I'm alarmed."

"It sounds like you're burned out," Lily said.

"Maybe." Alice sighed. "I think I need a change."

"What would you do in Hideaway Bay?" Lily asked.

Alice decided it wasn't the time to revisit the idea of turning the place into an inn. She was non-committal. "I don't know. I suppose I could find a job at a law firm there."

"There are only two firms in Hideaway Bay," her sister reminded her. "But you could always go up to Buffalo, plenty of law firms there."

Alice didn't treasure the thought of a one-hour commute each way either. But she wasn't going to worry about that now.

"Maybe I could take it easy for a while. Aside from the time I took for Gram's funeral, I haven't been on vacation in years," Alice said.

"Then that's what you should do. Sleep in, walk on the beach, go swimming. You've got another month here before it gets too cold to go into the water," Lily said.

"True."

"Can I make a suggestion?"

"Sure," Alice said.

"Don't resign yet, because you don't know how you'll feel in six months. See if you can take a leave of absence for say, three or six months."

Alice could practically see the expression on Mr. Billings's face when she asked for that. He'd probably fire her on the spot. But what Lily said made sense. Because Alice was exhausted and dissatisfied, her impulse was to walk in and hand in her resignation. But Lily was right: after six months in Hideaway Bay, she might be bored and itching to get out. Best to proceed with caution.

"Thanks, Lily, you're a good listener," Alice said. Their conversation turned toward the goings-on in Hideaway Bay, and Lily caught her up with all the local news. When she hung up the phone, she was full of relief.

It remained to be seen whether the partners would agree to a leave of absence. It didn't need to be said that this would scupper any chances she had of making junior partner this year or even next, but the last thing she wanted was more responsibilities at work. She needed to catch her breath, and Hideaway Bay was the place to do it.

With a quick glance at her watch, Alice hoofed it to one of the conference rooms for a meeting with Dennis Ballantine and the legal team. Everyone was there and seated when she pushed through the double doors, her right arm full of paperwork.

Everyone looked up when she entered.

"Apologies for being late," she said, slightly breathless from the run in high-heeled shoes. She took the nearest vacant chair.

Across the table sat Mr. Ballantine. He smiled, and then he winked at her.

What the hell was that? She looked around to see if anyone else caught it, but no one appeared to have seen it. Heat fanned out beneath the collar of her blouse.

Mel, the lead counsel, sat at the head of the table. He acknowledged Alice briefly with a nod and started the meeting.

Alice zoned in and out of the meeting, her mind on her plan to talk to Mr. Billings at some point today and ask for a leave of absence. When she looked up at one point, she realized Mr. Ballantine's gaze was on her, studying her. She ignored him, turning her attention to Mel, who was speaking.

After an hour in which she had to listen to the explicit details of the plaintiffs' complaints, the meeting was called to an end. With much relief, Alice stood.

As she headed for the door, she heard Mr. Ballantine call out her name. With her hand on the doorknob, she rolled her eyes, sighed, and turned around and smiled sweetly at him.

"Yes?"

"Are you up for a game of tennis on Sunday?" he asked.

"Oh, I'm sorry, I have other plans," she lied. She was done playing tennis with the Ballantines. As far as she was concerned, she'd already gone above and beyond.

"That's too bad," he said, brushing his bottom lip with his thumb and forefinger. His gaze raked up and down the length of her, finally coming to rest on her breasts. "Maybe the following weekend."

"Yeah, we'll see," she said tightly, trying not to squirm beneath his gaze. She didn't appreciate being looked at as if she were the prime offering at a buffet.

Before he could say any more, Alice slipped out the door. Instead of heading to her own office, she headed to her boss's.

Mr. Billings stood at his assistant's desk, going over some paperwork. The assistant nodded and said, "Yes, Mr. Billings."

"Hello, Alice. What can I do for you?" Mr. Billings said when he spotted her.

"Can I have a minute of your time?" she asked, shifting the heavy paperwork to her other arm.

"Is it billable or unbillable?" He laughed. This was a frequent joke of his, and it wasn't even funny the first time she heard it. Even his assistant didn't smile. Alice gave a brief, obligatory smile and then made sure it disappeared quickly.

Mr. Billings swept his arm out, indicating Alice should lead the way into his office. She sat, setting her stack of files down on one of the chairs as she took the other.

"Is everything all right, Alice?"

She crossed one leg over the other and looked her boss right in the eye. She folded her arms across her chest. "Actually, it isn't, Mr. Billings. I'd like to take a leave of absence for three months."

Dan Billings narrowed his eyes. "What?"

"I know the timing isn't the best, but I can bring my associates up to speed in no time," Alice said.

"Is this health related? Are you sick or something?" he pressed.

Alice looked away. "Not sick in the general sense . . ." Her voice drifted off. How did you tell your boss that you were burned out and that it had more to do with mental health than physical health? She was uncertain how that would be received. Probably not well.

"You can't leave now, not with the merger you're working on and more importantly, Dennis Ballantine's case."

To her, the merger was more important than the Ballantine case. She sighed, closed her eyes, and rubbed her forehead. "Again, I can have my associates up to speed in no time."

"We've invested a lot of time with Audrey and Dennis. You can't just swan off now!"

"I need some time off," Alice said tightly.

"I'm afraid I'm going to have to say no," Mr. Billings said. "When the merger is completed and the case with Dennis sorted, then I'll have no problem granting you time off."

Alice blinked. Those two things, independent of each other, might not be resolved until the following year. Could she wait until then? Continue at her current pace? She didn't think so.

She gave it one last-ditch effort. "About Dennis Ballantine . . ."

"What about him?"

"I'd like to be removed from the case."

Mr. Billings had taken the chair across from her. "Why? What's happened?"

Pressed, her argument began to lose steam. How could she come right out and say she thought their client was guilty of the charges against him?

"This isn't my area of expertise," she tried again.

Mr. Billings chuckled but it didn't sound funny. "I'm well aware of your area of expertise, Alice. But I'm asking you to stay on as a favor."

Her heart sank. She slumped slightly in the chair.

"Is it that bad?"

She opted for truthfulness. "I don't like how I feel when Dennis Ballantine is around."

The partner all but snorted. "I don't like how I feel when I'm with a lot of my clients, Alice. We don't have to like them; we're here to represent them."

She drew in a deep breath. "He may be guilty of the charges." Maybe this tack would work.

"It doesn't matter whether he's guilty or not; it's our job to defend him."

Maybe it didn't matter to him, but it mattered to Alice.

"Again, Mr. Billings, I respectfully ask that you remove me from his legal team."

"I'm afraid that won't be possible. We've created a great attorney–client relationship with him and his wife. You can't abandon ship right now."

"And you won't reconsider?" she asked.

"I'm afraid not."

Alice nodded and stood, picking up her paperwork from the other chair. "Very well. Sorry to have bothered you." Without a goodbye and without looking over her shoulder, she marched out of the room.

Chapter Eight

1959

Thelma

Junie and Barb arrived in the side hall of the Kempf household. They both looked so put-together, whereas Thelma always felt she needed a bath and a change of clothes. The plan had been to go to the high school dance.

Junie held up two women's magazines, *Woman's Day* and *Ladies' Home Journal*.

"My mother told me to give you these."

Thelma muttered thanks, took them from her, and laid them on the kitchen table. She'd begun to leaf through them—not read them—looking for easy recipes, nothing too complicated and nothing that required ingredients she'd never heard of or couldn't afford.

Her youngest brother, Johnny, tugged on her hand.

"What?" she asked.

"I lost my sock," he said. With a chubby finger he pointed down to his foot, which was bare.

"I'm not the department of lost and found," Thelma said. She tried to keep the irritation out of her voice, but it was impossible. What she would like to do is go out with her friends, but there was too much to do. "Go look for it. And get Mikey, because I have to wash your hair."

Thelma turned to her friends. "I'd love to go with you, but it's hair-washing night."

"But we were all going to go together," Barb said.

"I know, but I've got too much to do and I'm not ready," Thelma said. Her hair was a lost cause and she had nothing to wear. Besides, she had no interest in the dance. She heard some of the guys were playing baseball in the park later and if she got all her chores done, she planned to go down and join them.

"Can we help? And then you can get finished faster?" Junie asked.

Thelma thought about it. "Okay, come on."

Thelma had picked Fridays for hair washing because her father bowled on Friday nights, and it was one less person to manage in the house. The two younger boys needed their hair washed weekly, sometimes twice if they got into things.

Junie and Barb removed their coats and hung them on the kitchen chairs.

"Hold on while I round them up," Thelma said. As she ran up the stairs, she banged on the boys' bedroom door. "Come on, Frank, get in the shower."

"Yeah, I will," he said. But Thelma knew it would take her three more times before Frank moved. "And take the garbage out before Dad gets home."

"Yeah, yeah," he yelled.

"It's your funeral if you don't do it," she said.

She called for Del, who was upstairs in the attic. Del shared a room with Frank, but they fought so much that Del often sought refuge in the attic. She ran halfway up the staircase to the attic and called up. "Del, come down and jump in the shower now, because it'll take Frank half an hour to get off his bed."

"Okay, Thelma," he said.

Thelma often thought if it were only her and Del, everything would be easy-peasy. He was easy to get along with and never gave her a hard time, unlike the rest of them. Not that they meant to give her a hard time, but sometimes it was like herding cats.

On her way back downstairs, she grabbed a towel from the linen closet and a bottle of shampoo. She corralled

Mikey and Johnny into the kitchen, where her friends waited.

"Did you find your sock?" she asked Johnny.

"No," he whined.

"We'll find it later," she said.

She cleared off the counter, putting everything on the kitchen table temporarily, and hoisted Johnny up onto it. He lay down on the counter on his back, his head hanging over the sink.

"Who wants to wash?" she asked her friends.

"I'll wash," Junie said, stepping forward. "This is a good idea, washing their hair right here in the sink."

"It's a lot easier," Thelma said. She handed Junie a glass pitcher. "Fill this up with water to wet his hair."

Junie nodded.

"What can I do?" Barb asked.

"Could you fold the laundry?"

"Sure."

Thelma picked up the two laundry baskets from the top of the basement stairs and with a nod, indicated to Barb that she should follow her. She stepped into the small dining room off the kitchen. They never ate in there. Not anymore. When her mother was alive, they ate special occasion meals at the big dining room table: Christmas, Thanksgiving, and their birthdays. But a meal hadn't been consumed in here since the death of her mother. Since then, it had turned into a catch-all for things that needed to be put away. Every morning before her father left for work, he slapped his rolled-up newspaper against the doorframe of the dining room and barked, "Get that table cleaned off."

And Thelma would try and put some things away, but there were things she had no idea what to do with, things like the small pile of mail addressed to her mother. It wasn't that she was afraid to ask her father, she was more afraid that he wouldn't have an answer.

With her right arm, Thelma pushed back one of the piles on the table to clear some space. Barb's gaze swept around the room, taking everything in: the cluttered table and sideboard, the untouched china cabinet. Poor Barb, Thelma thought. Their worlds were entirely different. Barb, the daughter of a doctor, had a housekeeper, but in the Kempf household, Thelma was chief cook, bottle washer, and housekeeper.

"It's all mixed up," Thelma said, bringing Barb's attention back to the laundry baskets full of dark clothes belonging mostly to her brothers and her father. "If you can fold it, I'll sort it later when I get home."

"All right," Barb said. She pulled out one of the chairs and sat down, removing the first item—a striped shirt—off the top of the laundry basket. She held it up by the shoulders, appeared to consider it, and then slowly folded it. At that rate, she might get it all done by next year. Thelma rolled her eyes and stepped back into the kitchen.

Johnny hopped down from the counter with a towel wrapped around his head.

"Come on, Mikey, get up there," Thelma said.

Like a pro, Mikey hopped up onto the counter to wait his turn. He sat on the edge, his legs dangling, his heels hitting the cabinet doors below.

Thelma took Johnny by the shoulder and removed the towel, drying his hair with it, doing a thorough job behind his ears.

"Ow," Johnny whined.

Thelma ignored him and instructed, "Go on now and get your pajamas on."

He ran out of the room and his footsteps were heavy on the stairs.

"Why does he always sound like he's got army boots on?" Thelma muttered to herself.

Junie washed Mikey's hair and within minutes, he too was all set.

Thelma ran up the stairs just as the shower was going off. Del was finished. She banged on Frank's door.

"Come on, Frank, you're up!"

"Okay!"

Thelma dashed down the stairs again and straightened everything up. She wiped down the counters where any water or bubbles had spilled. She collected the wet towels and threw them down the laundry chute. She put everything back on the counter.

"Would you go get ready?" Junie said. "Barb and I will finish up here."

Thelma dashed back upstairs. The only positive in her whole living situation was she had her own room as Johnny had moved into the other room with Mikey. She closed the door behind her, making sure it was locked as Mikey was apt to walk in without knocking no matter how many times she'd scolded him.

Quickly, she shed her sweatshirt and dungarees and dug through her closet for something to wear. It didn't necessarily have to be nice or fashionable, but it did have to be clean. She found a half-decent skirt and paired it with a fresh blouse. She sat down on a rickety chair she'd rescued from the attic. Her hair was a lost cause. She yanked the brush through it, but the curls kept bouncing back up. She blew out a deep breath and her bangs never lifted from her forehead. There was no time; the dance had already started, so she grabbed a rubber band from the drawer and pulled her hair back into her signature ponytail. Barb had given her one of her old cardigans and she threw that on.

Down in the kitchen, Junie and Barb stood waiting for her. She yelled back up the stairs.

"Del, I'm going, keep an eye on things."

"Okay, Thelma, will do," he called. She knew she could count on Del.

She'd powdered her face, and Junie pulled a tube of lipstick from her pocket and handed it to her. Her father would hit the roof if he saw her with lipstick.

Barb stood back, one arm slung along her belly, the other with her elbow propped up on said arm and her chin cupped in her hand.

"We should do something with your hair, Thelma," Barb announced.

Next to her, Junie nodded, but Thelma shook her head. "We don't have time. Let's go."

Barb pulled a lavender ribbon from the pocket of her cardigan. Thelma scowled. Who carried hair ribbon around with them? Apparently, Barb did.

"Take the ponytail out," Barb instructed.

Thelma removed the rubber band, and her hair spilled around her shoulders.

"You should wear your hair down, Thelma, it's so pretty. It has so much curl."

Thelma snorted. "It's a rat's nest."

"You look like Susan Hayward," Junie said with an encouraging nod.

"You know what they say about a woman's hair being her crowning glory," Barb said.

Thelma scowled. "What?" What was Barb going on about? She read too many books, that's what her problem was.

"Never mind. Here, let me put this ribbon in your hair," Barb said, stepping forward.

Thelma took a step back. "I don't really do ribbons."

"Tonight, you do," Barb said with a smile.

Thelma wondered what had gotten into Barb, she usually wasn't so forceful. When the priest spoke at Sunday Mass about being meek and humble, Thelma always thought of Barb.

Her friend looped the ribbon around the nape of her neck and pulled it up to the top of her head, tying it into a little bow over the side part of Thelma's hair.

"That's lovely, Thelma," Junie said.

"Do you have a sweater?" Barb asked.

"Huh?"

"A sweater instead of a blouse? A pullover one?" Barb asked. Junie looked at her and frowned.

Barb turned to Junie and said, "It's only that Thelma has lovely shoulders and has been blessed with a couple of gifts that should be accentuated."

Junie had a fit of giggles and Barb joined her. Thelma rolled her eyes.

"Come on, this isn't beauty school, let's go," Thelma said. She was afraid of one of her brothers getting into mischief that would prevent her from leaving the house.

There was a nip to the spring air as they walked over to the high school. The air smelled like wet earth. Pretty soon, baseball would be starting up. She couldn't wait. She loved this time of year.

"Just think, one of you might meet the love of your life tonight," Barb said. Her voice was soft amongst the sounds of the city night. Cars went by, one honking, another with its muffler dragging. Then the fire alarm went off at the redbrick fire station one block up, and it added to the noise.

When they reached the firehouse, they stopped as the big garage doors had been pulled up, and they waited until the long red pumper and the other fire trucks bounced out of the bay, their sirens blaring.

"Be open minded, because you never know where you'll meet the love of your life," Barb said.

Thelma looked at her friend. "I do not plan to meet the love of my life in a sweaty high school gymnasium."

Barb crossed her arms over her chest and lifted her chin but remained silent.

"Who knows where we'll meet the love of our lives," Junie chimed in.

Thelma turned to her. "I thought Paul Reynolds was the love of your life."

Despite it being dusk, Junie's cheeks visibly reddened, and she shrugged. "That was nothing but a childhood crush."

All the fire trucks had pulled out, and the three of them walked past the station and continued on toward the school.

Thelma had never given much thought to "meeting the love of her life." When she actually had time, she only dreamed of him being rich—rich enough to afford a maid and a cook.

The high school was all lit up like a stadium when they rounded the corner. From two blocks away, they could hear the band playing. It was the last dance of senior year. Then they'd all be going off in different directions. Barb was heading off to college in Vermont, and Junie had her job at the drugstore. Thelma had gotten a job at a factory that made cardboard boxes.

"Hard to believe this is our last dance of the year," Junie said, echoing her thoughts.

"We still have the summer to spend together," Barb said.

Thelma hated change. In her experience, big change usually meant a worse outcome for her. They walked on in silence, Thelma leading the way. Junie and Barb walked behind her, side by side.

They made their way up the stone steps to the main entrance of the high school. Light spilled out from inside, and some kids loitered out front while others were streaming into the school ahead of them.

Thelma spotted Stanley Schumacher leaning against the stone balustrade of the school. She pretended she didn't see him. She had nothing against Stanley, but he tended to overdo things. And she wasn't going to be the butt of anyone's jokes. But Stanley had spied her and pushed off the wall, making his way to her.

"Hello, ladies," he said, pushing his glasses up his nose. To Thelma he whispered, "You look beautiful, Thelma."

She frowned at him and kept walking, not wanting to encourage his devotion.

"When someone pays you a compliment, you should be gracious and say thank you," Barb said at her side.

"Who are you? Miss Manners?"

"No, but you know how Stanley feels about you," Barb said.

"Everybody and their brother knows how Stanley feels about me," Thelma said.

"Why don't you give him a chance?" Junie asked.

"Stanley? Stanley Schumacher?" Thelma asked, rearing her head back and looking at her friends in disbelief.

"He looks at you with such adoration," Barb said. "I bet he'd always put you first." Her voice had a dreamy quality to it, and Thelma grimaced. She'd been friends with Barb for a long time, but she had to get her head out of the clouds.

Did they think someone like Stanley was the only guy she could get? Because she was tied to her home, raising her brothers? Because she didn't have nice clothes like Barb? Because her hair had a mind of its own? No thanks. With a grim set to her lips, she picked up her pace and pushed through the crowd to the gymnasium.

One thing was for certain: Stanley Schumacher was not the love of Thelma's life.

Chapter Nine

Alice

Alice supposed her decision to quit her job had already been made, while she sat in the office of the senior partner. It had become apparent to her that she could no longer work under these circumstances. The job was stressful enough without having to be used as a pawn in the grander scheme of things. As she walked out, she was already drafting her resignation letter in her head. It left her feeling both queasy and nervous.

She sailed into her office and asked Donna to follow her.

Her assistant had been with her for five years, and Alice valued her as both a colleague and a friend. Before she even put pen to paper, she wanted Donna to know of her plans.

Donna stood in the doorway as Alice leaned against the front of her desk.

"I wanted you to be the first to know that I'm resigning, effective in two weeks," Alice said.

Donna's eyes bulged in surprise. "What?"

"The truth is I'm burned out and I'm looking for more of a work-life balance," Alice told her.

Her assistant's shoulders sagged, and she whispered, "Oh no."

She hugged Donna and there were tears in both their eyes. After Donna left her office, Alice wrote up her resignation letter and forwarded it to the three partners, the office manager, and human resources. Ideally, she should have given them two months but anxious to leave, she gave them two weeks' notice. Once the decision had been made and the email sent off, the tension seeped out of her body. She felt better. Lighter. Freer.

Within an hour of sending those emails, the partners called an emergency meeting requesting her presence in the boardroom.

When Alice stepped into the conference room, the three partners were gathered around a long rectangular table with a glorious shine. The last time she'd met with them like this had been when they'd hired her, saying she was a "good fit" for the firm. How hopeful and excited she'd been back then at her prospects. Now she'd resigned, and all those hopes and dreams were nothing more than a pile of ashes.

The three partners regarded her as she walked in. Each wore an expensive hand-tailored suit costing more than the other, along with expensive cologne: subtle but wonderful. No one was smiling. She was sure this was the part where she found out her abrupt resignation meant she'd never work again in the city and there would be no reference. She didn't care anymore. She only wanted to go back to Hideaway Bay.

George Steadman was the oldest of the group, with a head of white hair and a perpetual tan courtesy of a winter home in the Bahamas. "Sit down, Alice," said Mr. Steadman.

She pulled out a chair from the table, avoiding looking at Mr. Billings. In two weeks' time, she'd never have to look at him or deal with him again.

"We want to discuss your resignation," said Allan Jones. He was the most serious of the three partners, all business, and although Alice hadn't had many dealings with him, she'd heard from his associates that he was extremely fair.

"When I leave in two weeks, I'll have handed off all my casework to other associates," she said firmly. She'd been back and forth on the phone with the office manager, discussing which cases would be assigned to whom. She'd be doing that for the rest of the day.

"Hold up, there, Alice," Mr. Steadman said, putting up a hand. "Your resignation has come out of the blue, and we'd like to know the impetus behind it."

Alice opted for honesty. "Mr. Steadman, to be frank, I'm burned out. Working seventy to eighty hours a week has taken its toll. There's no balance in my life."

"Why didn't you come to us?" Mr. Jones asked.

"I did speak with Mr. Billings this morning and asked for a three-month leave of absence but was denied."

Both partners swung their gaze to Dan Billings, who threw his hands up. "She's in the middle of a merger and then she's part of the legal team for Dennis Ballantine."

"Dennis Ballantine?" Mr. Jones repeated. "Alice's area is corporate law, not sexual harassment in the workplace."

"We'll get to that in a minute," George Steadman said, waving his hand. "Alice, the mental health of our employees is very important to me. Why do you think I spend so much time in the Bahamas? You cannot punish your body with a grueling schedule such as yours and not expect to burn out."

Dan Billings scrambled. "I told her she could take a leave as soon as the merger and the Ballantine case were resolved."

"Well, that's rich of you, Dan," Mr. Jones said, folding his arms across the table and looking over his shoulder at his colleague. "And when would that be? Sometime next year?"

"I'm sorry you didn't come to us first," Mr. Steadman said.

Mr. Jones ignored Dan and spoke directly to George Steadman. "I say let Alice take her three months' leave of absence, and we'll revisit the issue when she comes back. That would be . . ." He looked up at the ceiling. "That would be December. But we can give you until January, Alice."

Alice thought for a moment. A small voice at the back of her mind whispered that to take the leave of absence rather than resigning was the more sensible move. But she also knew that if the door was left open, she might come back after an extended leave and be right back where she started: working awful hours with no personal life. It was time to make a decision.

"I appreciate your offer, but I'm going to decline and still tender my resignation," she said.

"That's regrettable, but we respect your decision," Mr. Steadman said.

"We wish you well," Mr. Jones added thoughtfully.

"There is nothing we can do to make you stay?" Mr. Steadman asked, hopeful.

Alice's mind was made up. Even if they offered her a partnership now, she'd still resign. Her tenure at the law firm was over and her future, although unknown, was full of hope and possibilities. She shook her head and stood to indicate the meeting was over.

"If you change your mind, you'd be welcome back here any time. In the meantime, I'll personally write you a letter of reference," Mr. Steadman said. He and Allan Jones stood to shake her hand. Mr. Billings did not get up.

At the end of her two weeks, after Alice had packed up her office and said some last goodbyes to everyone, she carried out her box of belongings and took the elevator down to the parking garage beneath the building. It felt like when she was a kid and it was June and she was walking out of school on the last day, full of excitement and anticipatory joy.

I can't believe I did it!

Inside her apartment, she set the box down on the long console table behind the sofa. She looked around, feeling odd. It was strange to be at her home during the week in the middle of the afternoon. It was refreshing to see it in broad daylight.

She discarded her skirt and blouse, changing into jeans and a T-shirt and letting her hair down, thinking how relieved she was knowing that she'd never have to straighten it again.

Barefoot, she padded to the kitchen and made herself a cup of chamomile tea. She carried it with two lavender biscuits tucked against the cup on a saucer to the living room. She drank her tea and nibbled a biscuit, contemplating the view of the city outside her floor-to-ceiling windows.

Briefly, she considered calling Leon and announcing, "Hey, I quit my job and am now available twenty-four seven for a relationship," but quickly nixed the idea, thinking that that ship had sailed. And what a shame that was. It would have to be filed under missed opportunities.

Instead, she rang Lily. She knew her sister was at work, but maybe she'd pick up. She was in luck; Lily picked up on the first ring.

"Hi, Alice, how did it go?" she asked.

As soon as Alice had tendered her resignation, she'd called her sisters. Lily had been supportive. And Isabelle—in true Isabelle fashion—had railed against corporate America.

"I'm okay," Alice said. "Do you have time to talk?"

"Yes, I'm on my lunch break," Lily told her.

"I'm a little nervous, kind of wondering what I've just done and whether I've made a mistake but also excited at the same time," Alice said in a rushed voice.

"That kind of thinking is inevitable with the life-changing decision you've just made," Lily said. "I felt the same way myself."

Alice smiled. Lily sounded so much better than she had when she first arrived in Hideaway Bay, when she'd been hesitant, indecisive, and fearful as she dealt with both her husband's death and Gram's.

"When are you coming home to Hideaway Bay?"

This had been Alice's plan, to return to Hideaway Bay, but she hesitated. "I thought I should be looking for another job. Like right away."

"You can look for a job in Chicago from here if your plans are to remain in Chicago," Lily said. In the background, a dog barked. Alice laughed when she heard Lily say, "Leave the birds alone, Charlie!"

Alice supposed what her sister said was true. In the three weeks she'd been home for Gram's funeral, all she'd thought about was how she'd like to return to Hideaway Bay. But now here she was with a chance to return to her hometown, and she was hesitant. What was that, she wanted to know. Fear? Uncertainty? Or was the dream to return to Hideaway Bay only that? A dream.

"Come on home. It'll be nice to have you here," Lily said.

Alice blinked and pressed her lips together, suddenly overcome with emotion. She supposed she could go back for a few weeks and investigate the possibility of moving back permanently.

"Besides, Charlie misses you and your home-baked dog biscuits," Lily added.

Alice burst out laughing. "How is Clumsy these days?"

"Considering that he hasn't knocked anything over or broken anything in almost a week, I'd say he's doing great," Lily told her.

"He must be on some kind of streak," Alice said, smiling. "Tell him to buy a lottery ticket."

"Will do," Lily said. She paused and asked, "So will you think of coming home?"

"I will," Alice promised.

After her phone call ended with Lily, it didn't take Alice long to make up her mind. By nightfall, she was packing a suitcase and texting Lily that she'd be leaving first thing in the morning. It'd be faster and easier for her to fly back, but she wanted to have her car with her. Besides, if Lily could drive from California to New York with a Great Dane in the back seat, then she could surely handle the drive from Chicago.

Since she'd left Hideaway Bay months ago, she'd dreamed of returning, and now was her chance. It was an opportunity she had to take.

When she slid into bed near midnight, she sank into the mattress, letting it mold around her body. She stared at the ceiling. It was amazing how fast your life could change. In the blink of an eye.

Chapter Ten

1962

Thelma

Thelma would be the first to admit that after two years at her job at the cardboard box factory, she was bored out of her mind. She did the same thing every day: sort the boxes and pack them into larger boxes for shipment. All day long. Day after day. The wage was decent enough, but the sheer tedium was more than she could bear at times. But college was out of the question, plus she had no interest in furthering her education. College was for other people, people like Barb Walsh. Some of her friends had chosen secretarial school, but she had no interest in being chained to a typewriter either. And the last thing she wanted was to get married and have children. She was still living at home, raising her brothers, and cooking the dinners and washing and ironing as she'd been doing since she was twelve, and she was in no hurry to do that with a husband. She wanted to live a little. Have some fun.

There was a meeting after work about the company baseball team. She was going to try out for the men's team, and she didn't care what anyone said. She wasn't going to get stuck playing with a bunch of girls who played like girls.

She headed to the break room after punching out. A group of men were gathered for the meeting at two of the long tables at the back. Thelma grabbed a chair at the edge of the group. A few of them eyed her curiously but said nothing. On the other side of the room, the janitor mopped the floor, rolling his bucket along, a squeaky wheel groaning in protest.

She dared them to keep her out.

The floor manager, Bill Mason, stood at the front of the room. She knew of his reputation for being handsy with some of the girls, but he knew better than to try any of that stuff with her.

"Thelma, the girls' softball team already met last week," he said, hands on his hips.

All the men from the company who were seated in front of her turned in their seats to stare at her.

"I know that. But I want to try out for the men's team," she said. She folded her arms across her chest and crossed her legs.

Bill snorted, and some of the guys in front of her smirked and muttered beneath their breath.

Thelma rolled her lips inward. She was the best pitcher this side of the state. And everyone knew it. She wasn't going to be held back just because she wasn't a man.

"You can't try out for this team, because you're a woman," he said with a laugh, as if pointing out the obvious.

"So? So what?" she asked.

There were a couple of sniggers rumbling through the crowd.

"Come on, Thelma," he said with a look that said he was going to humor her. "You can't try out for the men's team."

"I know, you said that already. I heard you the first time. But you haven't answered my question. Why not?" she demanded.

"Because you don't have the right equipment," someone quipped up ahead. That resulted in a lot of laughter.

"Ha-ha, funny, you missed your calling," Thelma said with a roll of her eyes. "Don't quit your day job, Janek."

"All right, you've made your point, now time to leave." Bill grinned at her as if he were humoring a naughty child.

Thelma drew in a deep breath but did not budge from her seat. Finally, she stood and said, "Let me try out. Because I bet there isn't one man in here who could pitch better than me."

There were all sorts of shouts of indignation among the men. So predictable, Thelma thought. Furious when their own pride was wounded. Couldn't admit that a woman might be as good as them at sports, or perhaps even better.

"Give me one chance. If someone can outpitch me, I'll walk away and say no more," she challenged.

Murmurs continued through the crowd, but Bill didn't back down. "Come on, be a good girl and go home."

Thelma's eyes blazed in fury. "I'm not a 'girl.' Maybe you can't accept the fact that I'm the best pitcher here, or maybe all the little 'boys' here are afraid I'll put them to shame."

There were shouts and calls for Thelma to leave.

"Why don't you join the bowling team, that's co-ed," someone shouted.

Thelma glared at them. "I don't want to bowl; I want to pitch!"

"Sorry, Thelma, rules are rules."

Down but not defeated, Thelma held her head high and walked out of the cafeteria. She would join the women's softball team, and she'd make damn sure they won a championship this season.

As she headed out, someone called her name. She looked over her shoulder and spotted Bobby Milligan behind her. He was one of the guys who worked in the warehouse. She knew him to see him but other than that, she didn't know much about him.

"Hey, Thelma, wait up," he called.

Bobby was tall and lean with a weak chin and a set of sloping shoulders that gave him an air of defeat. He was not what Barb would call movie star material.

"Hey, Bobby, what can I do for you?"

"Look, if it was up to me, I'd let you pitch for the men's team. I've seen you play before for the city's women's league."

"You have?" She didn't think any man had ever paid attention to her. With her unruly hair and short bangs, she was not what you would call movie star material either.

"And I know for a fact that you'd be a better pitcher than the one we've currently got."

"Who's that?" she asked.

He placed both his hands on his chest and smiled. "Me!"

Thelma couldn't help herself; she burst out laughing.

"You're not a good pitcher?" she asked.

He shook his head. "Naw. I can get the job done, but I'm not going to set the world on fire."

Thelma wondered if this assessment pertained only to baseball or to his life in general.

"Look, can I take you out some time?" he asked.

Thelma reared back, unsure. "What, like a date or something?"

"Yeah, that's it."

She'd never been on a date before. Didn't go to her prom. Stanley Schumacher had asked her to the prom, of course, but she'd turned him down. Junie and Barb had offered to ask a fella of her choice on her behalf, but she'd scoffed at their suggestion, saying if she truly wanted to go, she'd ask her own date and not leave it to her friends. She didn't operate that way. What she didn't tell them was that her father had already told her there was no extra money for any kind of fancy dress. So, she'd skipped it when secretly, she would have liked to go.

But now, here was someone, a man, asking her out. And if you didn't focus too much on the weak chin, Bobby Milligan wasn't bad looking with his brown hair and hazel-colored eyes. It might be nice to go out on a date. It wasn't like she had to marry him or anything. It might be a nice change of pace from taking care of everyone and her daily grind at home and at work.

"Okay, when?"

"Friday night?" he asked. He stuffed his hands in his pockets and kind of shrugged so that his neck disappeared into his shoulders. Thelma looked at him and frowned.

"All right," she said.

He pulled out a little black book and Thelma arched an eyebrow. She hoped he wasn't some kind of player. He didn't strike her as the type.

"What's your phone number and address?" he asked, taking a pencil from his back pocket and scribbling down the information when she rattled it off. That's when she noticed he was still on the first page of his little black book, and she was the first entry. She smiled.

"The show?" he asked.

"Yeah, sure, that's fine," she said.

"You can pick out the movie. I don't care what we see," he said.

"Good. I'll let you know."

He grinned. "You probably want to watch some romance."

Thelma scowled. "Anything but that. I like crime, westerns and such." It's what happened when you lived with a houseful of men.

He nodded, satisfied. "Cool. I'll call you."

"Where are you going? And why are you wearing lipstick?" Thelma's father demanded when Friday night rolled around. He'd shuffled in from the kitchen with a ham sandwich on a plate in one hand and a beer and the newspaper in the other. His red hair had gone almost white.

"I'm going on a date." Nervously, she smoothed her hair down for the third time.

"With who?" he demanded.

"Bobby Milligan. I work with him," she replied. She opened her handbag and made sure she had everything: change purse, lipstick, handkerchief, and housekeys. All set.

Her younger brothers were stretched out on the floor, and they started making smooching noises and laughing. She grinned at them, but her father waved his paper at them and told them to be quiet.

"What do you know about this guy?"

"Nothing," she admitted.

"He's not related to those Milligans over on Pomona, is he? They're a tough crowd, and I don't want you getting mixed up in that," her father said.

Thelma shook her head. "I don't think so. He's not from the city. He's from the suburbs."

"A farm boy," her father said, nodding knowingly.

Thelma wanted to roll her eyes but refrained. To her father, everything outside the city limits was farmland.

"You can ask him any questions you want when he gets here," Thelma said as the doorbell rang. "That's him now."

Her father set his plate and beer bottle down on a TV tray and laid his newspaper on his chair. He stood there, stared at the door, and pulled up his suspenders. He pressed his lips together as if irritated by the interruption to his evening routine.

Bobby stepped forward, his coat practically hanging off his sloping shoulders like an old hanger that was no longer useful. Thelma frowned at him as he stepped into the parlor, his legs going forward and his upper body hanging back, like his legs were in one room and his torso was still in the other, lagging behind him. Had she not noticed this before? She winced.

"Good evening, sir, I'm Bobby Milligan," he said, extending his hand.

That would score him points with her father. She wouldn't have to listen to his continuous rant about how none of the kids these days had any manners. She caught herself smiling.

"I hear you're a farm boy," her father said, shaking Bobby's hand.

"Huh?" Bobby said.

Thelma had to intervene or this conversation would quickly go off the rails and her father would get annoyed with Bobby.

"I told Dad that you live in the suburbs."

Bobby looked over at her as if he were seeing her for the first time, and he smiled. Thelma caught herself smiling back.

"Oh yeah, right. No, not quite a farm boy, Mr. Kempf. My father works at the bank and my mother works in the schools out there in Cheektowaga," he said.

"She a teacher?"

"No sir, she works in the lunchroom," Bobby said.

"Are you any relation to those hooligans also with the last name of Milligan, over on Pomona?" her father asked, narrowing his eyes.

Bobby turned his head halfway as if considering it, and then answered, "No sir, my dad was an only child."

This seemed to satisfy her father and before he could launch into another volley of questions, Thelma interrupted. "Bobby, we better head off. We don't want to be late for the movie. I don't know about you, but I hate when I miss the beginning."

"Let's go."

The two men shook hands again, and Thelma's father asked, "What time will you have Thelma home?"

"Well, uh, sir, if it's all right with you, I'd like to take her for a burger after the movie."

"All right, but not too late, it's a school night," her father said.

Thelma scowled at her father. First, it was a Friday night and second, she'd graduated high school almost two years ago. Surely he knew that she'd been working at the cardboard box factory. Where did he think she went every day on the bus?

Before there were any more questions or inane statements, Thelma walked toward the front door, satisfied to see Bobby following her. She didn't like him in the way that Barb seemed to swoon over men, but she was looking forward to getting out of the house for a few hours. And she'd get to go to a movie, and there'd be popcorn and Pepsi. There were lots of pluses.

Chapter Eleven

Alice

As she'd done when she arrived home for Gram's funeral, Alice decided not to go directly to the house on Star Shine Drive. Instead, after she turned off the highway and sailed over the railroad tracks, she headed west along Erie Street, toward the lake, opting for a leisurely drive around Hideaway Bay. Her cheeks hurt from smiling so much. It felt good to be back. Despite it being mid-September, the air was warm, and Alice drove with the windows down, forgoing the air conditioner. Through the canopy of trees, she caught glimpses of the lake. She sang along to the music playing on the radio, tapping her fingers on the steering wheel. When she reached the end of the road, she veered left toward Main Street and slowed her car down to a crawl to take in all the sights.

With all the boutique shops and their different-colored awnings, Main Street reminded Alice of something old-fashioned and nostalgic, something out of a wonderful fairy tale. On her left side, there was Lime's Five-and-Dime with its blue-and-white striped awning. The Hideaway Bay Olive Oil Shop with its burgundy awning stood next to it. There was a red awning with a green wreath for Ye Olde Christmas Shoppe. As she drove slowly, she passed Bev's Bookstore; the Chat and Nibble, where Granddad used to take her for breakfast; and Cabana Sally's, a restaurant and bar that overlooked Lake Erie. The Pink Parlor had the best homemade ice cream, in Alice's opinion, and that would certainly be one of her first stops. When she reached the end of Main Street, she was at the town square, a plot of green space that held the town's gazebo and the war memorial. She circled around the square and headed back toward Star Shine Drive.

When she arrived, she pulled over to the curb to look at the beach and the lake. The beach was crowded, but the lake was calm and as shiny as blue glass, the sunlight hitting off of it causing it to sparkle and shimmer. There was a gentle roll to the surf as it slid into the beach and then retreated quietly back into the lake. Gulls cried as they circled overhead, and a speedboat revved its engine, slicing across the lake, bouncing as it went.

Alice pulled back out. Gram's house was in view, and she smiled. So many memories.

It was good to be home.

1994

Nancy

Alice's mother

"Shh, shh, Alice, don't cry," Nancy said as she bounced Alice gently on her hip. Even though she was only three, Nancy wondered if her youngest had picked up on the tension in their household over the last few weeks.

"When's Daddy coming back?" Isabelle asked.

"I don't know, Isabelle," Nancy said quietly. She stopped bouncing Alice and felt her eyes pool with tears.

Dave had done a runner. Left a note on the table one morning, saying he couldn't do it anymore. Nancy had read the note a hundred times, trying to discern some hidden clue as to when he might be back. The note was currently folded neatly in half and tucked into the pocket of her bathrobe.

"But he is coming home, isn't he? Like last time?" Isabelle pressed.

"I hope so," Nancy said with a forced brightness. He'd done this before, almost four years ago. When he came back, he cried and promised he'd never leave her again. Their reconciliation had resulted in Alice. Every time Nancy looked at her youngest, she was reminded of an earlier, happier time when promises had been made. But she supposed promises were made to be broken.

"He's never coming back," Lily shouted from the doorway of the other room. She stuck out her tongue at Isabelle. Alice stopped crying, riveted to her older sisters.

"Don't you say that, Lily!" Isabelle yelled, and she chased Lily into the other room. This resulted in shrill screaming from both girls.

"Girls, please," Nancy pleaded. She went back to rocking Alice in her arms. Alice whined and cried.

Nancy wondered if Lily might be right about Dave not coming back. He hadn't been gone this long the first time.

Isabelle and Lily continued to argue in the next room, and Nancy did not have the energy to deal with them.

For the first week Dave was gone, Nancy hadn't bothered telling her parents. She'd hoped he'd come back before they noticed. But then Isabelle had inadvertently let the cat out of the bag.

Dave's sister Miriam claimed she didn't know where he'd gone, but somehow Nancy doubted that. Could not believe that no one knew the whereabouts of her husband.

There was a knock at the door.

The shrill screaming stopped, and Isabelle reappeared.

"It's Daddy, I bet," Isabelle said, running to the door, smiling.

The door opened and Nancy's parents, Junie and Paul, stepped in. Isabelle's face crumpled and she burst into tears. Lily started crying for no apparent reason, and Alice howled in her mother's arms.

Junie approached Nancy. "Not a good day?"

Nancy shook her head and started crying as well. Alice removed her hands from around her mother's neck and stretched them out toward Junie. She blubbered, "Gramma!"

Junie took Alice in her arms and hugged her.

"Okay, who wants to go for a sleepover at Gramma and Granddad's house?" Paul asked. He patted Nancy's arm and whispered, "Chin up, kiddo."

Lily's tears dried up first and she jumped up and down. She ran to Paul, wrapped her arms around his waist and said, "I do, I do!"

"Are you sure, Mom?" Nancy asked. She would have been lying if she said she wasn't relieved at the thought of an unanticipated break from three crying, fighting girls.

"Yeah, we are. You need a break," Junie said. "Pack a bag for Alice."

"Girls, get your things," Paul called out.

Isabelle stood there leaning on one foot, her arms crossed in front of her. Her bottom lip jutted out.

"Isabelle, are you coming with us?" Paul asked gently.

She scowled. "No."

"That's too bad. We were going to the five-and-dime to get some saltwater taffy," Paul said, keeping a side-eye on her.

"I can't leave. What if Daddy comes home and I'm not here?" she asked him.

Paul sighed.

"Go on with Gram and Granddad," Nancy urged. "I'll be here if Daddy should come home."

Isabelle regarded her skeptically.

"We're going to make popcorn later," Junie said, carrying Alice on her hip.

"Okay, I'll go, but Mommy, you'll call me at Gram's house if Daddy comes home?" Isabelle asked.

Nancy nodded. "Of course I will." She hated Dave then—not sure she wanted him back—because more than anyone, it was Isabelle's who was going to end up with the broken heart.

Isabelle stomped off and as she headed up the stairs, she elbowed Lily, who was coming down the staircase, her overnight bag over her shoulder and a wide smile on her tear-stained face.

"Go on, Nancy, get a bag for the baby," Junie prompted.

"Oh right," Nancy said, and she took the stairs two at a time. When she returned five minutes later, Isabelle and Lily waited at the front door with their grandparents.

"Thanks, Mom and Dad, I really appreciate it," Nancy said.

"Why don't you call one of your friends and go out for a bit," Junie suggested.

"She can't go out because Daddy might come home," Isabelle piped in.

"All right, let's go," Paul said, holding the front door open and herding them out. As the girls cleared out with her mother, her father held back and asked, his voice lowered, "Do you need any money?"

Nancy shook her head, but tears filled her eyes. "No, Dad, I'm all right."

1997

Junie

Junie ran the dustcloth along the bookshelves in the living room, making sure to get the cloth in along the grooves of the top of the books. As she went, she picked up the knickknacks to wipe them and dust along the shelves beneath them. Of all the household chores, she detested dusting the most. She'd no sooner do it than everything would be covered in dust again.

The front door pushed open, and she was startled from her reverie. It couldn't be Paul; he'd only just left to go up to the shop on Main Street to get candy for the girls' Easter baskets. Her surprise grew when she spotted Alice standing there.

"Alice? What are you doing here?" For a moment, she was alarmed. Alice was only six, and Junie wondered if Nancy knew she was here. Had she walked the three blocks by herself?

"Are your sisters with you?"

Alice shook her head and remained rooted to the spot.

Junie set down the can of furniture polish and laid the dustcloth over the top of it.

She knelt down in front of Alice and took her hands in hers, marveling as always at how small and perfect they were. "What's wrong, Alice?"

And with that, a torrent of words and tears spewed forth. Junie remained on her knees and listened intently, never taking her eyes off of young Alice's face.

"Isabelle and Lily are fighting all morning and Mommy keeps yelling and they won't stop," she said through hiccups and sobs, and when she was finished, she drew in a deep lungful of air.

It pained Junie to see Alice upset. Of the three girls, Alice was the most sensitive. Things that wouldn't bother Isabelle or Lily would bother Alice. Like the normal part of growing up: the screaming and fighting among siblings.

Junie stood and put her arm around Alice's slim shoulders. "Well, you've come to the right place, because there's no fighting or screaming here." Junie pulled a tissue from the box on the coffee table, dabbed at Alice's eyes, and then wiped the little girl's nose. She stuffed the tissue into her pocket.

"First, let me call your mother and let her know you're here, and then we'll find something fun to do," Junie said. After she rang Nancy—who was by turns harried by the incessant fighting of Isabelle and Lily and then mortified that she hadn't even noticed Alice was gone—she ushered Alice into the kitchen.

Junie felt sorry for her daughter. Raising three children by herself had not been easy, and she struggled. But Junie was grateful they all lived in Hideaway Bay. At least she and Paul could help with the rearing of the girls.

The sound of a car pulling into the driveway alerted Junie to the fact that Paul was home with the Easter goodies. Wanting to intercept him before he brought all the candy inside, she leaned down to Alice and said, "Why don't you look in the pantry and see what you'd like for a snack."

Alice nodded and ran to the pantry door, using both hands to turn the door handle.

Junie stepped out onto the porch as Paul was popping the lid on the trunk. She trotted down the steps and met him at the car as he was lifting bags out of it.

"Wait until you see what I got!" he said gleefully.

Junie smiled. Paul loved this sort of thing. He was worse at Christmas. She laid her hand on his arm and said, "Don't bring it into the house yet. We have a little visitor."

"Huh?" he asked, setting the bags back down in the well of the trunk.

The front door opened, and Alice appeared on the porch and held up a box of Ritz crackers. "Gramma, can I have these?" Her face widened in a smile when she spotted Paul. "Hi, Granddad!"

"Hey, sparrow!" he waved. When Alice disappeared back into the house, he turned to Junie. "What's going on?"

Junie gave him the condensed version and he only blanched once, at the part where Alice had walked the three blocks to their house by herself. When she was finished, he nodded. “Okay, let’s get the coloring books out.”

They walked side by side into their house. Junie figured now that Alice had walked over here by herself, she might start popping in more regularly. And that would be fine. The door was always open.

“You know what? We could take her to lunch at the Chat and Nibble and then take her to the five-and-dime afterward.”

“Sounds like a plan.”

“Our sparrow is the sensitive sort,” Paul said. “She needs to be handled with care.”

Junie smiled at him. “My thoughts exactly.”

Chapter Twelve

1963

Thelma

"Hey, Thelma, lover boy is on the phone!" Del shouted up the stairs. She was in the bathroom, applying some red lipstick while she waited for Bobby to pick her up.

"Del, I'm going to kill you," Thelma muttered as she shot down the stairs to grab the phone away from him before he could say something inappropriate to Bobby. Just last week, Mikey had answered the phone when Bobby had called and had asked him if Thelma was a good kisser. She'd clapped him good on the ears for that.

"Bobby, are you on your way?" she asked. She was anxious to get out of the house. Frank had been in one of his moods again, sitting on the bed and staring at the wall. Mikey and Johnny were in poor humor, and even good-natured Del seemed irritable. The only one who didn't seem annoyed was her father. At the first sign of spring, he'd begun sitting on the porch, going through cans of beer like they were going to bring Prohibition back.

"Hey, Thelm, I'm not coming over tonight," Bobby said casually.

"Oh? Why not?" she asked.

"Think I might stay in," he said. "I'll call you tomorrow, all right?"

"Yeah, sure."

When she hung up the phone, she went back upstairs to wipe off her lipstick. As she rounded the corner, she realized she wasn't too upset about not going out with Bobby. She didn't know if she necessarily believed him about staying in for the night, and then she realized she didn't care either way. They'd been going out for six months, and maybe the relationship had run its course. She certainly didn't feel the same way about Bobby that Junie felt about Paul. Those lovebirds were sickening sometimes. The way they looked at each other. If Bobby ever looked at her like that, she'd check him for a fever.

As she sat on the edge of the tub, wiping the lipstick off, she wondered if he was losing interest because she'd given in to him two months ago and had sex with him.

He had pleaded, and she had been curious, wanting to see what the big deal was. Afterward, the mystery revealed, she concluded she hadn't really missed out on anything.

Would he dump her now that he'd had his way with her? She didn't care so much about that part but if he were to spread rumors about her to that effect, well, she did care about that. She'd have to issue a threat, and she knew Bobby was a little bit afraid of her, so she'd drive the point home. He'd had his way with her and yes, she had allowed it, but she wasn't going to be taken for a fool.

That was all figured out, but a thought popped into her head. A very disturbing one. A fine sheen of perspiration broke out on her brow despite the fact that it was not hot outside. She sat up and stared at the tiled wall of the bathroom.

"No," she muttered. She couldn't remember the last time she'd had her period. Had it been more than a month? Yes, it had. Mikey's birthday was a month ago, and she remembered her period was due and she'd hoped it wouldn't show up and ruin the day. She'd had a whole bunch of his friends coming to the house. And the last thing she'd needed was those terrible cramps. But her cycle had never showed, not then and not since.

"Oh my God," she muttered, and staggered to her bedroom, queasiness settling in her stomach as the implications of what she had done—what they had done—and the possible consequences began to settle around her.

She made it to her bed and lay on it. There weren't a lot of options for girls like her who found themselves in the family way. Only two, really: give the baby up for adoption or get married. Neither appealed to her, but giving up her baby appealed to her the least.

She did not want to marry Bobby Milligan. The thought of possibly having to spend the rest of her life with him made her want to cry. But what choice did she have? For there was one thing she was certain of, she was not giving her baby up for adoption. This was her kid, and no one was raising him but her. If Bobby refused to marry her, she wouldn't have to worry about anything because her father would probably beat the shit out of her.

She couldn't tell Junie or Barb. Barb was away at college and although she'd written Thelma, Thelma had never responded. She wasn't the type to write letters, and she figured she'd catch up with Barb when she got home. She imagined her friends would be horrified if they knew.

Marrying Bobby Milligan was a lateral move; she'd be exchanging one set of problems for another. But she might not have any say in the matter.

A visit to her local doctor confirmed her suspicions. She ignored the egghead when he set his lips firmly together and handed her two pamphlets, one about an adoption agency and the other regarding a home for unwed mothers. Right in front of him, she tossed them into his metal wastebasket.

"I won't be giving this baby up for adoption," she said curtly.

He regarded her with what appeared to be a mixture of scorn and sadness. But Thelma Kempf paid no attention to him. The sole purpose of her visit had been to confirm her suspicions. There was no reason to linger. She lifted her chin and walked out of there.

"Where've you been?" she hissed at Bobby in the corridor at work.

Bobby looked around, embarrassed. "Keep your voice down, Thelma."

She hadn't heard from him in more than a week. She'd broken down and called him once, and his mother, no fan of Thelma's, had answered. She lectured Thelma on the impropriety of girls calling boys. It was something only loose women did. If Thelma hadn't needed Bobby, she would have laughed in the older woman's face.

"Don't tell me what to do, Bobby Milligan," she snapped. Finally seeing him face to face caused her anger to rush up from within like a geyser. He was the cause of all her current problems. Since her mother died, the male sex of the race had been nothing but trouble for her. God, she hoped this baby was a girl!

"Look, I thought we should take a break," he said.

She narrowed her eyes at him. "Do you mean to tell me that you're dumping me?" Her voice rose with each syllable. Her fury was greater than her panic over the possibility that he wouldn't marry her.

"Cool down."

Now she wanted to punch him.

"Let's talk about this," she said. "Pick me up tonight at eight."

"I can't—can't make it tonight," he said, looking up and down the hall, probably to make sure no one was listening. "Another time," he said casually.

Thelma pointed a finger in his face. "Now you listen here, Bobby Milligan. You pick me up at eight so we can discuss this, or we can discuss it here at work for everyone to hear."

Bobby blanched at this. One thing he couldn't stand was "scenes," as he called them.

He threw up his hands. "Okay, okay, I'll see you at eight."

Chapter Thirteen

Alice

Alice had been home for a week when she decided to start looking for a job in the small town of Hideaway Bay. There were only two attorney's offices. The town wasn't big enough to support any more than that. And although she had enough money in her savings, she had worked since she was sixteen and knew nothing else. Despite Lily's encouragement to take a break and catch her breath, Alice felt restless. She had channeled some of that restless energy into baking and by the end of her first week, all the counters and the kitchen table were covered with cakes, brownies, and cookies, including a batch of dog biscuits, much to Charlie's delight.

"I've gone up a size in my clothes since I got here," Lily said, standing in the doorway of the kitchen with her hands on her hips.

Alice looked around the kitchen. Every available space was covered with baked goods, and she wondered if she might have a compulsion. She shrugged and went on beating her egg whites by hand. It took a while, but it was good exercise for her arms.

Lily looked over everything and despite her comment about going up a size, she picked up a chocolate chip cookie off one of the cooling racks.

"Alice, what are we going to do with all these baked goods?" she asked, pulling the cookie in half. The chocolate chips were still warm and gooey.

"Take a plate to Simon," Alice suggested.

Lily tilted her head to one side with an expression that read *Really?* "Even he can only eat so much."

"I suppose I could give them away."

Lily nodded enthusiastically. "Tonight's Tuesday night. Thelma's group meets every Tuesday at the parish hall."

Thelma was one of Gram's two best friends since childhood. She ran an informal card club for the widows and widowers of Hideaway Bay.

"You belong to that club, don't you?" Alice asked.

The egg whites started to stiffen. She added a quarter teaspoon of cream of tartar and continued whipping.

"Sort of. I don't go every week, but I am addicted to pinochle, and if I'm free I like to go over and play cards for a little while."

Alice was glad her sister was finding her way after the death of her husband. When they'd arrived in Hideaway Bay back in May for Gram's funeral, Lily had seemed so lost. But now, after making the decision to stay, finding a job she enjoyed, and starting up a side project making and selling beach glass crafts, Lily was settling in comfortably. Alice was happy for her.

"There's also that veterans' group that meets twice a week. I'm sure they'd love a donation of baked goods," Lily added.

Alice nodded. That's what she'd do. She'd drop a few platters off tonight for Thelma's group and then she'd investigate this veterans' group.

"How'd you hear about it?"

"Simon mentioned it to me," Lily said. "His friend the Colonel runs it."

"The Colonel?" Alice asked, picturing an old man with a string tie and a walking stick.

"Colonel Jack Stirling. He's a veteran. Afghanistan. Iraq."

Alice scrunched her nose. That couldn't have been pleasant. At the very least, the veterans deserved some homemade baked goods.

"They meet at the parish hall too," Lily said, picking up another cookie. "Maybe you should bake over at their kitchen since it seems like you'd be bringing their baked goods there anyway."

"Maybe I should."

"What's the plan for your day?" Lily asked, tossing the last bit of cookie into her mouth and taking one of the dog biscuits off the counter and giving it to Charlie. The Great Dane wolfed it down in one gulp without even chewing on it. Alice raised an eyebrow but said nothing.

"When I'm done here, I plan on going to the two law offices in town and asking them if they're taking anyone on."

"Well, good luck," Lily said. She headed out the door and called over her shoulder, "Come on, Charlie, time to go to work."

"Hey, do you want to go for dinner later?" Alice called out after her.

"Sounds good. You pick the place," Lily said.

"Cabana Sally's?"

"Perfect. Bye!" The screen door at the front of the house slammed behind Lily.

After the meringue was made and spread over the mini lemon pies, Alice donned her protective goggles, started up her kitchen blowtorch, and browned the tops of the little pies. When they were finished, she pulled the goggles off and pulled the rubber band out of her hair that held a loose ponytail in place. Her hair spilled around her shoulders and she looked over her creations, satisfied.

She made herself a cup of ginger-pear tea and settled down with a cranberry-and-almond cookie. She took a bite, rolling it around on her tongue to gauge the flavor. After the second biscuit was eaten, she declared it a winner. She grabbed the recipe she'd used and made her adjustments in pen, noting the date and the measurements she used.

Then she settled in with her cup of tea and Gram's old cookbooks and pile of recipes, taking her time, going through page by page. It was a delightful way to spend the morning, and she figured the attorneys of Hideaway Bay could wait until the afternoon.

After lunch, Alice straightened up and dashed upstairs to do her hair and put on a pair of khaki pants, a nice blouse, and a pair of sandals. She didn't want to go marching in there, resume in hand, wearing shorts and sneakers. This outfit was casual but business enough for Hideaway Bay.

For one of the last weeks in September, the midday sun was bright and fierce. Alice was sorry she hadn't brought her hat as her scalp felt hot. Depending on how long she was at these two offices, she might head off to the beach and go for a swim. When she'd left the house earlier, she could see that the beach was quiet, as was to be expected with the return of school.

Her first stop was the law offices of Stodges and Hindermarsh, the firm that had handled her grandmother's will. As with her previous visit with her sisters, the air conditioning had been set on "arctic," and Alice shivered as she stepped inside the main reception room. It was a small, pleasant area with the walls painted a pale pink on top and burgundy on the bottom, bisected halfway by white chair rail. At the ceiling was white cove woodwork, and white Bahama shutters covered all the windows. There were neutral-colored club chairs and a small two-seater sofa, and several green houseplants appeared to be thriving despite the cold atmosphere.

The receptionist, whose name tag indicated she was called Amanda, looked up from her desk and smiled.

"Can I help you?"

"I was hoping to speak to one of the partners," Alice said.

"Do you have an appointment?" Amanda asked.

Alice shook her head, thinking she should have known better than to just walk in off the street without an appointment. Time was money.

"Can I ask what this is about?" the receptionist asked.

"I'm Junie Reynolds's granddaughter. Mr. Stodges handled my grandmother's will. I've recently moved back to Hideaway Bay, and I was looking for work," Alice said. To illustrate the point, she waved her resume around.

Amanda held out her hand for the resume and stood. "Let me see if he has any time. Your name?"

"Alice Monroe."

Amanda disappeared through a door behind her, and Alice got a glimpse of a short corridor with white walls. She remained standing at the reception desk.

Within minutes, Amanda returned and said with a smile, "Mr. Stodges will see you now."

This buoyed Alice, and she followed Amanda back through the door. At the end of the corridor there were two doors opposite each other with gold nameplates. Mr. Stodges's office was on the left and Mr. Hindermarsh's was on the right.

Amanda gave a quick rap on the door to the left and stepped in. Alice followed her. Amanda held the door open for Alice and after she stepped into Mr. Stodges's office, Amanda left, closing the door behind her.

Arthur Stodges was as Alice remembered him from the reading of Gram's will, smartly dressed in a business suit, crisp white shirt, and blue tie, with cropped silver hair. He was a bit younger than Gram and had mentioned that he'd been the closing attorney when they bought the house on Star Shine Drive back in 1966.

Mr. Stodges stepped out from behind his desk and smiled, extending his hand.

"Alice, it's good to see you again."

Alice shook his offered hand firmly and then sat down in one of the club chairs in front of his desk. He had her resume laid out in front of him on the desktop.

She thought back to the time when she, Isabelle, and Lily had sat here, in these very same chairs directly across from him, and learned that Gram had left them her house.

"Amanda gave me your resume," Mr. Stodges said. "She says you're looking for a job."

"I am. I've come back to Hideaway Bay after living many years in Chicago," she told him.

"Chicago's a great city," he said. He looked through her resume, finally coming to the letter of recommendation from one of the partners of the firm. Mr. Stodges scanned the page.

"Your former boss sure has written a glowing recommendation," Mr. Stodges said.

She sat up straighter in her chair, feeling encouraged.

"You certainly have some nice qualifications, Alice," he said, looking up at her and smiling.

She could almost picture herself working here in this nice, pleasant little office. What a change it would be from the offices of the firm she used to work for. Something told her that she wouldn't have to kill herself in a place like this. That she'd still be allowed to have a life outside the office. It was close by, so she could walk to work. And there were some nice restaurants and cafés on Main Street, so there'd be variety for lunch. She'd bet she wouldn't have to eat at her desk every day. Yes, this would suit her perfectly.

She was pulled back from her daydreaming by something Mr. Stodges said.

"I'm sorry?" she said, shaking her head as if to dislodge something.

"I said, you're actually overqualified," the elderly lawyer said. "Your resume is certainly impressive, but we deal mainly in wills, divorces, and bankruptcies. A few drunk driving cases and real estate closings."

"That's all right. I'd be interested in that too," she said quickly.

He smiled benevolently. "That's gracious of you to say. But the truth of the matter is, we're an old firm—been around over sixty years—and we have plenty of work for the two of us, but we're really not in a position to take on a third partner."

"I wouldn't have to be a partner, an associate position would be fine too," she said. For whatever reason, a partnership didn't seem to be in the cards for Alice. She tried not to be discouraged, but it was almost impossible not to be.

"Alice, I wish we had a spot here, I'd offer it to you in a heartbeat," he said. He was letting her down easy.

She sighed and stood. He handed her resume back to her, and she took it from him and tucked it neatly into her purse.

"Can you tell me anything about the other firm in town?" she asked.

"Ben Enright? He's not here in Hideaway Bay proper but out on the main highway. Go over the railroad tracks and hang a left onto the main highway, heading toward the city. He's in a small strip plaza right after the thruway entrance." He stood from his desk and added, "You can try him, but he's a one-man show."

She nodded. She held out her hand to shake Mr. Stodges's and thanked him for his time.

"If we're ever in a position to hire another attorney, Alice, you'll be the first phone call I make," he said, following her to the door.

"I appreciate that," she said, and she bid him goodbye and left.

She walked away from the attorneys' office, waving to Sue Ann Marchek, who was placing a sandwich board advertising the day's deals out front of the Hideaway Bay Olive Oil Company, where she worked. Sue Ann was the daughter of Gram's other childhood friend,

Barb Walsh, and she'd recently moved back to Hideaway Bay as well. She waved back and gave Alice a big smile before stepping back into the shop. When they were younger, Sue Ann used to babysit them.

Although the second law firm did not sound promising, Alice figured she had nothing to lose and besides, it wasn't like her afternoon was all booked up. But she'd need her car, so she walked back to the house, went inside to grab her keys from the crystal bowl on the small table by the door, and headed back out.

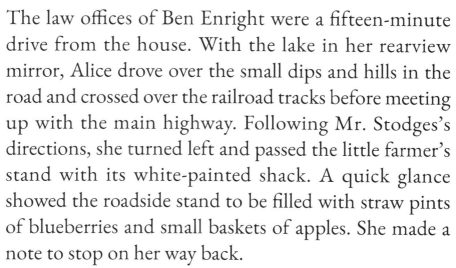

The law offices of Ben Enright were a fifteen-minute drive from the house. With the lake in her rearview mirror, Alice drove over the small dips and hills in the road and crossed over the railroad tracks before meeting up with the main highway. Following Mr. Stodges's directions, she turned left and passed the little farmer's stand with its white-painted shack. A quick glance showed the roadside stand to be filled with straw pints of blueberries and small baskets of apples. She made a note to stop on her way back.

The plaza was nothing more than a low-rent strip mall. She looked left to right, noting the occupants, all of whom shared a common flat metal awning. There was a big-box discount store, a hair salon, a shipping place, a discount shoe store, the law offices of Ben Enright, a dry cleaner, a florist, and a little café at the far end.

She parked her car in one of the spaces directly in front of the law office, noticing there were no other cars parked there, not like in front of the rest of the businesses. Some of the windows looked as if they could use a good washing, and the footpath in front of the stores was pockmarked with old gum.

She made her way to the office, noting the big plate-glass window with the words *The Law Offices of Ben Enright* painted in gold and edged in black. To the right of the window was a single column of blond bricks and next to that, a glass door with a heavy aluminum hand plate.

She pushed through, stepped inside, and looked around. She didn't know what she had stepped into, but it looked like it was a victim of terrible housekeeping. There was one main area with a reception desk, a cheap laminated version whose time had come and sadly, gone. The walls were covered with artificial paneling that was a little too eager with its shininess, and the one plant in the corner in a pot on the floor had died a long time ago, its leaves gray. In one corner of the drop ceiling, one of the rectangular tiles bore a disturbing water stain resembling a wet tea bag on a paper towel.

"Be with you in one moment," a male voice called out from an office behind the reception desk.

There appeared to be no receptionist, but the desk itself was covered with stacks of manila folders. The bookshelves behind the desk, the kind you would pick up at a discount warehouse and assemble yourself, were crammed with law books with papers and folders wedged into them.

The whole place was disheartening. She couldn't understand how anyone could operate like this.

Ben Enright—she assumed that's who it was—appeared in the doorframe, and his appearance matched the workspace around him. He was short and round, and his belly hung over his belt. He wore a white business shirt, and there was a spot on his loosened tie. He was in dire need of a shave. His hair was thick and pale blonde. Matching eyelashes framed dark brown eyes, and he was covered in freckles. It was difficult to estimate his age, but if she had to guess, she'd say he had at least ten years on her.

"Can I help you?" he asked.

Alice was afraid to ask for a job. He looked like he was more in need of a housekeeper than an associate.

"Well, um," she started, "I've recently moved back to town, and I was looking for a job."

His shoulders slumped and Alice wondered if he'd been hopeful that she was a prospective client. "What kind of job?"

"I'm an attorney," she replied.

"Did you bring a resume?" he asked.

"I did," she said, swinging her purse around until it was positioned in front of her. She dug through it, pulled out her resume, and handed it to him.

He unfolded it and began to read, heading back into his office. "Come on."

With no other choice, Alice followed him to the office at the back.

His workspace was a twin of the outer office in that it too could have been declared a disaster area. The desk was covered in stacks of manila folders and loose sheets of paper, giving it a disheveled appearance. A thick coat of grime covered the single window, but she could still make out that there was a long field of sparse trees behind the plaza. A trash can beside his desk overflowed with takeout containers, burger wrappers, and plastic coffee cups.

How could he even find anything in this mess? And once he did manage to lay his hands on whatever file he needed, how could he concentrate on his work? She wouldn't have been able to think straight. Briefly, she wondered if he even had any clients, but the number of files and piles of paperwork all over the place suggested he had, unless he liked to give the illusion of being busy . . . and messy.

"Sit down, Alice," he said. He looked up from her resume and asked, "May I call you Alice?"

"Of course," she said.

There were two chairs in front of his desk. One was occupied by piles of folders, and the other was covered in cat hair. She raised her eyebrow at this but sat down anyway on the edge of the cat chair.

Ben Enright sat in his chair on the other side of the desk, flipping to the next page of her resume and reading the letter of recommendation. He tilted his head back and forth and raised his eyebrows, his lips moving silently as he scanned the document.

He set her resume down on his desk, picked up a half-eaten hamburger whose wrapper served as a plate, and took a bite. He chewed for a moment before he spoke.

"I'm sorry, you caught me in the middle of lunch."

"Did you want me to come back?" she asked, looking over her shoulder toward the door.

"No, not necessary." He took another bite, chewed quickly, and swallowed. "Your qualifications are impressive, Alice, but I mainly work no-frills divorce cases and DWIs."

She didn't understand if he was saying there was a job in there somewhere. And she didn't know if she would take it or not. The conditions were certainly not . . . ideal.

"Are you looking for an attorney to join your firm?" she asked.

He shook his head. "Not really. But what I am looking for is an assistant."

Alice's heart sank. She didn't want to be anyone's gal Friday. It wasn't what she'd gone to college for. The other option was to drive an hour up to the city and circulate her resume there. But did she want a two-hour daily commute? She didn't think so. What she was looking for was more balance in her life. She found herself asking, "What do those duties include?"

"Well, as you can see, my office needs some organization."

That was the understatement of the year.

"Someone with a law background or a paralegal would be ideal," he said. "I'm a little bit disorganized."

"You don't say."

With that, he burst out laughing. "Look, right now I don't need an attorney, but we can talk about the assistant position if you're interested."

"Is it part-time or full-time?"

"Part-time at the moment but could go to full-time," he told her.

"What about pay and benefits?" she asked.

He launched into how he was a small, independent firm, which told her that it was going to be barely above minimum wage. Which it was. And there were no benefits except that she could make her own schedule; he didn't care when she came in.

To her own surprise, she took the job, if only to get his office organized. The law was a respectable institution and should be treated as such.

Alice didn't know who was more shocked that she accepted the position: him or her. But there it was. They agreed she'd stop in the following day and get familiar with the place.

As she was leaving—she told him not to get up, and he didn't—the door to the office opened and a man walked in using a cane, one of his legs appearing stiff. Judging by his salt-and-pepper hair and the laugh lines around his eyes, he was older than Alice by maybe ten years or so, and he smiled and nodded at her in acknowledgment. She returned the smile and as they passed each other, her going out of the office and him coming in, she heard Ben call out behind her, "Hello, Colonel, what brings you here?"

Now there could only be one Colonel in Hideaway Bay, and she assumed he was one and the same person Lily had mentioned to her earlier that morning. He was younger than she'd envisioned, but he did have a cane. She looked over her shoulder at him just as the Colonel looked over his at her. They smiled at each other again, and Alice turned her head and pushed through the door to the outside.

On her way home, she wondered what had just happened. The job was certainly beneath her ability and her experience. Not that Alice was a snob, because she wasn't. And it wasn't a great paying job, but she didn't need the money. But it was as close to the law as she was going to get in Hideaway Bay for now, and more than that, she felt compelled to help Ben Enright. He seemed overwhelmed. He was busy, which indicated he was a half-decent lawyer, or at least she hoped so. She liked that he did pro bono work for the county's legal aid department one day a week. Besides, it was only twenty hours a week, which would still leave her a lot of time to bake and to enjoy what was left of the warm weather. And who knew, maybe another job with the law would come up soon.

Alice rang Thelma later than evening and asked her if she knew anything about the veterans' group that met at the parish hall and, more importantly, would they be interested in some baked goods?

"What planet are you on that you have to ask if a man would be interested in food?" Thelma said with a laugh. "But all kidding aside, they meet on Tuesdays and Thursdays at eleven in the morning. They talk and drink coffee, and I'm sure they'd appreciate some baked goods to go with it. Colonel Stirling runs that group."

"Perfect. I'll drop some off tomorrow before I go to work," Alice told her.

"You got a job?"

Alice nodded, even though Thelma couldn't see her on the other side of the phone. "Part-time. With Ben Enright."

"You'll be practicing right here in Hideaway Bay? Congratulations! I'll start spreading the word," Thelma said.

"Not exactly," Alice said. "He's taken me on as more of an assistant. It's only temporary."

"That's what he needs. Have you seen the state of his office?"

"I have," Alice said. "I'm hoping I can help."

"I'm sure you will."

"Hey, will you come for dinner on Sunday evening?" Alice asked. She and Lily had discussed inviting Thelma and Sue Ann for dinner.

"Sure, what's on the menu?"

"Jeez, I haven't gotten that far," Alice said.

"When you figure it out, text me. I like to think about what we're going to have."

No pressure there, Alice thought, making a mental note to dash off a text as soon as she and Lily decided the menu.

The following morning, Alice assembled three platters of various baked goods: slices of banana bread, chocolate chip cookies, peanut butter fudge, cranberry-and-almond cookies, and her famous salted caramel brownies. She covered the platters with cling wrap, put them in the back seat of her car, and headed over to the parish hall, arriving fifteen minutes before the meeting was scheduled to begin.

There were a handful of cars in the parking lot. The parish hall was a low block building set right outside of Hideaway Bay proper, near the railroad tracks. She hoped she wouldn't be interrupting preparations for the meeting; she knew it was for veterans only and didn't want to intrude.

She popped her sunglasses on top of her head and carried one tray inside. In the outer vestibule, she saw the man with the cane she'd seen yesterday at Ben Enright's law offices. This had to be Colonel Stirling. He stood there, leaning on his cane, talking to a man a little bit younger than Alice, who was covered in tattoos and still sported the military-required short haircut. The young man was an amputee and had an artificial leg.

The man with the cane spotted Alice, and his eyes widened in recognition.

He held up an index finger to his companion. "Excuse me one moment, Brad." He stepped away and said to Alice, "Can I help you?"

"I'm Alice Monroe. I was told your group might be interested in some baked goods for your meetings." She held out the tray, then blushed as it occurred to her he might not be able to carry it and use his cane at the same time. But he surprised her by accepting the tray from her in his other hand.

"They look delicious," he said. "I'm Jack Stirling, by the way." Up close, his eyes were bright blue with flecks of gold. Deep lines ran on both sides of his mouth.

Gesturing with a thumb over her shoulder, she said, "I've got more in the car."

He grinned. "Bring them in. We'll eat them."

She nodded and headed back out to her car. As she pulled out the first of the two trays, she was approached by another young man wearing jeans and a T-shirt.

"The Colonel sent me out to see if you need any help," he said.

"That'd be great," she said, handing him one of the platters.

She followed him in, feeling a bit conspicuous although she didn't know why. Maybe because she felt as if she were intruding on their privacy. Maybe because she was uninvited. But they seemed friendly enough. It was a small group, only ten or twelve people, two of whom were women. Because of the small number of people and the poor acoustics, their voices boomeranged around the room.

Chairs had been placed in a loose semicircle in the middle of the hall, and there was a table to one side holding an electric coffee pot and an urn for tea. She arranged the platters of baked goods next to them, thinking she should have brought some napkins or plates. The Colonel approached her.

"Do you live here in Hideaway Bay?" he asked. He surveyed the platters on the table.

Alice nodded. "I do, for the next little while, anyway. I just arrived from Chicago. I'm over on Star Shine Drive."

"Where?" he asked with a puzzled frown. "If you don't mind me asking. It's only that I thought I knew most of the residents around here."

Alice smiled. "I live in Junie Reynolds's house. I'm her granddaughter."

"Of course!" he said. He lowered his voice and added, "I'm very sorry about your loss."

Alice could only nod, as the sympathy had made her throat tighten.

The Colonel continued. "Junie was a wonderful person. She and Thelma do—did—so much for the community."

"I know. Gram was really happy here," Alice said.

He laughed. "It's hard not to be."

As the other members of the group began to take seats in the circle, Alice figured that was her cue to leave.

"It was nice meeting you," she said.

"You too. And thanks for this." He waved his hand over the three dessert trays. "I'll make sure you get your platters back."

"No rush," she said.

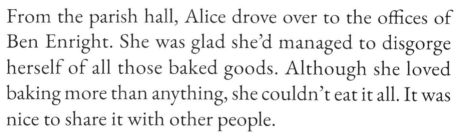

From the parish hall, Alice drove over to the offices of Ben Enright. She was glad she'd managed to disgorge herself of all those baked goods. Although she loved baking more than anything, she couldn't eat it all. It was nice to share it with other people.

The parking lot of the strip mall had a few cars parked in it, most of them in front of the big-box discount store. She pulled in next to a beat-up older-model sedan in front of the law offices. She guessed this was probably Ben's car, if his office and his manner of dress were anything to go by.

When she entered the office, she spotted Ben at his desk with a young man seated across from him. Ben saw her, his eyes widened in surprise, and he returned his attention to the young man.

Alice stood there with her hands on her hips, not sure where to start. The place was a mess. It was then she noticed there were no filing cabinets. The office could be tidied up quickly if things could be filed away. For the life of her, she could not understand how he could keep things straight in these circumstances. She thought she'd start with the reception desk and chair; both were covered in stacks and piles of folders and papers. It would take her about two months to go through every piece of paper and file. If she started with the desk and the chair, then at least she'd have a place to operate from. She picked up one set of files from the desk, noting the dust and grime that covered the area.

Sighing and seeing that Ben was still busy with his client, Alice popped out of the office and walked along the footpath over to the discount store, in search of cleaning supplies.

She returned twenty minutes later carrying a plastic bag of supplies in one hand and a newly purchased bucket filled with more supplies in the other. As she walked in, Ben was escorting his client out. He had his hands in his pockets, looking as disheveled as he had yesterday.

"Now remember, Chris, this was just an isolated, regrettable incident, that's all. Own up to it, take your punishment, and don't make the same mistake again. Because I can assure you, if you end up killing someone, the guilt will consume you."

Alice hoped Ben wasn't speaking from experience. She set down the bag and the bucket by her desk.

The young man nodded and said quietly, "Thanks, Ben."

"No problem, I'll see you at the courthouse."

When he left, Ben said, "DUI. First-time offense. Hopefully his last."

She nodded.

Ben scratched the back of his head and laughed. "To be honest, I didn't think you were serious about working here. I'm surprised you showed up."

"Why?" she asked with a frown.

"I thought this job would be beneath you. You certainly are overqualified."

Alice didn't take offense at his honesty. "It's not beneath me. If it were, I wouldn't be here."

"I kind of figured that out in the last few minutes," he said.

"Look, I know you don't need another attorney, but I can help you get all these files organized, and I know how they should be filed," she offered.

Ben put his hands in his pockets and rocked back and forth on his heels. He glanced around the mess that was his office. "If you can get this place organized, you'll get a prize."

Alice laughed. Despite his untidy appearance and messy workspace, she couldn't help but like the guy.

She regarded him for a moment and said, "I honestly don't know how you're able to find anything in here. How do you manage?"

He laughed. "I know it looks disastrous, but I prefer to call it organized chaos."

"More like disorganized chaos," she said with her hands on her hips. Her former bosses at the law firm came to mind, and she knew they'd be appalled at the state of things here. But that was okay; they were in Chicago and as far away as possible.

"The funny thing is, I look at it from this viewpoint and I know where everything is. I can lay my hand on a file in an instant." He snapped his fingers to illustrate his point. "There is a logic to it."

Alice folded her arms against her midsection. "The logic is illogical."

He didn't seem perturbed but simply shrugged. "It's a conundrum, for sure."

"However you define it, we need to overhaul it," she said.

"Maybe only tweak it."

"Well, right now I have nowhere to sit, so we'll have to do a bit more than tweak," she said. There was a sense of hesitation on his part, and she wondered if he was a hoarder. She hated to think what his home looked like.

"I better get started, I'm on the clock," she joked.

"Jeez, Alice, don't you think cleaning is beneath you?" he asked.

"Now who's being a snob?"

He laughed.

"I would like to purchase some four-drawer file cabinets for the space," she said.

"Oh," he said, blanching.

Suspecting that it might not be in his budget, Alice suggested, "How about I purchase them, and you can pay me back either in my weekly pay or monthly or whatever suits you."

His easy smile returned, and he said, "That sounds doable." His gaze bounced around at the burgeoning mess that was his office. "I'll let you get on with it."

Chapter Fourteen

Thelma

Thelma stood on her porch, ready for when Bobby would pull up to the curb around eight. She'd been filled with dread most of the day that he wouldn't show up. It annoyed her to no end that the possibility of her keeping her baby was dependent solely on the actions of Bobby Milligan. She swore to herself several times that going forward, she would never put herself in a position to be dependent on a man again. Never.

"Isn't Bobby coming in?" her father asked. He stood at the screen door, opened it, and stepped out. And like he always did, he looked to the left up the street, turned his head, looked right down the other side of the street and, seeming satisfied, looked straight ahead, his gaze settling on the house across the street.

Thelma tapped her foot against the porch floor and glanced at her wristwatch. It had been her mother's; Thelma had taken her mother's jewelry box as it meant nothing to the rest of them. There were a few pieces that stood as a reminder that she did indeed at one time have a mother. She wished she were here now. She could certainly use some guidance.

"Haven't seen Bobby around here much lately," her father said.

"He's been busy," Thelma muttered. It came back to her that Bobby had said he had plans tonight. He'd been lying low for the past week, and she wondered if he had started dating someone else. She'd get to the bottom of that, too, before the night was over.

"Maybe you could try to be a little nicer to him," her father said. "He seems like a decent enough sort of fella, and he has a job. What more could you ask for? You'll get farther with honey than vinegar."

Thelma was about to round on him when Bobby pulled up in his '53 De Soto. Why was it that she was the one that had to change? Why couldn't some of the men change? Be nicer, as her father had said.

She wished she didn't need Bobby, but that's the way it was. No marriage, and the baby would have to be placed for adoption. She could raise the baby by herself, right here in her father's home—he wouldn't throw her out, he needed her too much. She'd given that some thought.

But her child would grow up and be labeled a "bastard," and there'd always be whispers behind their backs for the rest of their lives. That wasn't good enough for her or her child.

"All right, Dad, I won't be late," she said, skipping off the porch as Bobby got out of the car.

She didn't want Bobby to start talking to her father. Invariably they'd end up talking about baseball, and usually it was a conversation she loved to partake in, but not tonight. Tonight, she needed to take care of business.

"Hey, Mr. Kempf, how are you doing?" Bobby called.

What was wrong with his voice? Thelma wondered. He sounded very "woe is me." *Well, just wait*, she thought.

"Did you catch the game last night?" her father asked Bobby.

"I did. It was a real barn burner." Bobby started to make his way up the driveway toward the porch. Thelma intercepted him, took hold of his arm, and steered him around.

"What?" he asked. "I was going to shoot the breeze with your father."

"Another time. We've got things to discuss." *And besides*, she thought, *once we're married, you can talk to him all you want.*

"Bye, Mr. Kempf," Bobby called out with a half-hearted wave.

He opened the car door for Thelma, and she slid in. As he walked around to the driver's side, she undid the button at the top of the side zipper of her skirt. When it was released, the tightness left, and she was able to breathe a little easier.

When Bobby got behind the wheel, he turned to her and asked, "So what did you want to talk about?"

She let out a breath through pursed lips. "Not here. Let's go somewhere else."

"Want to grab a burger?" he asked.

She shook her head. This wasn't a conversation to be had in a public place. And hopefully she'd be back home in no time. It made her a little sick to know that she had no choice but to marry this man. And to be honest, he would probably feel the same way when he found out. Finally, she said, "Go to Botanical Gardens and we can talk."

He nodded, started the car, which always took three tries, and looked over his shoulder before pulling out.

The Botanical Gardens was a park located roughly ten blocks from Thelma's house. Neither spoke during the entire ride over. As they drove into the park, they came face to face with the tri-domed Victorian glass conservatory, then, following the route of traffic, Bobby veered right and eventually pulled off to the side of the road and stopped beneath a giant weeping willow. In the distance, there was a small bridge, and Thelma spotted a couple leaning over the railing and throwing something into the water. They stood next to each other, their sides touching. At one point, the girl turned to the guy, brushed her hair away from her face, and laughed. For a split second, Thelma wished she was that girl and not the girl in the serious predicament that she was in.

"What did you want to talk about?" Bobby asked.

"I'm pregnant," Thelma blurted out. There was no sense in beating around the bush. She studied Bobby's face for his reaction.

All the color leeched out of his face and Thelma didn't think it was possible, but he looked paler than pale.

"Are you sure?" he asked.

"Yes. I've already been to the doctor," she said.

"So now the doctor knows?" he asked, panic in his voice.

"He was there, and he did perform the test," Thelma said through gritted teeth.

Bobby burst out crying.

Thelma looked up toward the ceiling of the car and let out a long, deep breath. *Oh no, not a crybaby*, she thought. *Please, anything but that.*

"I've been seeing Sheila—"

Thelma's head pivoted sharply. "Sheila Dunbar? From the office?" Anger coursed through her. Not only had he dumped her, but he hadn't bothered to tell her and had quickly moved on to someone else.

"She's a real nice girl," he said.

She couldn't believe him. Here she was pregnant, by him, and he was going to sing the praises of his new girlfriend.

"She doesn't say boo," Thelma said. She knew of the girl. When she'd first started working at the box factory, she'd filled out all her paperwork with Sheila. She'd been quiet but efficient. Kind of plain looking. Nothing stood out.

"Look, we'll have to get married," Thelma said.

If she'd thought he looked pale before, he'd now gone ghost white. Even his lips were white. He looked as if he was going to throw up. Apparently, marriage hadn't popped into his mind even though it was the decent thing to do. For the first time, Thelma was really scared. She had figured he'd marry her, offer right away. But he didn't. That began to sink in.

"Can't you give it up for adoption?" he asked.

"I'm not giving my baby up for adoption to be raised by someone else," Thelma said sharply. She wasn't going home until he agreed to marry her. "It's your child too, don't forget that."

"I don't think I want to get married," Bobby said.

"What?" Thelma said. She realized that it wasn't marriage in general, but it was her. Bobby didn't want to marry her. It amazed her how only a few months ago, he kept trying to push her skirt up, his hand roaming over her thigh. Well, as her mother used to say, the piper had to be paid.

"When's it due?"

"Stop calling it 'it.' I'm due in five months," she said.

"That soon? Again, I think you should give it up," Bobby repeated.

"No," she said firmly. "Whether you marry me or not, I'm keeping my baby. Make no mistake. And if you don't marry me, I will go into that office and tell your sweet Sheila that you've put me in the family way and then dumped me. Didn't do right by me. And everyone and their brother will know that you're the kind of guy who gets girls in trouble and walks away."

Bobby cried harder.

"So, here's what's going to happen. Tomorrow, we'll apply for our marriage license, get blood tests or whatever you have to do. We'll have to leave work early," Thelma told him. "When we have everything sorted, we'll go downtown to the justice of the peace and get married. Hopefully within a few days."

"That soon?"

"Well, yes, I'm going to be showing very soon," she said tightly, rolling her eyes.

They both went quiet and after a few minutes, she said, "You can take me home."

"Where will we live?" he asked.

"I'll find an apartment for us," she said. "Between the two of us, we should be able to afford rent and utilities."

"The apartments would be cheaper out in the suburbs," he said. "We could live near my parents, and they could help out with the baby."

Although she was relieved that he was now thinking in terms of the three of them, she did not want to live anywhere near his parents.

"We need to live in the city. I have to be near my father and my brothers," she said.

"Maybe we could move in with your father," he said.

Thelma didn't want that either. She wanted to get out of that house.

"We'll discuss it later," she said. She was tired and wanted to go home and go to bed. The effort of the conversation had cost her, and she wanted to put it behind her now. There was some relief knowing that he would marry her even if he didn't want to. After they were married, he could do what he wanted. She didn't care.

They didn't speak on the drive back to Thelma's house. When he pulled up to the curb, he put the car in park and she told him, "No need to come in."

"I was going to ask your father for permission to marry you," he said.

She was touched by the gesture, but she didn't want to drag this out. She wanted to be married and for it to be over with. Besides, she was afraid of her father's reaction when they told him they would be getting married in the next week.

In the meantime, she'd go up into the attic and start sorting through all the old clothes, bring down those that could be used for a baby. They'd have to be washed or cleaned up.

There was a lot to do and not a lot of time to do it.

When she stepped through the front door, her father was sound asleep in the chair, and her two youngest brothers were stretched out on the floor on their bellies, watching television. She picked up the wanted section of the newspaper, grabbed a pencil from the kitchen, and went upstairs to her bedroom. She plopped down on the bed, on her back, pencil to her lip, and she began her search for an apartment for her and Bobby.

It remained to be seen whether Thelma's father would show up to her wedding. He grumbled something about not wanting to take any time off from work. He'd probably already figured out the reason they were getting married. Even Del pestered her with "What's the rush?" Frank only looked at her and said nothing, and Mikey and Johnny continued to make smooching noises.

The following evening after her father came home from work and the dinner had been served, she took the car out to see Uncle Johnny and Aunt Linda. She would have liked them to come to the wedding. But maybe they'd hmm and haw too when they did the math and realized things didn't add up.

Aunt Linda's face was full of surprise when she opened her front door and saw Thelma standing there. Immediately, she pulled her niece into her embrace and hugged her tight.

"I'm glad you came over, but Johnny isn't here. He's down at the marina," she said, holding the door open for her. Thelma had heard that Uncle Johnny had taken up fishing in the last few years.

She stepped inside her aunt's house. It had been years since she'd been there. The furniture was all floral, and there were multiple cabinets housing all sorts of ceramic and fine china knickknacks. That wouldn't be for Thelma. Too much dusting.

Her aunt invited her to sit down, and Thelma took the center cushion of the sofa. This was a new piece; it hadn't been here when Thelma was last there.

Linda hurried off to the kitchen and put on the kettle. After the tea was made, she brought it out on a tray. There were matching cups and plates with cake on them. Thelma thought that was nice; someday she'd like to have a set of dishes where none of them were chipped or mismatched.

"What brings you out here? Wait until Johnny finds out you were here." Linda beamed.

Thelma wanted to kick herself for not coming out sooner. As soon as she'd gotten her driver's license at eighteen, this should have been her first stop. Uncle Johnny and Aunt Linda had always been good to them, and it wasn't their fault that her father was an oaf. Besides, Uncle Johnny was her mother's brother, and she didn't have too many connections left to her mother.

Thelma took a deep breath. "I'm getting married."

Linda put down her teacup and broke into a big, generous smile. She clapped her hands. "That's wonderful! Who's the lucky fella?"

"Bobby Milligan. I met him at work," Thelma said.

Aunt Linda went on about how weddings in the fall were so nice as it wasn't too hot, and no one wanted to look at a sweaty bride on her big day. Thelma had laughed at this.

"Actually, we're getting married Monday downtown at the justice of the peace," Thelma explained.

Linda's face went blank and then she asked, "How long have you been engaged?"

Thelma sighed. "About three days."

Linda stared at her and by her expression, Thelma could see that the pieces were quickly falling into place. Before she kicked her out of her home, Thelma said hurriedly in a somewhat shaky voice, "I wanted to know if you and Uncle Johnny would come. To my wedding, that is." She didn't know why, but she wanted someone from her family there. It was important to her.

Linda didn't say anything. She stood, and Thelma thought *This is the point where she kicks me out of her house*. But Linda didn't do that. She came around the coffee table, sat down on the couch, and took Thelma's hands in hers.

"Your uncle and I would love to go to your wedding. Nothing would make us happier."

Her kindness made Thelma want to cry. It took all her resolve and courage not to. She gritted her teeth hard and blinked the tears away. For the first time since the whole ordeal began, she didn't feel as anxious about it.

Aunt Linda made more tea and brought out more cake. "There is one thing, Thelma."

Thelma's cup paused midair and for a brief moment, she wondered if Aunt Linda was going to offer to raise her baby. No one was raising this child but her. That was the one thing she was certain of.

"What are you going to wear for your big day?"

Thelma shrugged. "Haven't decided. I'll look in my closet and see what I have there."

Her aunt sipped tea delicately from her china cup and seemed to consider this. She set her cup down on the coffee table and said, "If it's all right by you, Thelma, I'd like to buy you a nice dress for your wedding day."

"Aunt Linda, that isn't necessary," Thelma said hurriedly. She didn't want her aunt spending any money on her. She only wanted them in attendance.

Her aunt looked at her and smiled. "I'd really like to do this. I could pick you up Saturday morning and we could go get something nice and suitable."

"You don't have to . . ."

"I know I don't, but it would give me great pleasure," Aunt Linda said, her eyes bright.

Thelma decided it might be nice to have a new dress for the occasion, somehow mark the day as special. Junie was having a big wedding in the fall. And a hotel at a reception. There wouldn't be any of that for Thelma. She wasn't bitter about it; it was just one of those things.

Aunt Linda did pick Thelma up on Saturday morning and took her downtown to a dress shop. In the end, they chose a smart navy dress, which Thelma planned on getting a lot of use out of after the baby was born and she got her figure back to where it was supposed to be.

Chapter Fifteen

Alice

Alice settled into a nice routine of working and baking. She donated the baked goods to Thelma's group and the Colonel's group. If there were any coffee mornings to raise donations for a charitable cause, she baked for them as well. She spent her evenings sitting on the porch, researching information about turning Gram's house into an inn. Scouring the internet, she downloaded tons of brochures and information sheets of beachside inns, hotels, and bed-and-breakfasts across the nation, getting an idea of prices and what was on offer. She still hadn't mentioned it to Lily. She figured it was best if she researched the idea first to see if it was even feasible.

On her second week at work, Alice arrived at the strip mall to see that the lights were on inside the office, but the door was locked. She knocked and waited. When there was no reply, no appearance of Ben to let her in, she looked around the parking lot. His car, the older-model sedan she'd noticed on her first visit, was parked where it had been when she left the previous afternoon. She frowned and, tenting her hands over her eyes, she pressed against the glass door and peered inside. The light was definitely on in Ben's office. She stepped back, pulled out her phone, and called the office number. It rang inside until the voicemail picked up. All the while there was no movement in Ben's office.

"Everything all right?" said a voice behind her.

Alice spun and came face-to-face with the Colonel, looking casual in a blue chambray shirt and a pair of khaki-colored trousers.

"Oh, hi," she said. She rubbed her forehead. "Are you here to meet with Ben? His car is here, but he doesn't seem to be in the office."

"I am." He looked toward the parking lot and swung his gaze back to the office, peering inside through the glass door. Without a word, he fished a set of keys out of his pocket, found the one he wanted, and inserted it into the lock.

"Should you be doing that?" she asked. It seemed a bit forward to her. Almost presumptive. "I mean, he's probably just stepped out for a minute."

The Colonel unlocked the door and pushed it open, allowing her to go in first. "Unfortunately, this is not the first time I've had to access the office."

"Why do you have keys?"

He regarded her for a moment and said, "Because he trusts me."

She was about to question him further when he brushed past her, heading toward Ben's office. Over his shoulder, he said to Alice, "I can count on your discretion?"

"Of course, but why—"

He stopped inside the doorway of Ben's office, and she joined him. Ben was sprawled out, unconscious, at his desk, still wearing yesterday's clothes. She frowned, trying to make sense of the situation. There was a lingering scent of sweat and stale beer in the room.

Oh.

"Ben. Ben." The Colonel shook him several times to rouse him.

Ben lifted his head from his arms and mumbled something incoherent. His head lolled before collapsing back onto his arms. He continued to mutter into his arms, but what he said was incomprehensible.

The Colonel stood with his hands on his hips. "What are we going to do with you, Ben?"

"Has he ever done this before?" Alice asked.

"Yes, but it's an irregular occurrence."

"Has he gotten help for this . . ." She felt she didn't know Ben well enough to define his situation. If it was irregular, like every few years, maybe he was someone who couldn't handle his drink. If it was more frequent, maybe it was an addiction. But what did Alice know—her area of expertise was the law, not substance abuse.

"What should we do?" she asked.

"I'll take care of it," the Colonel said.

That said a lot about him as a friend, she thought.

"I'd like to help," she offered. "If I could."

The Colonel considered her for a moment. "You're not going to quit on him?"

She frowned and shook her head. "No, why would I?"

He made a point of looking around the office. The appearance of the place had improved, but there was still a way to go toward efficient organization. "Because his employees don't usually last too long."

Alice shrugged. What did he want her to say? The situation wasn't ideal but after finding him in this state, it was apparent he needed some help. She couldn't jump ship.

The Colonel broke into a lopsided grin. “You must be made of sturdy stuff, Alice.”

She blushed at the compliment. She nodded toward Ben. “So now what?”

“I’m going to take him home,” he said. “I’ll pull my car up to the front door and between the two of us, we should be able to get him in.”

“What about when you get him home?” Alice said.

He thought for a moment. “I’ll figure it out when I get there. If the neighbor’s around, he usually gives me a hand.”

“Why don’t I go with you and then you can drop me back here,” she suggested, and she added hurriedly, “That’s if you don’t mind.”

He shook his head. “Not at all. When Ben sobers up, I’ll talk to him about getting you some keys.” He looked around the office and said, “If this should happen again, if you come into work and find him in this condition, you can call me. He can’t stay here like this when he’s got a practice to run.”

“Sure,” Alice said.

“You’re an attorney, aren’t you? Chicago, I think Ben said.”

“Yes, there’s reciprocity between New York and Illinois.”

“That would be handy if you ever needed to step in for Ben.”

Prior to now, Alice would have dismissed that thought but looking at Ben passed out over the top of his desk, she had to agree with the Colonel.

"Well, we better get him home. Ben doesn't live too far from here."

As the Colonel left, he leaned on his cane, and Alice wondered how they'd get Ben into the car. But she understood that he had done this before. She would follow his lead.

The Colonel pulled his car up to the front of the building and left it idling. He came back inside and leaned his cane against the desk.

"Come on, Ben," he said, shaking him on the shoulders. There was some mumbling but no movement or shifting in the chair.

Alice stood on one side of Ben and looked across at the Colonel.

"Let's get him under his shoulders and stand him up," he suggested.

She put up her hand. "Wait a minute. Let's make it easy for ourselves." She glanced down at Ben's chair. It had casters on it.

"Let's wheel the chair to the front door. That way, the distance we have to carry him is less," she suggested.

The Colonel smiled. "I guess you'll be the brains of this outfit."

Alice laughed.

Between the two of them, they managed to pull Ben back from the desk, stabilize him in the chair, maneuver it out from behind the desk, and roll it toward the front of the office.

"Well, thank goodness it's a small office," Alice said, breathless from the weight of the man in the chair.

"Thank goodness, indeed," the Colonel said. He leaned against the chair for support, his cane hanging off the arm.

At the front door, they hesitated.

"I'm trying to keep his privacy and dignity intact—" he glanced at Ben. "Such as it is."

She nodded. "Let's roll the chair out, stand him up, and put him in the car."

"Okay."

Alice stepped in front of the chair and held the door open with her leg. She looked around. There were people going into the big-box discount store but not too many. In the immediate vicinity there was no one around. She pulled the front of the chair by the arms while the Colonel pushed it from behind.

She opened the passenger-side door of the Colonel's car and between the two of them, they managed to stand Ben up. The chair rolled backward slightly and, holding Ben beneath his arms, they turned him until he faced away from the front seat. She noticed the Colonel grimacing with the effort to get Ben into the vehicle.

Once he was in, Alice picked up his legs and swung them around until they were in the car. She stood, wiping an errant curl off her forehead.

As the colonel locked up Ben's office, Alice slid into the back seat. They kept the conversation to a minimum on the way to Ben's house, a bungalow located on a side road off the main highway, no more than ten minutes from the plaza.

Ben's next-door neighbor was outside, cutting his grass. When he spotted the Colonel and Alice trying to get Ben out of the car, he turned off his lawnmower and trotted over to assist.

The neighbor was sixtyish and built like a linebacker, all squares and rectangles. His forehead was a long rectangle while his chin was square. His trunk was wide and rectangular. A pink polo shirt hung off his solid frame and over a pair of floral board shorts.

"Baddie, this is Alice Monroe, she's Ben's new assistant," the Colonel introduced them. "Alice, this is Baddie Moore."

"Great to meet you, Alice, I'm Ben's stepfather, so this isn't my first rodeo," he said with a nod toward Ben. He shook Alice's hand, dwarfing it in his. "I was married to his mother, Marlene, for five years. Best five years of my life. Anyway, I promised Marlene I'd look after him after she died. So, here we are."

Alice smiled. Ben was lucky to have him.

"I'll take it from here," said Baddie. "Come on, buddy, let's get you inside and you can sleep it off."

He hoisted Ben up over his shoulder, and the Colonel and Alice followed him into the house. He seemed to know where to go and hauled Ben to a back bedroom.

Alice stood in the front room of the house and looked around. Surprisingly, it was relatively neat. But then there wasn't that much to mess up. The front room had a sofa and television and a bookshelf. There weren't any books on the shelves, but there were vinyl albums and stacks of CDs. The kitchen was another story. It was a dated '70s kitchen complete with loud wallpaper: oranges against a bamboo background. The avocado-colored appliances had circled from fashionable to out-of-date to horrid and swung back to retro. Dishes littered the sink. She moved to load the dishwasher when she was startled by a chirping noise. Her gaze followed the sound until it landed on a towel-covered cage in the corner. Gently, she removed the towel to find a peach-colored canary hopping from perch to perch, chirping wildly.

"Hello, little friend," Alice cooed. There was a water tray attached to the inside of the cage, but it was dry, and there was no food in the dish. Quickly, she remedied that by figuring out how to remove the water and food dishes without breaking them. At the sink, she rinsed out the water reservoir and filled it with fresh water.

She attached it to the cage and went on the hunt for birdseed.

The Colonel popped his head into the kitchen.

Alice closed the cabinet she was exploring. “I’m looking for birdseed to feed the bird.”

“Back hall.”

Alice popped out back with the food tray in her hand. The bag of birdseed leaned against the wall near the back door. She wasn’t sure how much to give him, so she filled it only halfway. She attached it to the bird’s cage and asked the Colonel, “How’s Ben doing?”

“He’ll be okay,” he said.

They were interrupted by the reappearance of Baddie, who filled the doorway.

“I’ll keep an eye on him,” he said. Not only was he big but he was loud and blustery. “Thanks for bringing him home.”

After the Colonel dropped her back at Ben Enright’s office, Alice went to work, continuing to organize the office and answer the phone the odd time it rang. She decided that although the job wasn’t ideal, she was needed here.

Chapter Sixteen

1963

Thelma

Aunt Linda and Uncle Johnny stood on the steps of city hall in the blazing sunshine as Thelma and Bobby crossed the street from the McKinley monument. After being embraced by her aunt and uncle, Thelma accepted the small green box Linda handed her. Inside was the prettiest corsage, and Thelma's mouth dropped open at the kind gesture. Aunt Linda took the corsage from the box and pinned it above Thelma's right breast.

"Every bride should have some flowers on her wedding day."

Uncle Johnny had tears in his eyes and said, "I wish your mother were here."

So do I, Thelma thought. *Every day.*

When Bobby had arrived on time at the house to pick her up, Thelma's foremost emotion had been a sense of relief. This was happening. They were going to get married, and she'd be able to keep her baby.

Bobby's parents flanked him as if they were protecting him. His mother stood with her lips pursed as if she were sucking on a lemon. His father remained stern. Neither of them acknowledged Thelma. When Aunt Linda tried to engage with Mrs. Milligan, Mrs. Milligan replied curtly, "This is nothing to celebrate. It's a shameful day."

"Aw, come on now," Uncle Johnny said in his usual good-natured way.

Thelma didn't care one bit that her future mother-in-law didn't like her. As far as she was concerned, after today, she'd never have to see them again. But she didn't like Mrs. Milligan speaking to Aunt Linda like that. Bobby stood there, shoulders drooped, looking like he wanted to be anywhere else but there. Looking like a man condemned to his fate.

They went inside, and Thelma looked around for her father. She tried not to let it bother her when she didn't see him. She'd thought for sure he'd come. It was the only time that day she would feel tears in her eyes.

Thelma and Bobby were called into the dark-paneled office of the justice of the peace. Aunt Linda served as her witness, and Bobby's father served as his. Mr. Milligan managed to lob off a parting shot right before the short ceremony began.

"I'm standing for him to make sure he does the right thing. The Milligans own their mistakes," he said proudly.

If one more person referred to her or her baby as a mistake, Thelma was going to start knocking heads together.

The justice of the peace stood in front of Bobby and Thelma as they faced one another. Thelma heard a noise behind her, and she turned her head and spotted her father slipping through the door. He'd put on the only suit he owned, the one he last wore for her mother's funeral. He looked old and tired. He nodded to Thelma and stood at the back of the room.

It was all right now. She could get married. Everything was in place.

As soon as the ceremony was over, her father slipped back out the door.

She looked at the thin gold band on her finger and a sense of optimism filled her. Maybe she and Bobby would be okay. Maybe one day, after the baby arrived and they continued to work, they might be able to have a house of their own. Maybe there'd even be more children. Because that was one thing Thelma knew she was good at: raising children.

The six of them gathered outside, and Bobby's mother kept looking at her watch. She said nothing to Thelma.

Aunt Linda announced, "I've made reservations for six at the Royal Pheasant downtown."

Thelma looked at her, gape-jawed. The plan had been to go back to her house and pack up some things. They couldn't get into their new apartment until the first of the month, so Thelma was still living at home and Bobby would stay with his parents. She hadn't thought to do anything after the ceremony to mark the occasion.

"We won't be joining you," Mrs. Milligan said.

Aunt Linda did not argue with her or try to convince Bobby's parents to join them. She said sweetly, "No problem, I'll change the reservation to four."

Bobby's parents left without another word. Thelma was relieved that they'd opted out; she wouldn't have to look at their sour faces across the table.

Thelma was more in awe of the restaurant than her actual marriage. She kept looking around, feeling out of place. When she looked through the menu, her eyes widened at the prices. There was no way they could afford this. Across the table from her, Bobby's gaze was frozen as he must have discovered the prices too.

"Now, this is our treat," Uncle Johnny said. "Order anything you want."

Despite her concern over the cost, Thelma ordered the steak after much encouragement from her aunt and uncle. It was only one day and she was going to enjoy herself, she decided. A lot of ground beef and chicken was consumed in the Kempf household. Uncle Johnny ordered a bottle of bubbly, as Aunt Linda called it. It was Thelma's first taste of champagne, and she rather liked it: it was light and fizzy and bubbly.

In the end, she was glad she went with the steak. It was so tender and delicious that she wanted to cry. She didn't know which she appreciated more: the taste of the steak or the fact that she didn't have to cook her own dinner for once. She could definitely get used to that.

Four months later, Thelma stood in the dairy aisle at the Park Edge grocery store and rubbed her belly as the baby kicked her several times in a row. She put milk, butter, and a carton of eggs into her cart and wheeled away. She looked down at her hand. Her once slim hands were swollen, and the thin gold wedding band Bobby had slipped on her finger months ago was now so tight she was no longer able to remove it. She felt heavy and cumbersome, she had a double chin, and her ankles were swollen—or at least they had been when she could still see them past her huge belly. She wanted it to be over with. She wanted her old body back.

She finished her grocery shopping, and the bag boy bagged all her groceries after she directed him where to put what. She liked all the dairy products in one bag and the dry and canned goods in another. She was sure he appreciated when she told him to put the eggs on the bottom so they wouldn't shift and break.

As she wheeled her cart out of the store, all she could think about was that after she'd put all her groceries away, she could put her feet up and take a short nap before Bobby came home from work.

It turned out that marriage to Bobby was more work than she anticipated. She was still going over to her father's house every day to get the dinner on, and it was easier if Bobby came over there to eat, because she wasn't cooking twice.

It took her father some time to get over the initial shock of their marriage. But within a month, Thelma's bump had grown considerably, and her father had been able to put two and two together. He remained silent on the subject.

"Thelma?"

Thelma turned in the direction of the voice and came face-to-face with Stanley Schumacher. Immediately, she reddened. She didn't know why she was embarrassed in front of him but for whatever reason, she was. People weren't stupid. She'd only been married a few months, and now she sported this huge bump in front of her. The reason for the marriage was obvious. The whole situation would certainly cure Stanley of his undying love for her. She was sure of that. No one wanted a loose woman for a wife.

"Thelma, how are you doing?"

She shrugged, trying to appear casual as if all the recent events of her life didn't bother her. *Never let them see you down*.

"You're looking well," he said.

"Are you being smart?" she snapped.

"No, Thelma, come on, you know me better than that," he said evenly.

She didn't know what to say. It felt awkward and all she wanted was to go home, but she couldn't seem to move her feet. "I got married to Bobby Milligan a few months ago." She knew he already knew as Junie had run into him and told him, but she said it for lack of anything else to say.

He nodded. "I know." He paused and looked around the Park Edge parking lot. "Bobby's not good enough for you, Thelma," Stanley said.

She'd arrived at that conclusion way before Bobby ever slipped that gold band on her finger.

"Stanley, that's my husband, don't speak against him," she said. The word "husband" still felt foreign on her tongue.

"Why didn't you come to me?" he asked. His pockmarked face was earnest.

She didn't understand. What would he have done, thrown her a baby shower? "Why? Why would I have come to you?"

"Because I would have married you in a heartbeat and raised your child as my own," he said. He shook his head as if disgusted with her and headed off inside the grocery store.

Thelma stood there for a moment, gripping her cart full of groceries, stunned. After a minute, she collected herself and pushed the cart toward her car. Shaking, she loaded her paper bags full of groceries into the back seat, then climbed into the front seat, maneuvering her big belly behind the steering wheel. She laid her head on the steering wheel and sobbed.

"It'll be good for you to get out," Bobby said. He sat below Thelma on the front step of her father's house. He leaned back and rubbed her leg.

"I know I promised Junie, but I'm not in the mood," she said. She was still upset about seeing Stanley earlier at the Park Edge. It had left her feeling upside down. It had her second-guessing everything, including all her decisions.

"Come on, I'll drive you over there," he said.

Reluctantly she stood, thinking she'd only go over and stay for a bit. She eyed Bobby, wondering why he was being so agreeable. Maybe he wanted to get rid of her.

It was a beautiful fall evening. It would probably be the last round of warm weather before winter arrived.

Two weeks ago, they'd gone to Junie and Paul's wedding, and Bobby had asked her on the drive home afterward if she wished she had had a wedding like that. She'd responded irritably that what was done was done. There was a part of her that didn't feel like she deserved a big affair. After all, she wasn't in love with Bobby, and she was pretty sure he wasn't in love with her. She supposed if they'd had a big church wedding and a reception at a hotel, she might have felt like a fraud. Junie was in love with Paul, and you'd have to be blind to not notice how Paul felt about Junie. She was happy for her friend.

There was no parking to be found on Junie's mother's street. Junie had said to meet at her mother's and for the life of her, Thelma couldn't understand why she couldn't go to Junie's new apartment instead.

"Someone must be having a party," she said.

"Street's full, I'll drop you off in front of the house," Bobby said, slowing the car in front of the Richards's house.

Thelma rolled out of the car, her hand on her big belly. Again, she had half a mind to get back into the car and go home. Bobby leaned over and said, "Call me when you want to come home and I'll come pick you up."

"Okay," she said. She waddled up the driveway and made her way up the front steps, breathless by the time she reached the porch. She realized that Mrs. Richards had a houseful of people, and she wondered if she'd gotten something wrong. Maybe she was supposed to go to Junie's new apartment, or maybe this was the wrong night. In the last month, her brain had been a little foggy. But it was too late; Bobby was already gone.

She pushed the doorbell and waited.

Junie appeared in the doorway and opened the door. When she did, the volume from inside the house increased.

"We're supposed to get together tonight, right?" Thelma said. She hesitated and did not cross the threshold, remaining on the porch even though Junie held the door open for her.

Junie nodded. "Come on, Thelma." Junie wasn't smiling; she was grinning. She held the door open wider for Thelma and, grumbling about how she didn't want to interrupt anything, Thelma finally stepped into the Richards's house.

Several things happened at the same moment as Thelma stood in the archway to the parlor. A group of people jumped up and yelled "Surprise," startling her. Mrs. Richards was there, along with Mrs. Krautwein from next door and Aunt Linda. There were a few girls that Thelma worked with on the line at the box factory and a few friends she had gone to school with. But when her gaze landed on Barb standing next to the fireplace, Thelma scowled and said, "Barb, what are you doing here? You're supposed to be in Vermont in college."

Everyone burst out laughing, and Barb and Junie rushed her, pulling her into their embrace.

It felt good to be hugged by her best friends. When they pulled apart, she asked, "What's going on?"

"It's a baby shower, what did you think?" Junie asked with a laugh. Junie appeared lighter, happier. Marriage definitely agreed with her. Thelma envied her.

She swallowed hard, trying to deal with her shock. She'd never expected anything like this.

"It was Barb's idea, and I'm sorry I didn't think of it myself," Junie said. "But under Barb's strict instructions, I organized everything here on a local level."

Thelma's gaze swung to Barb, with her future full of promise—one that was going to be vastly different from Thelma's. She was the one who had come up with the idea to throw a baby shower for her? Thelma was overwhelmed.

"Thank you," she whispered.

She looked around again, taking it all in. There were yellow streamers looped from one end of the ceiling to the other. A giant cardboard stork stood in the center of the dining room table, which was crowded with food and silverware and paper napkins with storks on them. Her stomach growled as she looked at all the trays of food. There were all sorts of baby decorations all over the place in shades of yellow. Stacks of gifts wrapped in baby-themed paper covered the surface of the coffee table. She couldn't believe it.

"Come on, we'll eat first and then you can open the gifts," Junie directed.

Her voice lost because of emotion, Thelma could only nod.

Barb guided her to the table by the elbow. "How are you feeling, Thelma? You look great!"

Thelma could only nod, as she was trying to register that this was something for her. That people had planned this for her. That her two best friends had made this happen. By the time she got to the dining room table, she'd settled down and decided that there were so few surprises in her life that she was going to enjoy this one. The rest of the women fell in line behind her. She picked up a plate and a set of silverware and looked at all the food laid out. There were potato and macaroni salads in big bowls and an aluminum pan of hot roast beef. There were barbecued hamburgers and fried chicken, and Mrs. Krautwein had made a pan of *glombke*. Smiling, Thelma picked up the large serving spoon next to the macaroni salad and doled out a scoop onto her plate.

Later that evening when Bobby picked her up, he was all smiles. "Junie and Barb swore me to secrecy!"

Thelma looked at him and her eyes glistened. Even he had been in on it. It turned out he'd given Junie the names and phone numbers of the girls at the factory that Thelma palled around with.

By nightfall, the group had been reduced to themselves, Junie, Paul, Barb, and Mrs. Richards. Thelma looked around at all the stuff. Junie and her mother had gifted them a stroller. Barb had given them a high chair, and Aunt Linda had bought them a maple crib with a gorgeous little lamb on the side of it. The rest was all baby clothes and receiving blankets and cloth diapers. There was a ton of stuff. And it was all brand-new. Thelma had been getting bits and pieces here and there from the thrift shops, but it was nice to have brand-new things.

They were able to pack most of it into their car, and Paul and Junie took the rest in theirs, following them back to their apartment.

On the way home, Thelma and Bobby were happy and excited at the thoughtfulness of their friends. For the first time since they'd married, Bobby seemed relaxed and contented. As Thelma looked out the window, she wished it could always be like this.

Chapter Seventeen

Alice

Alice made a trip to Lime's Five-and-Dime down on Main Street in the center of Hideaway Bay. She hadn't been there since she was a kid. Gram and Granddad used to take her and her sisters in there all the time for a bag of saltwater taffy. She used to love the banana flavor. Isabelle had favored the peanut butter, and Lily had always gotten a bag of lemon-and-lime.

The glass-fronted door beneath the blue-and-white striped awning had the words "Lime's Five-and-Dime" etched in gold on the glass, and when she opened it, she was transported back in time. If the last century, especially decades ago, had a smell, it could be found in here. She didn't know whether it was the age of the building or the old, scuffed wooden floors or the rows of bins laid out with every imaginable item. Plastic, tin, paper—you name it, it could be had at Lime's Five-and-Dime. From saltwater taffy to the plastic rain bonnets her Gram used to wear, it housed an odd compendium of things.

She'd heard that Mr. Lime was still running the place, but she thought that couldn't be possible. But as soon as she stepped into the store, she spotted him behind the counter, sporting his familiar blue-and-white striped apron. If she thought he was old twenty-five years ago, he was ancient now. The skin on his hands was gnarled, blue veiny, and covered in age spots. His face was gaunt, almost skeletal, the skin papery, and his eyes were wizened.

"Can I help you?" he asked, his voice a croak.

"Hi, Mr. Lime, how are you?" she asked.

His immediate response was a frown. "Do I know you?"

"Um, maybe you don't remember me—"

His posture stiffened and he barked, "There's nothing wrong with my memory, missy. Just because I'm ninety-eight doesn't mean I've forgotten everything."

Duly chastised, Alice's face reddened, and she stammered, "I meant no offense. It's only that I haven't lived in Hideaway Bay for years."

"All right, what's your name? Spit it out!"

"Alice—Alice Monroe," she said.

"Nancy's girl?" he asked, his expression softening.

Alice nodded quickly.

"Your mother died too young," he said with a shake of his head.

She agreed and nodded.

"Meantime, I'm pushing one hundred, and it appears the good Lord forgot about me," he said.

Alice wanted to laugh but refrained. Now that she recalled, Mr. Lime had been cranky when she was a kid. It was nice to know some things never changed.

"Were you looking for something specific?" he asked.

"Actually, I was. I'm looking for those paper lace doilies that you put on serving platters," she explained.

He nodded. "Follow me." Mr. Lime came out from behind the counter, and Alice stepped in behind him as he made his way slowly down an aisle and then turned right and headed up three rows.

He stopped in the kitchen section. Alice's eyes took in everything. There was a hand flour sifter, which she couldn't resist, and she picked it up and gripped the handle, pulling it and watching the plates shift. Although she normally used a sieve, she liked the thought of this and decided to purchase it.

"They should be right here," he said, staring at the empty plastic bin. Mr. Lime eyed her with the flour sifter in her hand. "What about a Bundt pan? Nobody seems to make them anymore. Fifty years ago, Bundt cakes were all the rage. Not anymore. But they might come back in fashion."

Alice nodded, picked up the pan and thought, why not?

"Come on, we'll go back into the storeroom and see if there's any back there."

If the front section of the store was a cornucopia for the eyes, the storeroom was something else. Alice had never been back there before, and she realized her mouth was hanging open. Two stories high, there was a skylight right in the middle of the ceiling that let in lots of natural light, illuminating the otherwise darkened space. Dust motes danced merrily in the shafts of light. Mr. Lime went along the metal shelves, pulling strings hanging in front of him, turning on single light bulbs.

"Now, I should have some here somewhere," he said, rooting around in the boxes.

Alice was distracted by Christmas decorations. There were boxes marked "aluminum trees," and there was a big plastic bin of popcorn art. She remembered her Gram had such decorations. She sorted through them, pulling out a Christmas tree, a Santa Claus, and a sign that read "Merry Christmas."

Mr. Lime looked back at her. "Those used to be all the rage, then they fell out of favor, and now they're considered retro. That's why I don't throw anything out. When you get to be my age, you'll see everything come back around."

Alice nodded, thinking he had wonderful treasures back there.

"Oh, here we are. Now what size did you need?" he asked. He held up a package each of large paper doilies and medium-sized ones. "I don't see any of the smaller ones."

"These are fine. I'll take a pack of each," Alice said.

"Good, now carry these out to the front of the store and put them in the bin where they go," he said, dumping several packages of paper doilies in her arms. "I'll ring these up for you."

She asked for a bag of banana saltwater taffy and a bag of lemon-and-lime for Lily.

From the five-and-dime, she went next door to the olive oil shop.

She browsed the wares, looking at the various dipping oils, trying to decide between two. Sue Ann Marchek approached and stood next to her.

"If it were me, I'd buy the two," she said. Alice always thought Sue Ann was so pretty with her chestnut hair with the sunny highlights and her bright, sparkling eyes.

Alice laughed. "You're a great saleswoman, Sue Ann." She set both bottles into the woven basket hanging over her arm.

Sue Ann folded her arms across her burgundy-colored apron, which had the logo of the store emblazoned on it in cream. “You’ve settled right back into Hideaway Bay. It’s like you never left.”

“That’s how it feels. Was it like that for you?” Alice asked.

“Not at first. I arrived in winter but gradually, it started to feel that way,” Sue Ann said with a smile, a dimple in evidence on the right side of her mouth. “But now it feels as if I always lived here!”

“Good morning, ladies,” said a male voice.

Alice turned her head to see the Colonel carrying a basket that held a bottle of balsamic vinegar and pink Himalayan salt. “Good morning.”

“Let’s ask the Colonel, get a different point of view,” Sue Ann said.

A slow smile appeared on his face. “Ask me what?”

“We were just talking about how, since we returned to Hideaway Bay, it feels like we never left. What about you? You’re a transplant, what do you think?”

The Colonel appeared thoughtful, and his gaze rested on Alice’s face. “It feels like I’ve always lived here. It feels like home.”

Sue Ann clapped her hands and crowed, “Perfect!”

“Excuse me, Sue Ann?” It was another customer. “I’m looking for that caramel-flavored popcorn topping?”

"We moved that display over here," Sue Ann said. She excused herself and led the customer to the other side of the shop.

"We have to stop meeting like this, Colonel," Alice joked. "Everywhere I go, you're there."

He grinned. It was a pity he was so much older than her, she thought, because he was quite attractive with his impish grin and his dark hair with the liberal amount of silver. Dashing was the word that came to mind.

"It begs the question, who's following who?" he asked with a slight tilt of his head.

"Indeed, it does," she said.

"How's Ben these days?"

The abrupt change of subject left her scrambling for a moment but she quickly recovered and said, "He's fine. Ben's a great guy, and he helps a lot of people. I just wish he would take better care of himself. So many people depend on him."

"Excuse me for using a cliché, but you can lead a horse to water, but you cannot make him drink it."

Alice broke into a smile. "My Granddad used to say that."

He grimaced. "I'm old, but I'm not that old."

Instinctively, she reached out and laid her hand on his arm. "I didn't mean it like that, Colonel."

He laughed. “I know, I was only teasing you. You know, everyone calls me Colonel, but it would be all right if you called me Jack.”

She held up the two dipping oil bottles. “Well, Jack, which one would you recommend?”

He chuckled again. He was so relaxed, she thought, and his smiles were generous and easy.

“I’ve tried them both and I’d recommend them both.”

“Sue Ann said the same thing,” she said with a sigh, putting the bottles back into her basket.

“It goes well with some nice crusty French bread. Or Italian,” he mused.

There was a moment of awkward silence whose chasm widened, and she didn’t know how to cross it.

“Look, Alice, I’ve been meaning to ask you something,” he said.

Relieved at the break in the silence, she smiled. “Ask me anything.”

“Would you go out to dinner with me?” he asked. His gaze locked on hers.

Alice’s mouth opened and stayed that way. She had not expected this. She liked Colonel Stirling. A lot. But not in that way. There was too much of an age difference.

“Uh, you know . . . I can’t . . . uh, no thank you,” she stammered. She did not want to hurt this man’s feelings. But going out to dinner with him to spare his feelings wasn't right either, especially if she wasn't interested in him that way. Better to nip it in the bud. Her mind scrambled for what to say. "It's just that . . ."

The Colonel held up a hand and smiled. "It's all right. No explanations are necessary."

She opened her mouth to say something but then closed it. Finally, she said, "I'm sorry."

He laughed, putting her at ease. "It was only dinner. It's not like I asked you for a kidney and you refused."

Hurriedly, she said, "But if you needed a kidney, I'd gladly give you one of mine."

A generous smile full of mirth spread across his face. "Let me see if I have this right: you'd rather give up a kidney than go to dinner with me. Ouch."

She immediately reddened. "I didn't mean it that way. I just meant—"

He held up his hand and laughed. "Seriously, it's all right, Alice. You're too kind, and I have to admit it's one of the quirkiest rejections I've ever had."

She didn't like thinking about him getting rejected. He was such a lovely man; surely there was someone for him. How could anyone reject him? Of course she answered her own question, reminding herself that she'd just turned him down only seconds ago.

"I better get going," he said. He held up his basket and said, "Time to check out."

It appeared he might say something else, and she waited. But finally, he said, “I’ll see you around.”

She nodded and watched him walk away. With nothing more to purchase, she made her way to the front of the shop to pay for her items. If she wasn’t interested in the Colonel, then why did she feel bad for saying no to him?

Chapter Eighteen

1964

Memorial Day Weekend

Thelma

Thelma bit at her nails, worrying about Donny. Not that he was sick, but only that he wasn't with her. And he was far away. She'd come down for an overnight in Hideaway Bay with Bobby and Junie and Paul and Barb and Jim. Barb was home from California and had brought her new boyfriend. And it wasn't like Donny wasn't in good hands. It wasn't as if she'd left him with her father or her brothers. Her beautiful chubby baby was with Aunt Linda and Uncle Johnny, and they'd told her that if she and Bobby wanted to stay the whole weekend out at Hideaway Bay, they could do that.

"Are we ready?" Junie asked, holding a tartan blanket under her arms. Paul came up to her and slid an arm around her neck, pulling her close and planting a kiss on her temple.

If Bobby ever did something like that, it would go one of two ways: Thelma would die from shock or she'd slug him.

Barb stepped out onto the porch with Jim behind her, his hands on her waist, propelling her forward. He'd graduated from college last year with a degree in history and had joined the Army right afterward.

Barb was lithe, her blond hair much longer, almost down to her waist, and already sporting a California tan.

Junie and Paul had rented the cottage for the week. Barb and Jim were staying with Barb's parents, Dr. and Mrs. Walsh, over at their family cottage near the green space with the war memorial.

Barb held up a large plastic jug. "I've made highballs for us, ladies. The guys can drink the beer."

Thelma would have preferred the beer but said nothing. Bobby stood out on the sidewalk talking with Paul. She watched him, curious. It amazed her to no end that you could be married to someone, and they were still a complete stranger to you. She couldn't imagine what he was talking to Paul about. She and

Bobby rarely talked at home. Outside of conversations revolving around Donny or what bill needed to be paid, there was nothing left to say. She didn't know if their mutual love of Donny would be enough to hold them together.

The air was warm, and she stood up from the porch step and brushed off the bottom of her shorts. After Donny, her figure had returned. The baseball playing had helped. She wore a pair of shorts with a sleeveless cotton shirt that buttoned down the front. She'd shorn her hair after she had Donny, and she felt this suited her better as a mother. It was easy because it was wash-and-wear. There was still enough curl to keep it interesting.

Barb had a stylish halter dress on. Thelma thought she looked like a movie star. Junie had also opted for shorts, and a cute top she had tied into a knot right below her bosom.

"Bring the cooler of beer down to the beach," Junie said to Paul.

Paul nodded and ran back into the house.

They walked along the asphalt, heading to the boardwalk just off of Main Street that led directly to the beach. Thelma half paid attention to Barb and Junie's conversation. Barb was telling Junie something about California. Thelma looked back and spied Paul and

Bobby carrying the cooler, and Jim had Barb's plastic jug of highballs on one shoulder.

Junie picked a spot on the beach where there weren't too many people around. She spread out the tartan blanket onto the sand as Paul and Bobby set the cooler down.

The lake was loud and rough, the surf crashing on the shore. The water itself appeared almost black in places. The sun bobbed in and out of clouds. Thelma was sorry she hadn't thought to bring her cardigan down to the beach with her. Hopefully, someone would build a bonfire soon.

Barb and Junie got comfortable on the blanket, leaning back, stretching their arms behind them and their legs out in front.

Paul lifted the lid on the cooler, took out three beer bottles, and passed them around.

"Damn, we forgot the bottle opener."

"I'll run back and get it," Bobby said, and he sprinted across the beach, kicking sand in his wake.

"Ladies, would you care for a cocktail?" Jim asked with a smile. He held up the jug in one hand and a stack of plastic cups in the other.

"Three, please," Barb said, smiling, and pointed to Junie, Thelma, and herself.

"At your service," he said playfully.

Thelma liked Jim. More than that, she liked Jim for Barb. They were well-suited for one another. And although she was no big believer in romance—not the way Barb was—no one suited the role of knight in shining armor better than Jim Eckhert. She was glad for Barb. There was nothing worse than being miserable in a marriage.

Jim handed each of them a drink, and Thelma sat cross-legged on the blanket in front of Junie and Barb.

"Are you all right, Thelma?" Junie asked, sipping her drink.

Thelma shrugged, not wanting to pull her friends down.

Barb gave her a sympathetic smile. "She misses her baby."

Thelma sighed. "I do. I mean, I know he's okay. Aunt Linda and Uncle Johnny are great. But well, there it is, I do miss him. We're so far away." If anything happened, it would take an hour to get to him. She tried not to think about it, and sipped from the cup Jim had given her. Watered-down whiskey.

"I'd be the same way," Junie said.

"Anything happening on that front?" Thelma asked. Junie and Paul had married the previous fall and more than anything, Junie wanted a baby.

Junie looked around to make sure no one was in earshot. Bobby had returned with the bottle opener, and he stood off a bit with Paul and Jim. The three of them yucked it up and laughed, drinking their beer.

"Nothing yet, but not for lack of trying!" She burst into a fit of giggles.

"I can't wait to get married!" Barb gushed, taking a swig from her cup.

"Well, there sure is a lot of fun in it," Junie said with a smile and a wink.

Thelma couldn't help it; she had to ask. "Do you enjoy it, Junie? The . . . you know." She tilted her head to one side, nodded and raised her eyebrows. If Thelma never had sex again, she'd be perfectly okay.

Junie reddened at Thelma's blunt question. "Of course, doesn't everybody?"

Thelma didn't answer. She set her cup down on the blanket and pulled at an imaginary thread. Why couldn't her marriage be like everyone else's?

A silence descended that threatened to cast a pall over the night.

"What about you, Thelma?" Barb asked.

"What about me?" Thelma asked. She hoped she didn't sound defensive. She hoped Barb wouldn't ask about her and Bobby's sex life.

"Do you want to give Donny a little brother or sister?"

Thelma colored. She felt the heat rise to her cheeks and stared down at the blanket. She lowered her voice.

"There won't be any more babies. You have to have sex to have a baby."

Junie and Barb looked at her, dumbfounded.

Embarrassed, Thelma looked away. She picked up her cup and downed the contents.

"Oh Thelma, I had no idea," Junie said softly.

Thelma shrugged and muttered, "It's all right."

"It's not, though," Barb interjected. "Sex is an important part of marriage."

Thelma snorted. "If that's true then Bobby and I are doomed."

"Not necessarily," Junie rushed to say. "Maybe you could get help."

Thelma lifted her head and her eyes widened. "What, like ask Father Harmon for tips? Or maybe Bobby's mother? We all know how she feels about me! Hell, we might even ask my father while we're at it." She didn't know why, but suddenly she was laughing hysterically and rolled on her side, holding her belly. Her friends looked at her, concerned. Thelma sat up quickly and cleared her throat. "Look, we should never have married, but we had to."

"Out in California, some couples go to marriage counseling," Barb offered.

Thelma scoffed. "I think it'd be easier to sort it out over a game of horseshoes."

This time Junie and Barb laughed with her.

Thelma didn't want them feeling sorry for her, and when they managed to pull themselves together, she said, "It's just how it is. Not all marriages are wonderful. Honestly, if I had to go back and do it all over again, it would play out the same because I can't begin to imagine my life without Donny." She paused and added, "Donny will probably be the best thing I do with my life."

Jim interrupted them, holding up the jug and asking if they wanted another round. All three women held their plastic cups aloft.

Chapter Nineteen

Alice

Alice arrived at work to find that Ben was not there yet.

After unlocking the door, she flipped on the light switch, the overhead fluorescent fixtures blinking into action, their background hum like white noise.

Things had improved in the office. The filing cabinets lined one wall of the reception area, and she had managed to either file or shred every loose piece of paper. Ben's own office was a work in progress. At least she'd cleared off the two chairs in front of his desk and, using a hand-held vacuum, had managed to get rid of the cat hair, mysterious origin unknown.

Even Ben had noticed, walking in one day and asking, "Am I in the right place?"

But that morning, he wasn't there. Alice set her purse in the desk drawer and checked the main diary. He had a court date that morning, and she wondered if he'd gone straight to the courthouse.

As she booted up her laptop, the front door opened and Ben's neighbor, Baddie Moore, walked in. Despite it being October, he wore a pair of fluorescent-blue board shorts and a bright-orange polo shirt.

She sighed. Baddie's appearance could only mean one thing.

"Alice, I was passing by, so I thought I'd stop to tell you that Ben won't be in today," he said. He fiddled with his car keys in his hand.

Her shoulders slumped. "Is he all right?"

He shrugged but gave her a reassuring smile. "He had a bad weekend. He's on a bender."

The episodes of drinking had increased considerably since her arrival, and she wondered if her being there had indirectly contributed. Did knowing that she was there holding down the fort fuel him to go on a binge? She hoped not.

"Does he need help?" she asked, which she realized was a stupid question as soon as she said it.

Baddie rested his bum against Alice's desk, stretching out his long legs and folding his arms across his chest. "Of course he does. He certainly has his demons. His mother and I were after him for years to get help."

"He doesn't want to?" Alice asked.

He shrugged again. "I think the prospect of getting help for his drinking overwhelms him. He doesn't know where to start. We've all tried."

That could be true, Alice supposed. She liked Ben; he was affable and easy to work for. He had some quirks, but that only made him more interesting. She felt compelled to ask, "How long has he been drinking like this?"

"I'm not sure, for as long as I've known him."

"Is there anything I can do?" Alice asked.

"We all want to help him, but he has to want to get help," he said, voicing what she already knew.

"I appreciate you driving down here to let me know about Ben," she said. "Let me give you my cell number in case you ever need to call."

The phone rang and Baddie pushed off the desk. "You better get that. Take care, Alice."

"Thanks, Baddie," she said, lifting the earpiece of the phone.

"The law offices of Ben Enright," she answered.

"Hi, this is Chris Metzger," said the voice on the phone. "I'm at the courthouse and Ben isn't here. My arraignment is today."

Alice could hear the panic in his voice. "Ben's been held up, Chris, but I'm on my way," she said as she stood from her chair, pulling her purse out of the bottom drawer.

She hung up the phone and quickly pulled his folder from the file cabinet. She hurriedly leafed through it, committing certain facts to memory. She shoved the file inside her shoulder bag and ran out the door, locking it behind her.

The courthouse was back in Hideaway Bay proper, located across from the town green. It took her only ten minutes to get there, and luck was on her side as she found a parking space right out front.

Chris Metzger was pacing the marble floor of the long corridor outside the courtrooms. He was the same young man she'd seen Ben talking to the day she'd started this job. There was a spark of recognition in his eyes when he spotted her.

"Are you even an attorney? I thought you were Ben's secretary," he said. His voice was almost shrill.

Alice nodded. "I am. I've worked with a big law firm in Chicago for the last seven years."

He did not appear convinced.

"Come on, let's go," Alice said, glancing at her watch. She stopped and said to Chris, "Remember, like Ben told you, this is a regrettable, isolated incident. Hopefully, this will be the only time you'll be in a courtroom in your life, Chris."

She opened the door and stepped inside the courtroom with Chris following her. A thrill coursed through her at being able to practice law once again, even if it was only temporary.

They took their seats. When the judge arrived and took his seat on the bench and initial formalities were dispensed, he asked Chris if he had legal representation. Chris looked at Alice, who stood and announced, "Alice Monroe, Your Honor, attorney for the defendant."

After a night of tossing and turning, Alice crept quietly out of the house at sunrise. The street was peaceful. Not quite time yet for school bus pickups. The streetlights were still on, bathing the early morning scene in a soft, monochromatic orange glow. She strolled across the street and walked along the beach. The sun was just beginning to climb up behind the houses. There was no one on the beach, which was how she liked it. It was like having the whole place to herself.

The water was murky with snowy whitecaps, and it thundered as it crashed against the shoreline. The air was cool, and she pulled her sweater tighter around her. As she walked, she thought of the day before when she'd gone to court for Chris. He'd been issued a hefty fine and would have to do community service. He'd seemed relieved. Her work at Ben's office had morphed into more than receptionist work, as she filed papers in the court for him and researched briefs, but standing in for him made her realize how much she missed practicing law.

She bent and picked up a piece of beach glass, tossing it into the pail she carried with her any time she headed for the beach. Lily was doing well with her beach glass crafts, and Alice wanted to help her. It amazed her how there seemed to be an endless supply. There was also the usual flotsam the early morning tide had thrown up on the beach: piles of tangled seaweed, a couple of dead fish, and a plastic bottle that she picked up and threw into her pail. The seagulls circled above her, their cries piercing the morning silence.

Alice walked as far as the town center and cut across the boardwalk that dumped her right at the corner of Erie Street and Star Shine Drive. From there, she turned left onto Star Shine Drive and headed toward home. She had a few things to do before she went to work.

Her thoughts drifted to the Colonel. After she refused his offer of dinner, she'd feared that it would be awkward between them, but it hadn't been. He'd been so good-natured about her refusal that it had made her feel worse for turning him down. But he was too old for her, wasn't he? She saw him regularly as she continued to drop off baked goods for his veterans' group meetings, and he remained friendly. Perhaps going forward, they could be friends.

Satisfied with this conclusion, she climbed the steps to the house. The streetlights had long since gone off.

Alice and Lily covered the porch furniture with black plastic tarps. Since Lily had converted the shed into a craft room, the furniture would have to remain on the porch throughout the winter. It was not a problem; Gram had always kept the furniture on the porch year-round. The cushions had been brought in and carried upstairs to the second floor, where they would be stored in a spare bedroom until spring. Alice looked forward to the winter in Hideaway Bay. It had been a long time since she'd spent a winter here.

The wind picked up and whipped an edge of the tarp out of her hand.

"We'll need something stronger to secure it," Lily said.

"Let's use some rocks from the garden," Alice suggested with a nod toward the front gardens and the decorative rocks placed along the beds.

"Good idea."

Using the foot of the chair to secure the tarps momentarily, Alice and Lily bounded off the porch and began to lift some of the rocks from the garden. Alice lifted one up, turned it over, and saw it was covered in worms. "Yuck!" she said. She placed her rock back where it was. "We need another idea. What did Gram used to do?" she asked, wishing she could remember.

Lily shrugged. The underside of her rock was also covered with worms and with a grimace, she set it gently back down in the flower bed.

"What about bags of sand?" Lily asked. "We could fill gallon bags. They'd keep the tarps from going anywhere."

"Good idea," Alice said.

She ran into the house and grabbed the box of gallon-sized freezer bags from the pantry in the kitchen. Lily put the lead on Charlie, and the three of them crossed the street to the beach. The lake was navy-black and heavy crested with white sea foam. The sky was dark gray, and off on the horizon it looked practically black.

"Storm coming in," Alice said with a nod toward the horizon.

"We better hurry," Lily said, opening a bag and scooping up sand with it. They quickly filled up the bags and carried them back, a couple in each hand. Charlie loped behind them, stopping along the way to sniff at various things.

As they crossed the street, they spotted a woman exiting her house on the corner of Star Shine Drive and Erie Street. The older woman had short silver hair and wore a pink checked tabard over her cardigan and slacks. She was hunched over her walker as she made her way down the driveway, battling the fierce wind.

"Oh my gosh, is that Martha Cotter?" Lily asked.

"Nooo, it can't be. I thought she was dead," Alice said.

"Where is she going in this weather?"

"Good question."

Both women lingered a moment on the sidewalk across the street from their house to watch the elderly woman. Lily squinted. "That *is* her. I thought for sure she'd be dead by now."

"Didn't she have a daughter or something?" Alice asked. Alice's memory was hazy, but she thought she remembered a teenaged daughter being there when she was younger.

Lily looked at her. "She did, that's right. I forgot about her. But she left a long time ago. We were kids."

"We'll have to ask Thelma about her."

"I can't believe she lives in that big old house all by herself," Lily said, referring to the grand Victorian that stood on the corner. It was by far the largest house on Star Shine Drive, the most elegant and well-kept. The house had been painted in three shades: pale green, cream, and forest green for the gingerbread trim.

"I've always liked that house," Alice said. It certainly was grand with its high-pitched roof, ornate trim, stained-glass windows, and bay windows. She often wondered about the history of the place. Who had had it built, and had the Cotters always lived there? Martha Cotter was the only resident of the house that she knew of. She wished Gram were here so she could ask her.

Together, they watched the elderly woman make her way slowly to the end of the driveway, bracing herself against the sudden gusts of wind, to the mailbox that stood at the curb. With one foot in the street and the other on the curb, Martha leaned forward and grabbed the edge of the mailbox, pulling it open and reaching inside. With her mail in hand, she closed the box, gingerly put both feet on the asphalt, and made her way slowly back up the driveway before disappearing through a side door of the grand house.

"She doesn't look well at all," Alice said.

"No, she does not," Lily said.

Alice collapsed on the sofa in the front room across from Lily. She was tired and wasn't in the mood to bake. She only wanted to chill out. She might look for a romance on Netflix later. After they covered the porch furniture, they'd spent the rest of the afternoon raking up the leaves that covered the yard. All you had to do was push them to the curb and the town would pick them up, a service courtesy of their taxes.

Lily was parked at the other end of the sofa with her laptop open in front of her. Charlie was curled on the floor at her feet, snoring and farting.

"Since you've been back, you haven't mentioned one word about turning the house into an inn," Lily said, reaching down and scratching the top of Charlie's head.

Any thoughts of turning the house into an inn had been put on the back burner. Alice sighed and blew out a puff of air that lifted her hair off her forehead. "I'm still in the research phase."

"Research is important."

Alice replied carefully, "And besides, I know you're not keen on the idea, and neither is Isabelle."

"Only because Isabelle isn't here." Lily shrugged. "I wonder if the house is big enough. There are only five bedrooms upstairs, and we need to sleep somewhere."

"I thought we could renovate the attic and add some more bedrooms," Alice said.

"You don't think it would be kind of hot up there in the summertime?" Lily asked.

"Maybe. To be honest, it feels like a pipe dream. And besides, I'm happy doing what I'm doing." As Ben's drinking increased, so had Alice's workload. She hated to think she was benefitting from his problem. She'd still rather see him get help. But she felt as if she was doing important work and keeping his business going in the meantime.

"What are your plans with your apartment in Chicago? Are you going to keep it and rent it out? Or sell it? " Lily asked.

"After Christmas, I'm going back to Chicago to put it on the market."

"That's wonderful. I'm so glad you made a decision."

"Me too." Alice looked around the living room. "It feels right."

"I know what you mean," Lily said with a smile.

"Can I ask you a question?" Alice asked. She pulled up her legs beneath her and sipped from her wine glass.

Lily looked up from her laptop. The images on her screen were reflected in her reading glasses.

"Do you know what you want to do yet in regard to selling or keeping the house?" Alice asked.

Lily shrugged. "I'm not sure yet. I'm settling in here, and I'm leaning toward keeping it. But how would that work?"

"That's a good question. I can't see Isabelle wanting to keep it. What purpose would it serve her?" Alice said, thinking out loud.

"That's it. I can't picture Isabelle ever returning to Hideaway Bay, can you?" Lily appeared thoughtful for a moment and said, "Although the two of us came back, so I suppose anything is possible. If Isabelle wants to sell it, then what?"

"I've given this some thought," Alice said, proceeding with caution. Although Lily's financial situation had improved somewhat since all the difficulty she'd had after her husband's death, she wasn't swimming in cash.

"I could buy Isabelle out of her share of the property," Alice said.

Lily shifted uncomfortably in her seat. "That's probably what would have to be done. It wouldn't be fair for Isabelle not to get her share. But I wouldn't be able to contribute."

"I know, Lily. That's okay. I could buy her out and the two of us could live here."

Lily bristled. "That wouldn't be fair. You'd own two thirds of the house and I'd own one third?"

"It wouldn't mean anything until we went to sell it," Alice said.

"But what if decisions had to be made? About upkeep, remodeling. Then what?" Lily asked. A frown appeared on her face.

"As far as that goes, everything would be fifty-fifty. We could even draw up a contractual agreement if it would make you feel better," Alice suggested.

"I trust you, Alice, but I know how these things play out. Feelings get hurt and people get angry and before you know it, family members aren't talking to one another."

To put her sister at ease, Alice said, "Look, we don't have to make a decision about anything until next May. Let's put it aside for now."

Lily nodded, went quiet, and stared at her laptop screen.

Buoyed by the fact that Lily was leaning toward keeping the house but at the same time wanting to reassure her, Alice looked around and smiled. "Everywhere I look, I see memories of Gram and Granddad."

Lily smiled. "Me too."

Chapter Twenty

1967

Thelma

I have no business doing what I'm about to do, Thelma thought as she wheeled the stroller around the block. *I'm a married woman, for crying out loud.* But then she reminded herself that she always did what she wanted to do. Besides, this was important.

Until a few years ago, she'd never heard of Vietnam in her life. And even when American troops headed over there, she'd still not been interested. It just wasn't in her busy sphere of motherhood, working and trying to scrape money together to pay the bills. She was still raising her younger brothers as well as Donny. As incredible as it seemed, her father was only getting ornerier with time. But when Frank was drafted, she'd gone over to Barb's house and asked her to show her where the country of Vietnam was on the map. After Barb got over her initial surprise at Thelma asking her for something, she'd taken her to her father's study and pulled a giant atlas off the bookshelf, opening it across her father's desk. When Barb pointed it out, all Thelma could think was it was so far away.

And Frank had gone off. Frank, the sibling closest to her in age, who was slow-moving and got to things in his own time. Who spent most of his time sitting on the edge of his bed, staring at the wall. Who she could never count on to help out with anything at home. But when he went off, looking uncertain, with his cowlick of red hair sticking up and looking around like he was trying to find a gate at the airport, she worried about him more than she'd ever worried about anyone before. She and Bobby drove him to the train station with her father in the back seat with Frank. She'd packed a lunch for him, and hugged and kissed him goodbye. Bobby and her father had shaken his hand.

He'd glanced around, his face red, and slowly made his way to the train. She couldn't help it that she called out after him, ran to him, and pulled him into her embrace again, whispering, "Stay safe."

You couldn't get away from the war, not even at home. Junie's neighbor, Mrs. Krautwein, lost a son at the battle of Dak To. Her own cousin, Dickie Kempf, was reported missing in action. She'd pushed Del to go to college; she had a plan. If he got drafted, he could use a college deferment like Barb's older brother had.

Frank came home a year later. Grateful that he'd come back in one piece, she'd gone to Mass, and she hadn't been in a church since she'd been in high school.

But this was a different Frank who'd returned from Vietnam. Sometimes, his hands shook, especially when lighting a cigarette. Sometimes he had a fifty-yard stare as if he wasn't present. And he spent more time than ever sitting on his bed and staring. When Thelma had suggested to her father that maybe Frank should see someone, like a doctor, her father had brushed her off, angry. "There's nothing wrong with him. He served his country, now leave him alone."

The heels of her penny loafers tapped along the sidewalk as she made her way down the street. It was a beautiful fall day. The leaves on the big trees that lined the street had turned rich shades of orange and gold with a smattering of red. The air was crisp, and she had pulled out her wool coat. As she turned onto the driveway of Stanley Schumacher's house, she parked the stroller, fluffed her hair with her fingers, trotted up the three steps to the front door, and rang the bell. Inside, a television blared.

Earlier that morning before Bobby headed off to work, he'd casually mentioned to Thelma that Stanley Schumacher had been drafted and was leaving in the morning. They were all gathering at the neighborhood bar later that evening to send him off. She'd been in the middle of washing breakfast dishes, her arms wrist-deep in bubbly dishwater when this piece of information landed at her feet. Stanley Schumacher had been part of the background of her life for as long as she could remember. Not that she'd always been happy about that, but he'd been there. And now he was going off to that god-forsaken place. It bothered her. When Bobby had muttered with a laugh, "He won't last five minutes over there," Thelma had rounded on him and sneered, "What do you know? You're here."

To which Bobby replied, his lunch pail in his hand, "You're a viper, Thelma."

Before she rang Stanley's doorbell again, she fluffed her hair one more time, knowing it was futile. Her hair always looked the same: red and messy.

Stanley's older brother, Ralph, appeared in the doorway. Like Stanley, he was short and thin, but unlike Stanley he didn't wear glasses or have a pockmarked face.

"Can I help you?"

"Is Stanley here?"

"Yeah, hold on," Ralph said. He disappeared and shouted, "Stanley, your dream girl is here."

Thelma rolled her eyes and stepped off the porch, because Donny had dropped his bottle and it had rolled off the driveway and into the grass. The toddler pointed at it, and she picked it up and handed it to him. She pulled a handkerchief from her coat pocket and wiped his runny nose. She caressed his cheek and smiled at him. "You're a good boy, Donny." The little boy smiled in return.

Stanley stood on the porch, watching her. His brother yelled something inaudible from inside, to which Stanley responded, "Shut up, Ralph, or I'll clobber you!"

He looked up and down the street and bounced down the steps.

"Thelma, what are you doing here?" he asked. His smile was broad and generous, like someone whose horse had just come in. He put his hands in his pockets.

"I heard you're leaving tomorrow," she said.

He nodded. "That's right. Catching the train to Fort Dix in New Jersey."

That's where Frank had gone.

She felt at a loss for words, which was an unfamiliar feeling for her. What did you say to someone heading off to war? Small talk seemed trite. And her usual acerbic tongue didn't seem called for either.

Stanley nodded toward Donny. "How's he doing?"

Thelma smiled. Any mention of the boy always brought an automatic smile to her face. She couldn't help it. "Good. He's a great little boy."

"Thank God he looks like you and not Bobby," he joked.

She laughed.

"They're having a little get-together down at Big Al's later," he said, his eyes searching her face.

"I can't," she said.

There was an almost imperceptible sag to his shoulders.

"It's hard to find a sitter these days, and I've got my brothers tonight," she said hurriedly. She didn't want him to think she didn't value his effort. Or that she didn't want to be there. Actually, she would have liked to go down to Big Al's and have a beer with Stanley and see him off. But she was married now, and it wouldn't be right.

It was funny. She knew of Stanley's adoration for her. Everyone and their brother knew how Stanley felt about her. It was always there. And if she was honest with herself, she'd have to admit that there was something empowering about knowing there was a man out there who thought you were the bee's knees no matter what you did or what you said or how you looked. She'd taken it for granted, assumed she'd always have that.

"Are you happy, Thelma?" Stanley asked. He no longer smiled but watched her intently.

She'd never really thought about it, so she shrugged and asked, "Are you?"

When he mimicked her shrug, they both laughed.

Donny began to fuss, and Thelma took it as her cue to leave. "Look, I wanted to wish you well."

"I appreciate that."

"Well, good luck," she said, wheeling the stroller away.

"Take care of yourself, Thelma," he said quietly. "I'll see you when I get back."

She nodded, swallowing hard. She hoped he would come back home safely.

With a smile, she pushed the stroller to the end of the street. Stanley stood at the end of the driveway until she rounded the corner, and he was no longer in sight. Feelings she could not identify filled her and nagged at her.

Chapter Twenty-One

Alice

"Any word on Isabelle?" Thelma asked. She, Alice, and Lily were seated around the dining room table at the house on Star Shine Drive, having just enjoyed their Christmas dinner. There'd been a lovely ham speared with pineapple rings and maraschino cherries. They'd also served mashed potatoes, corn, and green bean casserole. Alice had dug out Gram's recipe for candy gravy, and it had tasted just like Gram used to make it. After the dinner plates were cleared, they served Christmas cookies, and Thelma had declined the offer of eggnog in favor of instant coffee.

Alice and Lily had invited Thelma over as her granddaughters had gone out to Arizona to spend the holiday with their parents, leaving Thelma alone. She'd been asked; they'd tried all sorts of things to get Thelma to go with them, but she'd remained adamant that she wasn't leaving Hideaway Bay.

"We were hoping Isabelle would come home for Christmas, but she's in Australia," Lily explained. "She thinks she might pop home for Gram's anniversary in May."

Although Alice had been disappointed when Isabelle told them she had no plans to come home yet, it was wonderful to be back in Hideaway Bay for Christmas and to spend it with family. There had been a moment of hilarity earlier that morning when Lily gifted her with a pair of fleece pajamas, a cookbook, and some products for the bath. She had given Lily practically the same thing: fleece pajamas, a book on sea glass, and some bath salts.

"That's Isabelle, always traveling," Thelma said evenly, helping herself to another snickerdoodle from the platter of homemade cookies. "So tell me, Alice, are you dating anyone?"

Alice arched an eyebrow at the sudden shift in conversation.

"No, I haven't been on one date since I've been here," she said.

"Really?" Thelma asked. "A girl as pretty as you? I thought they'd be beating a path to your door once you came home."

Alice laughed. “No, sadly, that is not the case.” Her gaze landed on the holiday centerpiece on the table. It was so festive with its tall, slim red tapers set amidst green boughs with little gifts, bells, and red velvet bows attached to it.

“But she was asked out on a date,” Lily said in a singsong voice, smiling. “She said no.”

Thelma looked back and forth between the two girls. “Who? Was it Ben? Although I can’t see you with Ben. He’s not your type.”

Alice wished Lily hadn’t brought the subject up. She fooled with the edge of her napkin. “No, it wasn’t Ben. It was the Colonel.”

Thelma’s mouth opened slightly, and her eyes widened. “Jack Stirling? Really? He’s perfect for you!” Then she scowled. “But you said no?” She seemed shocked.

Alice squinted and made a face of displeasure. “He’s a little old for me, don’t you think?”

Thelma snorted and coffee flew out of her nose, splattering the tablecloth. Immediately, she picked up her napkin, dipped it in her water glass, and dabbed furiously at the tablecloth.

“Leave it, Thelma,” Lily said. “I’m taking the tablecloth to the dry cleaner’s after the holiday.”

Thelma chuckled. “I must admit, Alice caught me by surprise with her statement. At my age, I didn’t think I could be surprised anymore.”

“You don’t think he’s a little old for me?” Alice asked.

Thelma took a delicate sip of her coffee as she eyed the platter of cookies again, deciding on an iced cutout. “How much older is he than you?”

Alice shrugged. “I’m not sure, but I think he’s in his forties, which puts him at least ten years older than me.”

Thelma looked up to the ceiling and appeared to consider this. “Yeah, he’d have to be. Because he retired from the military after he’d put his twenty years in, and that was several years ago. Two tours in Afghanistan and Iraq. He spent time in the Helmand province.” She shuddered at the thought of it. “Maybe he needed a change. Understandable.”

“You don’t think ten years is too much of an age difference?” Alice asked.

Thelma looked at her, nibbling on the cookie. “Sure it is, if you’re nine and he’s nineteen. Then the age difference is a problem. But not now. Besides, that doesn’t matter because obviously, you don’t like him that way, or the age difference wouldn’t matter to you at all.”

“I do like him, but as a friend,” Alice clarified.

Lily stood and asked, “Thelma, more coffee?”

"One for the road, please," she said, handing Lily her cup. "Look, Alice, I'm the last one to be giving anyone advice on romance. But sometimes you need to explore opportunities." She paused. "I'd imagine the Colonel would be a good catch"—she leveled her gaze at Alice—"for the right person."

Alice tucked that away for future reference.

Chapter Twenty-Two

1970

Thelma

"I'm ten dollars short for the gas bill," Thelma said to Bobby before he left for work.

Her husband was hunched over his bowl of cereal, his cornflakes soggy at this point. He stopped chomping, seemed to consider what she'd said, and shrugged.

"What does that mean, exactly?" she barked. She made a quick peanut butter and grape jelly sandwich for Donny. There were still a few minutes before she needed to wake him for school.

Sunlight filtered in through the cream-colored curtains at the windows, giving the kitchen an opaque look.

Slowly, Bobby turned to face her. A small drop of milk had gathered in the corner of his mouth. He shrugged again, as if he was adding emphasis. “I don’t have it,” he said plainly.

“Okay, but we need to get it,” she said, lifting her eyebrows.

Every month it was the same thing. Not enough wage to last the entire month. Her stomach did a slight turn, as it did every month. That queasy uncertainty of worry, trying to head off a shutoff notice but also unable to pull a rabbit out of a hat. Last month, she’d swallowed her pride and asked her father for a loan to pay the gas bill. Currently, she was giving him five dollars every week from her own paycheck. She couldn’t ask him again. Thank God summer was coming and the gas bill would naturally drop. She’d have a few months of not worrying until the heat was turned on in the fall and the cost would rise again.

Bobby returned his attention to his cornflakes and picked up the speed with which he ate, going from spooning his cereal into his mouth to shoveling it in, anxious to finish, anxious to leave their apartment, anxious to get away from her.

Finished, he carried his empty bowl over to the sink and laid it on the counter, even though she had a dishpan of sudsy water sitting in the sink.

"I borrowed from my father last month, I'm not asking him again," Thelma said, not finished with the subject.

"Okay," Bobby said. He turned to walk away, picking up his lunchbox.

"Maybe you could get another job," she suggested. Bobby was still at the cardboard box factory. He'd been promoted to assistant manager of the warehouse. The promotion had sounded great until they looked at his paycheck and saw no difference. Thelma had left the factory after Donny was born and had taken a job in the deli at the Park Edge grocery store. She worked all the hours God gave her.

"I'm not getting another job," Bobby said. "I'm already working a full-time job."

"I meant something part-time," she said quickly. "In the evenings."

"Why don't you dip into the savings?" he said casually.

That was his answer to every shortfall. But Thelma was determined not to touch their meager savings. It would be too easy, and then they'd be left with nothing. Then what? Besides, she had plans: She hoped they could buy a house. And Donny was going to college, that much she'd determined already.

Her brothers came to mind. Her youngest brother, Johnny, had gotten a job with the fire department. Turned out he was a great test-taker. Thelma was proud.

Frank still lived with their father, and it appeared to be an arrangement that suited them both. Del had gone to college and was living in Virginia, and Mikey had a job at the steel plant's coke ovens. It was a relief. Now that her brothers were all sorted with their lives, she felt as if finally, she could live her own life.

With no resolution as to how the gas bill was going to be paid and no further word, Bobby picked up his lunchbox and headed off to work. Muttering to herself, Thelma went into the living room and cleaned up the blankets off the couch where her husband slept at night. As she folded them, she paused, holding them in her arms, and thought, *This is no way for a husband and wife to live.* But it had been like this for so long she couldn't remember when they'd ever slept in the same bed.

Standing in the middle of her tiny living room with the small television with the rabbit ears and the vinyl ottoman and the coffee table with a mark of red nailpolish and the second-hand couch, Thelma crushed Bobby's bedding to her chest and let her mind drift.

Almost thirty, what did she have to show for anything? No house of her own, no life of her own. Would it be like this in ten years? Twenty years? Would they still be in the same apartment? Living with nothing more than an uneasy truce between them? With Bobby sleeping on the couch? No wonder he was always complaining about his back.

Looking around again, she thought there had to be more to life than what she had. There had to be. Just because they had to get married didn't mean they had to stay married.

"What is this?" Bobby asked, holding up the notice from her lawyer.

"I want a divorce," she said easily. She sat at the kitchen table, folding clothes. She felt like she'd been doing laundry her whole life.

It had been two weeks since she'd asked him about the gas bill. When there had been no solution forthcoming, Thelma had dipped into their paltry savings account and paid the bill. She hoped that wouldn't form into a habit. But something had shifted inside her when she had to withdraw that money. It was as if all the years chipping away at what was left of her inside had finally chipped everything away, and she'd made her decision. There was no sense in prolonging their agony.

"Why?" he asked. He looked like he was going to cry.

"This isn't a marriage, Bobby," Thelma said. She squared the corners of a towel and logrolled it.

"No marriage is perfect," he said.

"I know that. But we're ill-suited to one another."

"Is there someone else?" he asked. "Has that Stanley Schumacher been coming around here?"

"No," she said with a scowl. "Don't be ridiculous."

"I heard he bought some old rundown restaurant down in Hideaway Bay," Bobby said, watching her face.

She'd heard that too. After his year-long tour in Vietnam, she'd run into him a few times. He'd been polite, but had told her he was moving permanently down to Hideaway Bay. He told her that he'd promised himself if he survived his tour of duty, he'd do something positive with his life. Knowing firsthand that he was the tenacious sort, she did not doubt his vow for one minute.

"Then why a divorce? I try and stay out of your way, Thelma," Bobby whined.

She rolled her eyes. "And that should tell you right there that we're not meant to be together."

There had to be more to life than just existing in a marriage. And Thelma felt she deserved some peace. She'd raised her brothers. She didn't believe in chasing happiness; it was a feeling that was too elusive, too hard to nail down. But she wanted peace and contentment, and everything Bobby did aggravated her. The way he chewed a banana made her see stars. His lack of ambition bothered her. The fact that he was happy raising their son in an apartment angered her. She hated that she had to depend on him. If they were going to be stuck in an apartment, she might as well be alone. The one thing she was not afraid of was raising Donny by herself.

"We made a mistake and we paid for it," Thelma said evenly. "But I can't do this anymore. I don't want to do this anymore."

"What about Donny? You don't think he might miss his dad?" Bobby glared. It was the angriest she'd ever seen him. She was relieved he was capable of strong emotion, so all was not lost.

She stood from the table, picking up the laundry basket of folded clothes and balancing it on her hip. "My mind is made up, Bobby. We're getting divorced."

Chapter Twenty-Three

Alice

Alice's eyes widened in surprise when she saw that it was Jules Milligan walking into the office. She jumped out of her chair.

"Jules! It's great to see you," Alice gushed, holding her arms open and pulling the other woman into her embrace.

Jules was Thelma's granddaughter, and she and Alice had gone to school together. Although after Alice moved away, she and Jules kept in sporadic touch. Jules worked in town.

Alice pulled back but kept her hands on Jules's arms. "You look great!" she said. And her friend did. Jules hadn't inherited her grandmother's red hair; instead, she sported a sleek, shiny ebony-colored bob. Jules's mother was Native American, and Jules favored her side of the family, blessed with dark eyes, high cheekbones, and a deep complexion. Alice had always been in awe of her friend's natural beauty.

"Granny said you were working here," Jules said.

"I am," Alice said. "There aren't a lot of law offices in Hideaway Bay."

"I guess not," Jules said with a laugh. Her eyes sparkled, and Alice remembered what good fun Jules used to be. There was a momentary pang of sorrow at how she'd lost touch with her over the years.

"What brings you in here?"

"Actually, I need a lawyer," Jules said. Her smile disappeared and the sparkle dimmed in her eyes.

"Is everything all right?" Alice asked, searching her friend's face.

Jules lowered her chin and stared at the ground. "I'm here to file for divorce."

"Oh, Jules, I'm sorry to hear that." Alice squeezed her hand. "Come and sit down." Alice led Jules to Ben's office, where they would be afforded privacy. Immediately she was grateful for two things. First, that the office, though still looking a little beaten-down, was at least clean and organized. And second, that she'd bought a proper coffeemaker.

She got the machine started, and as it gurgled on its stand in the reception area, she took the liberty of sitting in Ben's chair.

"Granny suggested I come see you," Jules said.

Alice decided to be upfront right away. "I'm not officially working here in that capacity—as an attorney, I mean—but I help out as needed," she said.

Jules slumped in her seat. "Oh, I wanted to get this underway."

"Even though Ben isn't here, I can get your particulars down and at least get the ball rolling," Alice said. "How's that?" When Jules nodded, Alice stood and said, "Let me get your coffee and we can start from there."

After she poured it, she handed a mug to Jules, who took it with both hands.

"How long have you been married, Jules?"

"Not long, only five years."

Alice took out a clean manila folder and a pencil. "Do you still go by Milligan?"

"D'Amico is my married name."

She wrote Jules's name on the tab, then grabbed a sheet of paper for taking notes. "Can I ask what happened?"

"It isn't working out, and I can't see wasting any more time on this," Jules announced. "We're two totally different people."

"Is there anything specific, or is it more a case of irreconcilable differences?" Alice asked.

"I think he's having an affair," Jules said quietly. She lowered her head and stared at her coffee mug as if it held all the answers.

"Think or know?" Alice asked.

Jules sighed. "I know he's having an affair. With a work colleague."

Alice nodded.

"He was away on business a few weeks ago and when I called him late at night in his hotel room, Jenna answered the phone. He claims they were going over details of their business meeting, but at eleven thirty at night? And even if that was true, why would she answer his phone? He said it was because they have the same phone, and she picked his up by mistake."

"You don't believe him?" Alice asked.

"I wanted to give him the benefit of the doubt, but it doesn't sit right with me."

"Have you tried counseling?" Alice asked. She felt compelled to ask this. It always seemed sad to her when a marriage broke up.

"We did about two years ago," Jules said. She shifted in her chair and crossed her legs at the ankles. "But it didn't work. Not that it was bad counseling—it's that Richard refused to go anymore. Said it was a waste of time."

Alice scribbled some notes. There were no children, both were working full-time, and the marriage was less than five years old. She asked further questions such as their address, where they worked, contact numbers, dates of birth.

"Does Richard know you are filing for divorce?"

"No, Granny said to blindside him," Jules said. Somehow, Alice could picture Thelma saying that.

"When I told her that I suspected Richard of cheating, she told me in no uncertain terms to 'dump his ass,'" Jules said. Here she smiled.

Alice could also picture Thelma saying that.

It was sad when a marriage broke down irretrievably. Despite her own parents' failed relationship, her grandparents' marriage had given her hope that happy endings were possible.

"It's hard not to be disappointed when you're on the verge of a divorce, but you'll get through this. Everything's going to be okay."

Jules laughed and for a moment there was that twinkling in her eyes again. "Alice, it's so good to have you back in town. And even better to see that you're still wearing your rose-colored glasses!"

Chapter Twenty-Four

1974

Thelma

Thelma arrived home from her shift at the Park Edge grocery store. As soon as she removed her smock, she took potatoes out of the bag from the lower cabinet and laid them on the table. Donny would be home from school in a few minutes. There'd been a sale at work, and she'd picked up some cube steaks for them for dinner. She was also going to make stewed tomatoes as they were one of the few vegetables Donny liked. She made them like her mother did, or as much as she remembered, mixing a can of tomatoes with some salt, pepper, and sugar, then breaking in pieces of white bread and adding a pat of butter to the pot.

It was only the two of them now. It had been three years since the divorce, and they were doing all right. They lived in a two-bedroom apartment within walking distance of her work and Donny's school.

She couldn't believe he was ten.

She missed Junie since they'd moved out to Hideaway Bay last year. It just wasn't the same. She even had to admit to missing Barb. She never thought she'd say that. So much so that she'd called her about six months ago and now, they spoke once a month on the phone. Barb was doing well. Thelma had been surprised when she admitted she wasn't crazy about living out on the west coast and would have preferred to come home.

She heard the door slam as Donny arrived home from school.

"Jeez," she muttered under her breath. If she'd told him once, she'd told him a thousand times not to slam the door. She was about to say as much, but forgot all about it when he appeared in the kitchen, his left eye red and swollen.

She dropped the paring knife and ran to him. With her finger, she gently lifted his chin to get a better look.

"What happened?"

Donny didn't say anything at first. But Thelma guessed.

"Lester Mulhouse again?"

He nodded, his chin quivering.

"It's all right, Donny, we'll get you fixed up in no time," she said reassuringly. "Sit up there and I'll get you some milk and cookies."

She wrapped some ice in a washcloth and had him hold it against his eye. Lester Mulhouse had been the bane of their existence for the past year. And her ex, Bobby, was useless in this department. Desperate, Thelma had signed Donny up for boxing lessons with a former welterweight champ downtown. She'd had to take extra shifts at the grocery store to pay for it. After three lessons, the welterweight had pulled her aside and said, "He's not a fighter, mother, and he's not going to be one. He just doesn't have it in him."

He'd gotten that from his father, because Thelma knew she could stand her own corner. But it wasn't like she could go to school with Donny. And they had the rest of grammar school and then high school. At this rate, the poor kid wouldn't survive.

The following morning, Donny was slow to get out of bed. His eye was completely swollen shut and dark purple in color.

Thelma poured him a bowl of Frosted Flakes and filled the bowl with milk.

"Do I have to go to school? Can't I stay home?" Donny whined.

"No, you have to go to school," Thelma said. Although in her heart she wanted to keep him home with her, she knew that wasn't the answer. She hadn't told him that she was going into the school again to talk to the principal. A fat lot of good it had been doing. "How are you going to go to college if you don't go to school?"

"Will I get beat up in college?" he asked, picking up his spoon and looking up at her out of his one good eye.

"Nope," she said firmly.

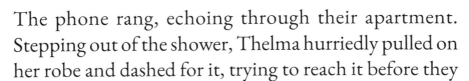

The phone rang, echoing through their apartment. Stepping out of the shower, Thelma hurriedly pulled on her robe and dashed for it, trying to reach it before they hung up.

"Hello?"

"Hey, Thelma, it's Bobby," said her ex-husband.

Thelma braced herself. This weekend was Bobby's weekend with Donny. If he was canceling again, Thelma was going to go through the roof. She couldn't stand the disappointment in Donny's face when she told him.

"What time are you picking Donny up?" she asked, cutting him off at the pass.

"Huh? Oh yeah, I won't be able to see Donny this weekend," Bobby said.

"What? Why not? You missed the last weekend," Thelma said, her voice rising. She stood there twirling the long cord of the wall telephone around her finger, dripping water on the floor.

"I know, but we've got some family events with Diane's family," he said.

Within a year of their divorce, Bobby had remarried, a girl named Diane. She came across as sweet and of course because she didn't fall pregnant before she married Bobby, his parents thought she was the cat's meow. Apparently, Diane, Bobby, and their two girls spent a lot of time with the elder Milligans out at their house, dinner every Sunday. In their short marriage, Thelma had only been out to the Milligans' house one time and even then, it hadn't been by invitation. She'd gone with Bobby to see them one afternoon. They'd barely acknowledged her or Donny, and never offered a refreshment. When they left, she'd told Bobby that neither she nor Donny would ever grace that doorstep again. They didn't go where they weren't wanted.

"So? Take Donny with you. He's family," Thelma snapped.

"You know it's a busy time of year with graduations and communions and christenings," he said evenly.

Boy, he was clueless, she thought. But she said. "What will I tell Donny?"

"Just tell him I'll see him next time," he said. Then he added, "And tell him I'm sorry."

"I'm not the messenger boy—you can apologize to him the next time you see him!"

He must have sensed that Thelma was about to go on a tear because he said hastily, "I gotta go, Thelm."

"Wait a minute, Bobby," she said. "Donny's getting bullied at school again."

"Is he?" He said it so casually, as if she'd mentioned something trivial like Donny had the day off from school or he had a new set of pajamas. Thelma saw murder.

"Yeah, he is, and what are you going to do about it?"

"Well, Thelma, there isn't much I can do, as I don't live with him," Bobby said. Bravely, he added, "You were the one who wanted a divorce."

"It didn't take you long to get over it. You had a new girlfriend within two months of us getting divorced," she practically spat.

"Please don't drag Diane into this," he said.

There was a thing or two she'd like to say about Diane, but she bit her tongue.

"And I got your check, and it was short, Bobby," Thelma said, deciding this was the more important battle instead of slagging his new wife.

"Oh yeah, about that, that's all I'll be able to give you now," he said. "I've got two kids and, well, it's expensive raising kids."

She clamped her lips shut to stop from shouting at him. Composing herself, she said, "No shit. But you're forgetting one thing: Donny is your kid too." She slammed down the phone. Tears pricked the backs of her eyes. She was furious, but she'd be damned if she was going to let her ex-husband get the better of her.

She wiped up the small bit of water off the floor and headed back to the bedroom, where she dried herself and yanked her clothes on, muttering. Thelma hated not having control over a situation. She knew this wasn't Bobby. It had to be Diane. As soon as Bobby put a ring on her finger and they started having kids, he began to pull away from Donny. She didn't care if she never saw the man again, but she wanted Donny to know his father. And begrudgingly, she had to admit that she wanted Bobby to be involved in his son's life. She knew better than anyone what it was like to grow up without a parent, and she wanted to spare Donny that. But she couldn't force Bobby to take an interest in their son. If it was Diane who was pulling his strings then shame on him. But then, he'd always been weak.

Her flurry of thoughts was interrupted by a knock at her door. She dashed out of the bedroom and opened the door to find her mailman, Ward, standing there with a package in his hand.

"Got a delivery for you, Thelma," he said, handing her the box.

"Thanks, Ward," she said, taking it from him. "Wait a minute, I have some mail for you." She grabbed the two stamped pieces off the counter and handed them to him.

He took them from her, looking at them, scanning the addresses like he always did. Thelma bit her tongue. It was an invasion of her privacy and what was worse, he was so blatant about it, but Thelma thought him basically harmless. Besides, whenever there was a package to be delivered, he always trudged up her back stairs to bring it to her when he could have left it in the side hall.

"Thanks again," she said, closing the door.

As soon as she'd seen the package, she'd recognized the familiar handwriting of Barb. Several times a year, she sent packages for Donny and on his birthday and at Christmas, she always sent him a gift plus a card with money inside. She was too generous.

Thelma opened the package and pulled out two outfits and held them up. There were two pairs of pants with matching striped shirts. One was in navy and the other in burnt orange. She fingered the tag, checking the size, and smiled at the correct choice. This was timely, as he'd just put a hole in the knee of his pants.

"She never forgets my kid," Thelma muttered to herself, folding the clothes carefully and laying them back in the box.

She was lucky in that she had two very good friends she could always count on. She'd wait until later that evening and call Barb after Donny had gone to bed. The long-distance rate was cheaper in the evenings and on the weekends. She'd like to catch up with her friend.

Chapter Twenty-Five

Alice

Alice stopped and picked up a few groceries from the chain supermarket along the highway on her way home from work. As she pushed her cart out of the store, she glanced at the cork bulletin board on the wall near the exit. For whatever reason, she loved reading all the notices, some homemade and handwritten, others professionally done. There was everything from art classes to all-season radials for sale to photocopied pictures of a missing dog with the phone number along the edge of it. She studied the photo, decided she hadn't seen the dog anywhere, and went on to the next notice. This one caught her attention. It was professionally done, set against a bold blue-and-white background, and called for volunteers for a community cleanup of the beach in April, which was only weeks away. It was sponsored by Hideaway Bay's Department of Community Events. Alice pulled her phone from her purse and snapped a photo of it. The meeting was next week at the parish hall, and she'd definitely be checking that out.

After Christmas, Alice had gone back to Chicago and put her apartment on the market. The decision had felt right. Although her job situation was not ideal and she would have preferred to be practicing law full-time, she loved being back home in Hideaway Bay.

The following week, she drove over to the parish hall after dinner for the meeting. The parking lot was full of cars. They were just over the St Patrick's Day festival, where corned beef and cabbage had been served at the parish hall to raise funds for the 4th of July fireworks committee. That had been a lot of fun.

The lot was so full that Alice had to drive around to the back. It was raining when she stepped out of her car, and she had to run around to the entrance at the front to avoid getting too wet. When she stepped into the outer vestibule, the volume of noise from inside the hall increased dramatically. There was a good buzz going on. Alice removed her raincoat and shook it off, draping it over her arm.

Inside, she found a vacant chair at the back and sat down. She looked around and waved at a few people.

Baddie Moore swiveled in his seat, put up his big mitt in greeting, and mouthed "Hi." Thelma spoke to the Colonel at the front of the room.

Chris Metzger, the young man she'd represented in court on his DUI charges, approached her with a smile. "Hey, Alice."

She gestured to the empty chair next to her, inviting him to sit down. "I'm happy to see you here," she said.

"I was assigned to the Department of Community Events by the judge," he said with a shrug. "I've got to do two hundred and fifty hours of community service as part of my sentence."

Alice already knew all this, but maybe he needed to say it.

"How's it going?" she asked.

"Fine, I actually like it. The Colonel runs a tight ship, but he's fair and he's got a lot of great ideas," Chris enthused.

"The Colonel?" she said. "What does he have to do with this?"

"He's the director of community events for Hideaway Bay."

This surprised her. How did she not know this? On reflection, she realized she'd never thought of him as having a job. She thought of him as a veteran who ran a support group. But she supposed he must work;

Thelma had mentioned that he'd retired from the service.

"Anyways, I wanted to say thanks, Alice, for your help," Chris said.

Alice nodded and their attention was drawn to the front of the room by the Colonel calling the meeting to order.

First, he thanked everyone for showing up and congratulated them on recognizing the importance of keeping the beach clean. He explained that the major spring cleanup would take place the following weekend and then they'd rotate every weekend with teams of two keeping it up until the snow fell.

"We supply everything from gloves to garbage bags to litter-grabber sticks. Remember, don't pick up sharp objects with your hands and if you find needles or syringes, they need to be disposed of in a sharps container."

After he went over everything, he said, "Now, I've had to cancel next month's meeting, but I'll give you the bullet points before we end tonight." He grinned and said, "I'm going to the home opener for the Boston Red Sox."

"New York Yankees!" Thelma called from the front row.

The Colonel grinned and said, "We can't all be perfect, Thelma." Thelma slapped her thigh and guffawed, and there were titters that spread through the crowd. Alice found herself grinning.

Chris leaned over and whispered, "He's a huge baseball and football fan. He has season tickets to the Buffalo Bills. Said he hopes they win a Super Bowl while he's still alive."

Alice smiled.

But their attention was redirected toward the Colonel.

"So, we're all set for the cleanup. Sign your name on the sign-up sheets. We'll see you Saturday!" He smiled at the crowd and continued. "On to other business. I do have some great news for Hideaway Bay residents. An anonymous donor has gifted a plot of land on Erie Street. After much debate, it's been decided—with the donor's approval—that the land will be used as an allotment to grow flowers and vegetables. There are a lot of residents who don't have access to land to grow gardens, so this will be for them and for all of us. Nothing's been finalized yet, but there's enough for a community garden, and someone has suggested making a garden for bees and butterflies, which I think is a great idea. Stay tuned. We'll cover it more in the first meeting in May.

Alice was excited about that as well. That's what she loved about small town life: there were a lot of community events that brought everyone together.

Afterward, as she leaned over a table, adding her name to a sign-up sheet, the Colonel approached her.

"Alice, I'm glad you've decided to join us," he said.

"I'm looking forward to it," she said truthfully.

"Great. Will you just be doing the big cleanup, or do you want to be part of the weekend roster going forward?"

"You can put me on the weekend roster."

"That's great. Usually, I pair a new volunteer with someone who has done it before. There are teams of two and we rotate. We never have to do more than two weekends in a row. It usually works out to once a month."

"Sounds perfect," she said.

Another resident approached Jack from behind and Jack said quickly to her, "I'll see you Saturday, Alice," before turning his attention to the other person.

Chapter Twenty-Six

1974

Thelma

"Hideaway Bay is a great place to raise kids," Junie said as she and Thelma sat on the porch of her house on Star Shine Drive one Friday evening.

Thelma didn't need to be told that, but she liked that her friend confirmed it.

It was late spring; the air was warm and the sky was blue and Thelma always marveled at how quiet it was out here as compared to the city. It would be a lovely place to raise a child. But she wondered how she would afford it.

"You can look for work here, and the rent will be cheaper. You'd be able to rent a small cottage for you and Donny," Junie said encouragingly.

From their spot on the porch, they watched Donny and Nancy riding up and down the street on bikes. You couldn't ride your bike down the middle of the street in the city, not unless you wanted to get hit by a car.

When Thelma had called Junie to tell her about the trouble she was having with Donny being bullied at school, Junie immediately invited the two of them out for the weekend so they could figure out what to do. Those had been her words.

Paul had picked the two of them up after he'd gotten out of work on Friday evening, and drove them out. It was good to be out here, she thought. It was like being on vacation but with your best friend and your kid.

Thelma voiced her fears. "I'm afraid I won't be able to get a job or find a place that has rent I can afford."

"You will. And if you don't, you can stay with us and save some money."

Thelma swung her head around and stared at Junie. "I can't do that! You've got your own family now."

"Don't be ridiculous," Junie said. She leaned back in her rocker and smiled. "I would love it if you moved out here. We could see each other all the time."

Thelma had to admit that the idea appealed to her as well.

"You know Stanley owns the Old Red Top Restaurant down at the end of Main Street? Paul and I were in there last week for Texas hots, and he has a sign up in the window advertising for a waitress."

Thelma grimaced. "Do I want to work for Stanley? Of all people?"

Junie shrugged. "He's all business now. Owns a few cottages that he rents out during the summer months. He'd give you a job."

"That's what I'm afraid of," Thelma said with a grin, and they both burst out laughing.

When they stopped laughing, Junie said, "Tomorrow after breakfast, we'll go look at some places for rent, just to price them."

"Isn't Paul working?"

"So?"

"How will we get there?"

"We walk everywhere in Hideaway Bay. Remember, growing up, when we used to walk up and down South Park Avenue every night? That was practice."

It sounded like a good plan, and Thelma felt a little hopeful on behalf of her son.

Thelma clung to Donny's hand. She loved nothing more than she loved her kid. He was the only person in her life that she could look at and have her heart fit to burst with love until it hurt. She could even overlook the fact that he'd inherited his father's weak chin. His hand was firmly in her grasp as were all aspects of his life. And it was because of him that she was going to Stanley Schumacher for a job.

She remembered how Stanley had asked her, after she'd married Bobby, why she hadn't come to him. He'd said he would have done right by her. She'd thought about that on and off over the ensuing years. But now she was going to put it to the test. To see if he was still willing to help her. But first, she would have to ask, and that would involve swallowing her pride. If it were only her needing help, it would be more difficult because sometimes her pride was a big chip on her shoulder, and she couldn't see around it. But when it came to her child, she was willing to do all sorts of things, not least of all, swallowing her pride.

Earlier that morning, she and Junie, with Donny and Nancy in tow, walked up and down the streets of Hideaway Bay, looking for a place to rent. She'd seen a little house not far from Junie's and while she went to the restaurant, Junie stayed home to call the number on the for-rent sign.

With the weak, watery May sun high in the sky, she and Donny marched down to the red-topped building owned by Stanley Schumacher. Everyone knew—and had been surprised by—the success Stanley had made of himself. No one was more surprised than Thelma. She never would have thought it of him back in the third grade when he'd sat behind her in class and made pulling her braids a kind of sport. But still, she had to give him credit where credit was due. Surely by now, he'd outgrown his crush on her. But she hoped not so much that he wouldn't give her a job.

The restaurant was busy. It was a bright place with white tiled walls and booths covered in vinyl the color of butterscotch. Most of the seats were filled, and the waitresses flew around the place with either trays or pots of coffee in their hands. In the background she could hear the sounds of a radio.

Stanley was on the grill line when they arrived. He spotted her through the pass-through window. She lifted her hand and waved. With a nod, he stopped what he was doing, said something to the other line cook, and exited the kitchen.

"Mom, you're hurting my hand," Donny said at her side. Thelma looked at him and muttered, "Sorry." She loosened her grip.

Stanley regarded her warily. He was no longer scrawny but more wiry and lean. The acne was long gone, but his face still bore the tell-tale pockmarked scars, like the craters on the moon.

"Hey, Thelma," he said. He appeared cautious. He nodded to Donny. "What happened to you, kid? How'd you get the shiner?"

Before Thelma could answer, Donny chirped, "Lester Mulhouse hit me."

"On purpose?"

"I guess so."

Thelma cut them both off, not wanting to get into the fact that her son was being bullied. It was something she'd handle. Something she was going to fix. Permanently.

Her palms were damp, and her throat was dry. This surprised her. Before today, she'd never been nervous with Stanley Schumacher. But now that she was dependent on his generosity, she was jittery. She wiped her hands on the sides of her pants.

"I'm here to apply for the job."

"What job?" Stanley asked. He pushed his glasses up on his nose.

"The one you have advertised in the window," she said smartly.

"That's a permanent job, Thelma. Not just for the summer. I need a waitress. Full-time, year-round."

She lowered her voice. "I need a permanent job."

"In Hideaway Bay?" Stanley couldn't hide his surprise.

"Yes, I'm going to move down here."

"Really?" His eyes lit up. "That's great news."

Thelma nodded.

Stanley glanced at Donny and seemed to draw his own conclusions. "There's a good school system down here."

"That's what Junie said."

He nodded. "Can you start Monday?"

"Wait a minute, Stanley, don't you want me to fill out an application? Don't you want references?"

Stanley laughed and folded his arms across his chest. "References? Thelma, I've known you all my life. And you can fill out the paperwork on Monday."

Thelma felt lighter as if a great burden had been lifted.

"Have you got a place to stay down here?" Stanley asked.

"That's where I'm going next," Thelma said.

"Look, I've got a cottage that I rent, a two-bedroom house. It isn't much, but the rent would be affordable," he said, and then he added quickly, "If you'd like to take a look at it."

"I would."

He nodded. "Good." Then he turned to Donny and said, "Young man, how would you like a Texas hot?"

"What's that?"

"A hot dog with special sauce."

Donny looked to his mother, who nodded. When she went to pay for it, Stanley waved her away.

Thelma got angry.

Stanley pressed his lips together. "Would you relax, Thelma? It's a hot dog, for Pete's sake. Not a marriage proposal."

"Yeah, make sure it stays that way, Stanley," she warned.

He rolled his eyes and walked away, but not before muttering, "If you ever gave me a chance, maybe you'd see the real me."

That little statement hit her hard. Not enough to do anything about it, but it was something to think about.

Donny settled into his new school and liked it. At least he wasn't being bullied. He even made a new friend, and Thelma encouraged him to bring his friend over whenever he wanted. Then one day, Donnie took off on his bike with his friend, Sammy, and Thelma stood on her front step, watching him ride off without her. He looked over his shoulder and waved at her. Thelma smiled and waved back. This was Donny beginning to pull away from her, as it should be. But it tugged at her heart. Although Donny was her life, she didn't want to be his. That wouldn't be right. She wanted him to have a life of his own. But with every step he took away from her, a little piece of her heart went with him.

It turned out that she liked working at Stanley's Old Red Top Restaurant. She definitely preferred it over the cardboard box factory or the grocery store. She'd be the first to tell you that she wasn't curing cancer at the Old Red Top, but she liked the banter she exchanged with the customers, especially the regulars. They didn't seem to mind her tough-talking, sometimes blunt manner. One of them, a favorite of hers, a World War I vet who had no teeth left and had to have his meals pureed, called her a character. She took it as a compliment.

The little cottage on Starlight Drive, which ran parallel to Star Shine Drive, was small, but it was a proper house and much better to raise a child in as opposed to the apartment they'd lived in in the city. She could just make out the back of Junie's house from her front stoop. The rental had a small yard and an old garage, but for her it was perfect.

At first, she was hesitant about working with Stanley. Initially, he'd told her she could work her shifts around Donny's school schedule, but Thelma had refused. She did not want to be treated any different than the other waitresses. That would go over like a lead balloon with the other girls if she was getting special treatment. She worked her shifts just like everyone else. Junie had been a great help. If Thelma had to work, she'd drop Donny over at Junie's home so Donny and Nancy could walk to school together. If a waitress called off for the afternoon shift, Junie would pick Donny up from school and he'd stay at her house until Thelma finished her shift. She knew he was well taken care of over there and he'd get a hot dinner from Junie. She was grateful to her friend. For the first time in a long time, Thelma was happy.

Stanley kept any mention of his undying love for her to himself, maintaining a strict employer-employee relationship. And Thelma was relieved about that. She didn't want to constantly have to tell him no or turn him down. But Stanley never pestered her to go out, never asked her for a date, and Thelma wondered if working with her day-to-day had tempered his enthusiasm for her.

She had no interest in another relationship. She was perfectly content to stay single for the rest of her life. From raising her brothers to cooking her father's dinner every day and then the whole disaster with Bobby, Thelma had had her fill of men. Not that some of the customers didn't ask her out. Some of them did. And she always said no, but it seemed that Stanley was always aware when a customer showed interest in her.

"If he's bothering you, I'll ban him," Stanley had said to her.

Thelma laughed. "No, Stanley, you don't have to do that. I can fight my own battles."

And Stanley would nod and return to his position on the grill line, spatula in hand.

But despite her having her fill of men and swearing them off, she loved her boy Donny heart and soul, and was determined to give him a happy childhood. On her time off, they did fun things. They went to the beach a lot, and she took him to the movies. She indulged him and took him twice to see *Herbie Rides Again*. They got their Cokes, their large bucket of popcorn with extra butter, and one box each of Milk Duds and Junior Mints. They were first into the large theater with its red walls and red velvet seats. Donny picked out their seats.

Yes, she decided, her decision to move out to Hideaway Bay had been the right one.

Stanley stood on the grill line, tending to the burgers and dogs and singing along with the transistor radio he'd set up in the grill area.

Before calling out her order, Thelma watched him for a moment. "Kung Fu Fighting" played on the radio and Stanley sang along, happily unaware of her presence as he sang into his spatula and did what she surmised to be karate moves. He put his heart and soul into it, and Thelma laughed. When he looked up, she rapped her knuckles on the stainless steel counter and yelled, "Two Texas hots with mustard and onion and a side of fries."

"Coming right up," he yelled back. The song ended, to be replaced with Redbone's "Come and Get Your Love," and Stanley flipped the spatula into the air, caught it, and began to sing in earnest while locking his eyes on Thelma's. He wiggled his eyebrows at her.

Thelma burst out laughing. She loved working here at the restaurant. It was fun. Stanley didn't take himself too seriously, but everyone knew he was the boss.

She turned from the counter to find Mel Byrnes standing there. Although she hadn't lived in Hideaway Bay long, she recognized him as the town's realtor.

"Does Stanley have a minute?" he asked.

"Hold on," she said. She leaned against the counter, peering through the pass-through. "Stanley, Mel Byrnes is here to see you."

"Okay, thanks, Thelma," Stanley said. He handed his spatula off to Gus, one of the new line cooks.

Thelma turned back to Mel. "Would you like some coffee?"

"Yes, please, black if it's not too much trouble."

As she poured him a cup, Stanley walked out from the kitchen.

"Hey, Mel, what can I do for you?" Stanley asked, reaching over to shake Mel's hand.

"A property has come up. It's a fixer-upper but with a lot of potential. You were the first person I thought of."

Thelma handed Mel his mug of coffee.

"Good man," Stanley said. "Come on back to my office and show me what you got."

Carrying his cup of coffee and his briefcase, Mel followed Stanley to the back of the restaurant.

Thelma's gaze followed Stanley. He was a man that was definitely going places.

Reluctantly, Thelma had agreed to let Donny go camping for a week with Bobby and Diane and the girls. She'd been hesitant at first, but Donny was so excited at the prospect of sleeping in a tent and sitting around a campfire, roasting marshmallows, that she couldn't say no. She only hoped that Bobby wouldn't bail on him like he'd done in the past. If he disappointed Donny over this, she'd wring Bobby's neck.

Donny had only been gone two days when Thelma found herself up at the crack of dawn, wandering around her cottage like a zombie. She was a little lost without him. In the kitchen, she put the kettle on, walked through the house, and opened the drapes of the front living room window. The sun was just coming up behind the house. Birds twittered loudly as if they were engaged in some kind of competition. Out of the corner of her eye, she spotted Stanley walking down the street, hands in his pockets, looking around at the sky and the house across the street. When his gaze swung over to her cottage, Thelma stepped back, hiding behind the drapes. She waited a few seconds, looked out again, and saw him turn at the end of the street and head in the direction of the beach.

When she'd taken the job at the restaurant and then the cottage from Stanley, she'd braced herself for an onslaught of propositions from Stanley. But they never came. He didn't show up at her door unannounced, which was one thing she had feared. And at work, he didn't show any favoritism. He was always kind to Donny and had an easy way with him when Donny showed up after school to wait for his mother to finish her shift.

Thelma chewed her lip and narrowed her eyes, curious as to what Stanley was up to. He certainly wasn't heading in the direction of the Old Red Top. The whistling kettle interrupted her thoughts, and she dashed back to the kitchen to turn it off. She ignored her waiting mug with the spoonful of instant coffee and headed back to the front of the house and out the door, closing it behind her. She didn't bother locking it. There was no need to, not in Hideaway Bay.

Folding her arms across her chest, she walked in the direction she'd seen Stanley go. When she reached the end of her street, she turned right and headed toward the beach. She crossed Star Shine Drive and there was no sign of Stanley. As she walked along the wooden boardwalk, she thought this was a fool's errand. Even if she saw him, what was her plan? He'd know that she'd followed him. And she certainly didn't want to fill his head with the wrong ideas.

She was about to turn around when she heard him call, "Thelma?"

She spotted him about ten yards down the beach, sitting in the sand, his ankles crossed, his arms over his raised knees. He looked in her direction and beckoned her with a wave.

Feeling as if she'd been caught spying, Thelma gave up and strode toward him, kicking up sand in her wake.

"What are you doing out here this early?" Stanley asked, looking up at her.

She ignored his question as she realized she couldn't come up with an answer quick enough. "I was about to ask you the same thing."

"Sit down," he said, and he patted the sand next to him.

Thelma settled down next to Stanley, folding her knees up and hugging them to herself.

"I come down here every morning at sunrise," he said, turning his head to look at her.

"You do?" Thelma asked. She drew in the sand with her finger, resting her chin on her knees.

"I do."

Neither said anything for a moment.

"Where's Donny?" he asked. He always asked after her kid.

"He's with his father and Diane camping for a week," Thelma said, her voice full of disapproval.

"That'll be good for him," Stanley said. "Boys should go camping and fishing and all those things. My old man used to do all that stuff with me and Ralph."

Thelma snorted. "I don't know about that. But at least he didn't cancel this time."

Stanley already knew that Bobby had bailed at the last minute before. Thelma sometimes griped about it at work when she had to try and get a sitter at the last minute.

When Stanley didn't add anything, Thelma said, "Bobby will never get a father-of-the-year award."

"Maybe not," Stanley agreed, "but he still is Donny's father."

She bristled.

He laughed. "I can feel you getting your hackles up, Thelma."

"Just because he's his father doesn't mean he's his father," she said.

Stanley regarded her for a moment and said quietly, "At the risk of my own personal safety, I'm going to give you some unsolicited advice."

She narrowed her eyes at him and waited.

"Don't say anything negative about Bobby to Donny. Kids are pretty smart, and he'll figure it out for himself and draw his own conclusions." Stanley said.

Thelma bit back her response. After a few moments of silence, she changed the subject.

"So what do you do at the beach when you come here? Just sit here in the sand?"

Stanley pointed to the horizon. It was various shades of blue and hazy, indicating a hot day was coming their way.

"See the trawlers and boats out there?"

She squinted and quickly looked at Stanley, wondering if he had the eyesight of a hawk before returning her attention to the horizon. Sharpening her focus, she caught sight of the ships.

"I like to watch the ships and boats out on the lake. I find it relaxing," Stanley said. "See that trawler there? The long one with the black hull with the red stripe?"

Thelma nodded.

"I'm guessing that traveled all the way in from the St. Lawrence Seaway. I wonder what it's carrying, where they're headed, that sort of thing."

He turned to her. "I wonder if they can see me sitting on the beach and if they wonder who I am or what I'm about. Do you ever think about things like that, Thelma?"

This was a side of Stanley she was unacquainted with. She was used to pestering Stanley from the third grade. She was used to the savvy businessman who ran a successful restaurant and owned rental properties throughout Hideaway Bay. And she knew the Stanley who always asked after Donny and kind of looked out for him. But this Stanley she did not know.

"Oh, I wonder all sorts of things," she said.

He waited expectantly. His arms were tanned beneath his short-sleeved orange-and-yellow plaid shirt but beneath the tan, she could see the freckles that covered his arms. How had she never noticed them before?

Thelma snapped up her head and said, "I wonder how I'm going to pay the phone bill, I wonder if Frank is all right, and I wonder what I'm going to make for dinner for Donny."

Stanley burst out laughing and slapped his knee. "Thelma, you're a hoot."

"Yeah, I'm a hoot all right," she said with a wry grin. She stood, brushing sand off her bottom.

"Where are you going?"

"I've got to get ready for work," she said. "My boss is a real stickler, and I don't want to lose my job." She winked at him and pivoted on her heel to head away.

"Thelma?"

She looked over her shoulder as Stanley said, “While Donny’s away, you could meet me down here. At sunrise.”

He looked so hopeful that Thelma couldn’t say no. Not this time. She smiled and said, “We’ll see.”

It was all she could give him. She thought she might pop down the following morning and surprise him. But Donny arrived home later that day, unexpectedly. Apparently, one of Bobby’s girls got sick and they returned early. And Thelma didn’t meet Stanley at sunrise, though she wanted to.

Chapter Twenty-Seven

Alice

There was a great turnout for the beach cleanup on Saturday. Alice waited on her porch and when she spotted people assembling, she headed across the street. Lily had wanted to go, but Simon was on a deadline for a book he was writing and had asked her to work overtime.

It was a dull April day with intermittent misty rain. The text that had been sent out earlier that morning said the event would go forward, rain or shine. Alice chose a bright yellow rain jacket with a navy lining. She slid her phone in her pocket as she neared the group. There were plenty of people she recognized: Sue Ann and Della, the owner of the olive oil shop. Mr. Lime was there from the five-and-dime. He was all decked out in a clear rain poncho that had a hood. Alice wondered if it was an item he sold at his store.

Jules was there, and Alice gravitated toward her. She did not bring up her impending divorce; it wasn't the time or the place. Behind them, the Colonel was talking to some of the members of his veterans' group. Alice couldn't help but listen as one of them asked him about his trip to Boston to see the Red Sox home opener. The Colonel told them about the few days he spent there: how he went to the JFK Presidential Library, had a beer at the Cheers Restaurant, went on the Freedom Trail, and made a stop at the Sam Adams brewery. Alice raised her eyebrows. He sounded like a great travel partner.

"Um, earth to Alice, earth to Alice." Jules waved her hand in front of Alice's face.

"Huh?"

Jules laughed. "I asked how Isabelle was and if she's coming home soon."

"Oh, sorry," Alice said with a quick shake of her head. "I was distracted."

"I can see that."

"I haven't spoken to Isabelle in a few weeks. She said she might come home for Gram's one-year anniversary, but she wasn't sure." It was not lost on Alice that the anniversary of Gram's death was only weeks away, and the three of them had to make a decision as to whether to keep the house or sell it.

"She's got the life, that's for sure," Jules said.

"It suits her," Alice said. She looked around. "Hey, where's Thelma? I thought for sure she'd be here."

Jules grimaced. "Granny's got gout. Her big toe is killing her."

"Is there anything I can do?" Alice asked.

"Nah, Maria and I are popping in a few times a day to make sure she doesn't need anything."

"Okay. Would she like some baked goods?"

Jules snorted. "Granny has more than one sweet tooth. I'm sure she wouldn't say no."

Alice laughed. "All right, I'll drop something off to her tomorrow then."

The Colonel called everyone to attention, showed them a diagram of the beach divided up into sectors, and assigned everyone a partner. Alice was partnered with Jules, who was a veteran of this affair.

Chapter Twenty-Eight

Christmas 1974

Thelma

Thelma stood on one of the seats of the vinyl booth to hang green garland along the top of the windows of the restaurant. It was almost seven-thirty, and she'd picked up an extra shift because one of the girls had called off. She didn't mind staying; she was already there. Besides, because it was her second shift, she'd be the first one out and if it was quiet, she could be home by nine-thirty.

She'd called Junie, who said it was no problem for Donny to go to her house after school. Junie'd made a big pot of beef stew earlier that morning so there was plenty to go around. She'd even asked if Thelma wanted her to save her a bowl, but Thelma laughed and said no. She'd eat at the restaurant like she did every day.

The staff Christmas party was scheduled for the following week. Thelma couldn't wait. Other than hanging out with Junie, she didn't have much of a social life. But she loved living in Hideaway Bay, even in the winter. It was bleak but it was still beautiful.

The Christmas Party was going to be held one evening after the dinner rush. They were closing right after the dinner hour and then they'd have the place to themselves. One of the other waitresses had told her that it was a lot of fun and that Stanley gave out Christmas bonuses—cold, hard cash. Thelma hadn't wanted to ask how much those bonuses were, but she hoped she wouldn't be disappointed. She had her heart set on buying Donny a brand-new bike for Christmas.

She stood on the seat, watching the snow fall outside in the bright exterior lights. She wished she could see the beach but beyond the parking lot, there was only darkness. This was going to be her first Christmas in Hideaway Bay and she was excited, even if Donny no longer believed in Santa Claus.

After Thelma tacked up the garland, she hopped off the booth and bounced up onto the adjoining one, tacking that bit of garland up. Stanley didn't seem to care what the waitresses did as far as Christmas decorations went, as long as the customers were happy.

She'd already stenciled snow on the windows and granted, they'd need a blowtorch come January to get it off, but she'd deal with it then. The other waitresses, Trixie and Betty and Angie, had decorated an artificial aluminum Christmas tree with red ornaments and red garland. Angie had looped sparkly red-and-gold garland along the ceiling, hanging great big ornaments from it. They'd strongarmed Louie, the dishwasher, into affixing exterior lighting to the front of the place. Stanley had had an intercom system installed and currently, Bing Crosby was crooning a Christmas song over the speakers.

She loved this job. She liked the rattle of coins in her pocket at the end of the day, and she liked the people she worked with. But more than anything, she liked the fact that Donny loved his new school and had friends. It had been a long time since he had come home sporting a black eye or some other bruise.

The door opened and the bell above it tinkled, signaling a customer. Thelma put the tacks aside and left the garland hanging. She recognized the new customer as Carol Rimmer, the town librarian. She'd had to take Donny to the Hideaway Bay public library a couple of weeks ago for a Thanksgiving project for school. Not knowing her way around the library, she'd asked Carol, who had been really helpful. She was an attractive woman: warm brown hair with even warmer eyes. Her looks fit her job description. Her voice was well-modulated and when they'd been at the library, she'd spoken to Thelma and Donny softly.

Carol lingered at the counter, glanced around, and checked her watch.

Thelma approached her, grabbing a menu from the stack next to the cash register on the counter.

"You can sit anywhere," Thelma advised her.

"I'm not here to eat." Before Thelma could question her, the librarian asked, "How did Donny do on his project?"

"Great, he got an A," Thelma said, glowing with pride. Turned out Donny was a straight-A student, a trait he'd gotten from neither of his parents. Must be a recessive gene.

"Can I help you?" Thelma asked.

"I'm here to meet Stanley," Carol said. Her smile was shy, and Thelma noted she'd said she was there to "meet" Stanley, not see him.

Thelma had just opened her mouth to respond when Stanley appeared from the back of the restaurant, where he had an office. He was bundled up in a coat and carried a pair of winter gloves in his hand.

"Hi, Stanley." Carol smiled at him.

"All set?" he asked.

"I am," Carol said. She looked back at Thelma. "We're going to dinner and then a movie. *The Towering Inferno*. Can't wait."

It was a movie Thelma had wanted to see. She loved horror films and disasters. Her voice had left her as she tried to process this new development.

"Come on, Carol, we don't want to be late," Stanley said, putting his hand on the small of the librarian's back and escorting her out.

"See you tomorrow, Thelma," he called.

Slowly, Thelma climbed back up onto the booth to tack the next piece of garland above the window. As she did, she spied Carol getting into Stanley's car. He had a nice car, a blue Chevy Impala with a white top. He leaned across the front seat and kissed Carol. As Thelma watched this, she stood there in the booth, unable to move.

Stanley had a girlfriend?

Carol was everything Thelma wasn't. She was educated, she was soft, and she was pleasant. None of those things could be ascribed to Thelma. And most of all, she had nice hair. Of course Stanley would be interested in someone like Carol. He'd finally woken up. Stanley had a lot to offer the right woman.

In almost thirty years, she'd never seen Stanley with another woman. From time to time, she'd heard of him dating different girls, but she'd never actually seen it for herself. And since he'd moved out to Hideaway Bay, he'd been too busy working eighty-hour weeks to see anyone. It never occurred to her that Stanley might want to marry and have a family of his own. Never occurred to her that he'd see another girl. Thelma was so used to taking it for granted that Stanley carried a torch for her that to see him with another woman left her shaken. She didn't know what bothered her more: the fact that he was going out with someone or the fact that it bothered her that he was. This was a new, unfamiliar, unpleasant feeling.

When she'd tacked up the last bit of garland, she stepped down, returning the box of tacks to the shelf below the counter. She looked around the restaurant and, seeing it practically empty, she told the other waitresses she was leaving. It was snowing outside; there wouldn't be too many more customers now.

"Are you all right?" Trixie asked. She was the newest waitress, graduated from high school the previous June. She favored thin eyebrows and bright-blue eye shadow.

"I am. I think. I think I might be coming down with something."

Hurriedly, she got her coat and purse from the back room, not bothering to empty her pockets of coins, not caring, deciding she'd do it later. Quickly, she bundled up in her coat and wrapped her scarf several times around her neck. She patted her pockets, checking for her gloves, and headed out, a headache growing in size.

Her car had been parked in the lot for more than twelve hours, and it was covered with snow. She slid into the driver's seat, the coldness of the interior making her shiver. It took three attempts at starting it for the engine to turn over. When it did, she got back out of the car, grabbed the snow brush from the back seat, and ran around the vehicle, swiping errantly at the snow that covered the windows. It was cold out, and her nose ran and her eyes stung. When she slid back inside and slammed the door, the car shook.

Thelma felt sick to her stomach. She wanted to vomit. Her reaction to Stanley seeing someone scared her. She didn't know what it meant, if it even meant anything at all. She'd always thought Stanley would be there in the background, adoring her like he always had. But it hadn't been fair to him to keep him in the background. If anybody had done that to her, she would have been furious.

But Thelma refused to think about what it meant, about any feelings she might possibly have for Stanley. How could that be? He was a nuisance! He was a pest! But that train of thought quickly derailed. Yes, back in school, he was all those things but if she was honest, he was not any of those things anymore.

As her older car continued to run and the defroster belted cold air at the windshield, Thelma moaned and slumped forward in her seat, resting her head against the cold steering wheel.

Do I have feelings for Stanley?

Christmas came and went, and Thelma learned that Stanley was seeing Carol regularly. She'd come into the restaurant to meet him, or he'd leave early to take her out to dinner. Thelma made no big deal about it, pretending that it didn't bother her.

"I'm heading out early, taking Carol to lunch," Stanley said, pulling on his coat. There'd been ten inches of snow the previous night and by now, with Christmas over, it was beginning to get old.

Thelma didn't look up from the menus, adopting an air of indifference. There were index cards with the day's specials on them, and she was inserting them into the plastic sleeve of the menu.

"We've got everything under control," she told him, finally looking up.

Stanley stood there for a moment as if he wanted to say something.

With a nod, Thelma said, "You better get a move on. The driving is slow today with all the snow."

With an exasperated sigh, Stanley turned and left the building. Thelma exhaled the breath she'd been holding after he closed the door behind him. She watched as he made his way to his car. He looked straight ahead, hands in his pockets, as if he had something on his mind.

January 1975

"Do you have to go to the library for this?" Thelma asked Donny when he arrived home from school.

Of all the places, did it have to be the library? The last person she wanted to see was Carol Rimmer. She didn't think she could stand to hear her gloat about Stanley and all the wonderful things they were doing: going out to dinner, going to the movies, going sledding and tobogganing while Thelma sat home, alone, no one wanting to take her out.

"Where else can I get information on the Mayan empire?" Donny asked.

"Did you look in Junie's encyclopedias?" she asked, exasperated.

"Yeah, I already did when I was there yesterday. There wasn't much. Besides, Miss Carol is a great resource," he said enthusiastically. Why couldn't he have been more interested in sports, Thelma lamented. But she didn't mean it. She was proud of his scholastic achievements, especially since academics had never been her strong suit.

"All right, let's go now because I have to get home and get dinner," Thelma said. She wanted to get it over with.

When Thelma had told Junie about the librarian dating Stanley, Junie had regarded her and said, "Well, there goes another missed opportunity."

"Why are you driving so slow, Mom? If you were driving any slower, we'd be going backwards," Donny complained.

"The roads are icy," she lied. They'd been plowed, and the snow that had covered the roads was flattened.

Donny ran ahead of her into the library and, dragging her feet, Thelma followed him.

This was nothing like the old city library Barb and Junie used to go to. This single-story building was newer, the words "Hideaway Bay Library" affixed to the blond bricks in big silver letters on the right side of the entrance.

To Thelma, all libraries smelled the same: of paper and books and wood and dust. She wasn't a reader, other than the daily newspaper, but she knew Junie spent a lot of time in here. As did Barb when she was home.

Donny stood at the desk, talking to Carol, explaining what he was looking for. When Thelma approached the desk, Carol's back stiffened, and her lips rolled inward in a tight smile.

"Hey, Carol, how are you?" Thelma asked.

"Fine," she said without looking at Thelma. She smiled briefly at Donny, stood from her desk, and told Donny to follow her. The two of them disappeared among the metal shelving of books. Thelma hung out at the desk, her hands in her pockets.

The two of them returned, each carrying some books in their arms. Donny nodded toward a table and the two of them set down the books. Thelma groaned. Her son was getting planted. She didn't want to hang out at the library with Stanley's girlfriend.

Carol and Donny bent over the books. Carol was friendly and encouraging toward Donny, opening books, flipping through pages, and showing him where to look for his information. Donny looked up at her in awe. Apparently, the librarian had quite a following.

Thelma folded her arms across her chest and huffed. If Donny was planning on staying for a while, she'd go home and start the dinner and return to pick him up later. She started to make her way over to him to let him know.

Carol turned away from Donny and spotted Thelma approaching. Her smile disappeared, and she pressed her lips together. She patted Donny on the shoulder and walked back toward her desk, ignoring Thelma as she passed her.

Thelma couldn't help but ask, "Is everything all right, Carol?"

Carol slowly turned her head toward Thelma. At first, she didn't reply and Thelma pressed, "How's it going with Stanley?"

"We broke up," Carol said tightly.

Thelma paled and backpedaled. "I'm sorry, I didn't know," she stammered. Her heart full of hope, she asked, "Did Stanley break up with you?"

"No, I broke up with him," Carol said.

"You did? Why?" Thelma felt compelled to ask.

"You're really going to ask me that?" Carol asked.

"I'm sorry, you're right, it's none of my business," Thelma said, and she took a step away from Carol. For someone who had initiated the break-up, she sure was bitter about it. Sometimes Thelma didn't understand the members of her own sex.

"I'll tell you why I broke up with him," Carol said, her voice shrill.

Thelma looked quickly around the library to make sure no one was in earshot.

"All Stanley can talk about is you. You're the best waitress, you're the best mother, and he goes on and on," Carol said, her voice plaintive, rolling her eyes toward the ceiling.

"He does?" Thelma said in disbelief.

"Oh, come on, Thelma, don't be coy. You have to know how he feels about you."

Thelma felt the heat rush to her cheeks. There was a narrow sliver of opportunity here, and she decided she wasn't going to blow it.

She laid her hand on Carol's arm, whose eyes widened.

"I'm sorry, Carol."

Before the other woman could respond, Thelma walked over to Donny and asked him if he could wait here at the library, assuring him she'd be back soon.

He nodded without looking up from his books on the Mayan Empire.

Thelma flew out of the library and down the few front steps, oblivious to the ice and snow. She could drive over to the Red Top but her heart raced and besides, it wasn't that far from the library, only a few blocks. She could surely manage that.

For January, the sky was a deep blue and the late afternoon sun, though watery, was bright and did throw some heat on her face. It was beginning its descent into night. The air was crisp and cold and the snow beneath her feet crunched with every step she took. By the time she reached the Old Red Top, she was breathless and her face was sweaty. She pulled off her winter hat and her red hair sprang up.

She pushed through the doors of the workplace she'd grown to like and even love in the last eight months.

Her gaze swung around the restaurant. The place was almost full. There were a lot of senior citizens who liked to come in for the early bird dinners and their discount prices. The Christmas decorations had all been taken down and put away until next year.

Trixie approached her, holding a coffeepot in her hand. The one for decaf as told by its orange handle.

"What are you doing here, Thelma?" she asked.

"I'm looking for Stanley," Thelma said easily. For a moment, she wondered if she was crazy. If her idea was stupid. Maybe she should go home and think about this. It would give her just enough time to come to her senses and stop this nonsense that she was about to embark on. But her feet kept moving forward.

With a nod over her shoulder, Trixie said, "He's on the grill line."

She hardly got the words out of her mouth before Thelma brushed past her, heading in the direction of the grill line. Through the pass-through, Thelma spotted Gus but not Stanley, but she could hear Stanley saying something to Gus and then laughing. Automatically, she smiled.

How had it taken her so long to see Stanley? Really see him? There was a sense of panic within her, wondering how it would have turned out if she'd not woken up to the possibility of him. To the certainty of him. It made her sick inside to think she might have missed this in her life.

How had she never noticed him? How had it slipped by her? Why hadn't she really looked at him and what he had to offer: the chance for Thelma to be loved for being herself. Why hadn't she looked past what she thought irritated her?

There was such an upward rush of emotion within her she didn't know if she could contain it. It was as if all the veils had lifted and she'd had a glimpse of the other side. And it was beautiful.

She pushed through the stainless steel butler door. Gus, a big bear of a guy and a veteran of the Korean War, stood at the grill, turning a few hot dogs. There was a well on the counter that had individual containers of Stanley's homemade Texas hot sauce, homemade chili sauce, and a pickle relish.

Stanley turned to Thelma and his smile disappeared, replaced by a puzzled frown.

"What are you doing here, Thelma? It's your day off," he said. He stepped closer to her, spatula in hand. His white apron was dirtied from the daylong cooking, and his white business shirt beneath it was rolled up to the elbows. His pockmarked skin shone from the unrelenting heat of the kitchen.

There was the smell of onions frying and the sound of bacon and hot dogs sizzling on the stainless steel grill. A transistor radio stood on a shelf in the kitchen with its antenna listing right. With its white industrial tile walls and brick-red tile floor, the grill line was as unromantic a place as you could imagine.

Thelma could not stop the tears that welled up in her eyes.

Stanley frowned. "Thelma, what's wrong? Is it Donny?"

She laughed. Her whole life had been distilled down to this moment. Never had there been more on the line. Because at the end of the day, the cost was going to be someone's feelings. Someone's heart.

It was now or never.

She approached him, her walk purposeful and expedient, her mind made up.

"What's going on?" he asked. He hadn't moved, still stood there regarding her, holding the black spatula in his right hand.

The other line cook, Gus, stood behind him, rolling the hot dogs on the grill, flipping a couple of burgers, all the while whistling and trying to be inconspicuous.

Thelma smiled at Stanley to reassure him. She nodded. When she was directly in front of him, she lowered her voice to a whisper and said, "I love you, Stanley Schumacher."

His sudden wide-mouthed grin was beautiful for how breathtaking it was.

"Well, it's about time!" he said, his voice full of excitement. He tossed the spatula on the counter, pulled her quickly into his embrace, dipped her until her back was horizontal with the floor, and planted a kiss on her lips.

Tears slipped from Thelma's eyes as she laughed, sinking into the kiss, her body relaxing, feeling as languid as oil. Kissing him as if they'd always kissed and as if they'd keep on kissing forever.

From behind them, Gus and one of the busboys started clapping. Trixie, watching through the pass-through window, started laughing and clapping as well.

Stanley pulled Thelma up, wrapped his arms around her waist while she slid her arms around his neck, and continued to kiss her amidst all the hooting and hollering.

Chapter Twenty-Nine

Alice

Baddie's text arrived as Alice was sifting through the morning mail. Once again, Ben would not be in the office. His binges were happening with alarming frequency, and he seemed to be surviving on a diet of fast food. She had a sick feeling in her stomach that it would not end well.

As much as she'd got the office where she wanted it, which was to say organized and clean, there was not much to be done about Ben's workspace. It had quickly gone back to its default state: disastrous. Alice had decided it wasn't a hill she wanted to die on. She made sure to empty his garbage can every evening to keep it from overflowing and to prevent the strong smell of takeout from leeching into every nook and cranny in the room. In the mornings, she tried to arrive five or ten minutes before Ben did so she could spray air freshener around the place, and when Ben wasn't there, she'd prop the door open to air it out a bit.

There were no court dates scheduled for the day, but there were two appointments in the calendar, which Alice knew she was well able to handle. The first was due to arrive shortly.

From where she sat, she had a good view of the battered, older-model sedan pulling into the parking lot, and she wondered if this was Ben's upcoming appointment. The car looked like a graduate of a demolition derby. The driver wrestled to get his door open, and when he got out and slammed it shut, the whole vehicle shook and rattled. But Alice soon forgot the car as she took in the questionable-looking driver. He was young, maybe early twenties, and he was tall and lanky. His jeans had rips and holes in them, and on his feet were a pair of black Nike sneakers. He wore a black leather vest over a black short-sleeved T-shirt, and his dark hair was styled in a mullet.

He approached the law office and pushed through the glass door, and Alice froze. Dark, vibrant tattoos covered his arms to his wrists and snaked up from beneath the collar of his T-shirt, wrapping around his neck. His dark eyes were made to appear darker with the heavy black eyeliner he wore. Studs lined both ears and the top of his right eyebrow.

She managed to find her voice. "Can I help you?"

"I'm Avery Winslow, I have an appointment with Ben," he said.

She extended her hand. "I'm Alice Monroe, an associate of Ben's. But he won't be in today."

Avery's shoulders slumped. "Really? Man, that's not cool. He already canceled on me once."

"I am sorry," Alice said.

"Is it that he doesn't want to represent me? I mean, I'm not an ideal client but he assured me on the phone that it was no problem."

"What was no problem?"

"I have no money and I need a lawyer."

"Maybe I can help you," she said. Speculation ran rampant in her mind as to what he needed an attorney for, and she wondered if it was a drug-related charge. But then she told herself that it wasn't fair of her to stereotype him. She reminded herself of her ordeal with Dennis Ballantine. Appearances weren't everything.

"Are you a lawyer?" he asked.

"I am," she said.

As there was no one in the office, she said, "Have a seat and tell me why you need a lawyer. But first, can I get you some coffee or tea?"

"Yeah, sure, tea if you have it."

"I do," she said, wheeling back on her chair and standing up.

She filled the kettle with bottled water and set it on the hot plate she kept next to the new coffee maker. She was a tea drinker herself and knew that microwaved hot water for tea was just not acceptable. She turned on the hot plate and within seconds, the ring was red with heat. She opened the small wooden box that held a variety of tea bags.

"I've got a selection. Green, chamomile, peppermint—"

Avery folded his hands together and leaned forward in his chair. "Any chance you have some rooibos?"

"I do," she said, looking at him. Appearances were definitely deceiving.

"Did you ever read that Alexander McCall Smith series?" he asked. His eyes were a deep blue and appeared intelligent.

The question surprised her. "About the lady detective in Botswana?" Avery nodded. "No, I haven't. But my grandmother read all the books." Those books still occupied space on the shelves in the living room.

"That's the one. She drinks rooibos tea and I thought, what the hell, I'll give it a try." He smiled. His teeth were straight, and he had one gold one in the front. "Turns out it's pretty good."

"I would have guessed you were a coffee drinker."

He scrunched up his face. "Nah, it gives me acid reflux." To emphasize his point, he rubbed his knuckles along his sternum.

"I find it quite bitter tasting myself," she added.

"Exactly. Any time you have to add all sorts of flavors and shit to it to be able to drink it, that should tip you off right away."

"I agree," she said. It was nice to find a like-minded individual when it came to matters of coffee and tea.

The kettle whistled and Alice poured boiling water over his teabag. She made herself a cup of peppermint tea. "How do you take it?"

"Black."

She steeped the teabag, then removed it and laid it on an old, chipped saucer she kept for that purpose. She handed him his cup and he said, "Thanks." She fixed her own and walked back to her desk and sat.

Avery took another sip of his tea and balanced his cup on the arm of his chair.

"You're new here," he said, leaning back in the chair and clasping his hands over his abdomen.

"I am. I'm back from Chicago."

"What'd you do there?"

"I worked for a law firm downtown. Corporate law, mostly," she said.

"Nice. I didn't know Ben had another attorney on staff," he said.

Alice pressed her lips together. “Unfortunately, no. I was hired more in an assistant capacity.”

“Aw, come on,” he said.

“There aren’t a lot of positions here in Hideaway Bay,” she said truthfully.

Avery fisted his hand and did a few air pumps with it. “Fight for your rights, Alice!”

She laughed. “I’ll keep that in mind. Now, what brings you here?” Alice pulled out a manila folder. On the tab, she wrote in her neat scrawl “Winslow, Avery.”

“As I told Ben over the phone, I’m a songwriter. Also, the lead singer for the band Rock, Paper, Scissors. We’re from town.”

Alice nodded, taking notes.

“We cut some demo tapes of the songs I’ve written,” he explained. He picked up the teacup and sipped from it.

Alice waited for him to resume.

“Somehow, my work has been recorded by another artist,” he said. “Almost song for song, word for word. And I want to know if I can sue for damages.”

“How do you know this?”

“It’s all over YouTube, they’ve gone viral.”

“And you say you wrote the songs,” Alice said.

“I did. I’ve got all the original notes and scores for the lyrics and the music,” he explained.

Alice paused and Avery, sensing her hesitation, said, "I can give you our demo tapes, which are dated, and give you links to this band on YouTube. They're making a fortune on my work."

Alice's forte was not copyright law, but as soon as Avery left the office, she'd be brushing up on it.

She didn't want to burst his bubble, so she started with, "Copyright is tricky to prove, Avery."

"I know that," he said. "That's why before we recorded the demo tapes, I registered all the songs with the US Copyright Office." He watched her expression and asked, "Would that help?"

Alice smiled. "It's a good start."

Out of curiosity, she asked, "What made you decide to copyright your material?" Avery Winslow couldn't be more than twenty-two, twenty-four at most. To know to copyright his creative work was quite forward-thinking.

Avery scratched the back of his head, frowning. "It was my uncle, actually. He lived with my mother and me. He said I should protect my work and get it copyrighted. Said my music was worth protecting."

She nodded. "That was good advice."

"He even paid for the copyright. I didn't have that kind of money then. I was only eighteen and working a part-time job."

She asked a few more questions so she'd have something to start with. After half an hour, when she was satisfied, she told him she'd look into it and be in touch.

Avery stood with his now-empty mug in hand and lifted it in a salute. "Thanks for the tea, Alice."

"No problem."

Avery exited the office and walked to his car, his right hand in his pocket. He looked around the parking lot. When he got to his car, he wrestled with the driver's-side door a good few minutes before finally giving up and trotting around to the passenger side and getting in. He slid over, started his engine, and pulled away.

Alice watched him, her mind churning. It might not be downtown Chicago, but at least she met interesting people.

Chapter Thirty

1975

Thelma

Thelma went through everything on the counter but couldn't find the gas bill. That was the problem since they'd moved into their new house in Hideaway Bay. She didn't know where everything was. Before they married in July, Stanley had insisted they buy a new house where they could start their marriage off on the right foot. She hadn't really cared; she'd assumed Stanley would simply move into her rental place. After all, he owned it. But he was adamant that they have a house with a proper yard for Donny.

They'd bought a two-story house on Seashell Lane, one of the side streets. And although it didn't have the view of the lake like Junie's house did, Thelma loved it. It was big and spacious with a bright kitchen. Stan had surprised her by putting her name on the deed alongside his. At first, she balked, saying she had no money to contribute to the purchase of it—Thelma hated owing anyone anything—but Stanley reminded her that they were a team.

"I'm your husband, Thelma, nothing is separate. What's mine is yours and what's yours is mine."

She snorted. "I bring nothing to the table."

"I beg to disagree," he said solemnly. This was a different Stanley than the one she was used to. There was no humor or joking in his voice. "I have more than enough money, and you bring yourself and Donny with you. As I see it, you're getting the short end of the stick."

She turned around so he couldn't see her face, emotion overwhelming her. "Well, I'll pull my fair share around here." It came out harsher than she intended.

He came up behind her and placed his thin hands on her shoulders. "I've no doubt about that, Thelma. You're going to be a great wife to me."

He'd left for work, and she'd gone to call up the stairs for Donny to get up for school. After that, more than once, she thought about that deed. How her name, Thelma Schumacher, was right below Stanley's. She'd never owned anything substantial in her life. That deed meant a lot to her.

But back to current reality. She put aside thoughts about that missing gas bill and opened the freezer, trying to decide what to cook for dinner. Finally, she pulled out a pack of stewing beef and threw it into the kitchen sink to thaw. Sighing, she went through the pile of bills again, her frustration mounting. She had to get the gas bill paid or there'd be no heat. And it was getting colder outside. She didn't like this feeling, one she was too familiar with: the worry of getting a bill paid on time and the humiliation when the shutoff notice arrived.

Stanley arrived in the kitchen, whistling. He was dressed and ready to go to work. Thelma gave him a quick once-over to make sure his clothes were clean and pressed. She'd do the same with Donny later.

"I'll see you later at the restaurant," Stanley said. He leaned in to peck her on the cheek, but she was distracted, standing there with her hands on her hips and looking around the kitchen.

"What's wrong, Thelm?" he asked, pulling on his jacket.

"I've misplaced the gas bill. It was due to be paid today, but I can't find it." She tried to keep the panic out of her voice but failed.

"Oh, I paid that last week."

A mixture of anger and relief flooded through her. She rolled her eyes. Sometimes her eyes hurt from rolling them so much. “Why didn’t you tell me?” she demanded.

He shrugged. “I don’t know. I wrote out a check and dropped it off at the gas company.”

She started to shake.

Stanley stepped forward, reaching out for her, but she pulled away.

“Thelma, tell me what’s going on,” he said. His voice was firm. That was one thing she had learned about Stan. Just because he’d been over the moon about her since they were nine years old didn’t mean he was a pushover.

“I’m used to paying the utilities. I’ve always paid all the bills. It made me panic, thinking they were going to shut off the gas.”

Stanley smiled. “They’re not going to shut off the gas.”

She nodded. She knew that, but after living paycheck to paycheck for so many years, it was hard to turn off that feeling.

“Let’s sort this out right now,” Stanley said.

Thelma nodded again. All this newness disturbed her, made her feel as if she were standing on shifting ground. She didn’t like it one bit. For a fleeting moment, she wondered if she’d made a mistake. Maybe she should have stayed in the rental with Donny. There were too many unknowns with this new marriage.

"You've got to remember that I've always been single," Stanley said. "If I didn't pay the bills, they didn't get paid. I thought you'd like me to take over."

Narrowing her eyes, Thelma glared at him. No man was going to boss her.

Stanley put his hands up and lowered his voice. "Hear me out."

She crossed her arms over her chest and leaned against the counter. She couldn't wait to hear his explanation. It would probably be something about how he was the man or, worse, how it was his money. And if that was the case, she'd pack her bags, get Donny, march right out of the house, and never look back.

Stanley put his hands on his hips. "You have spent your whole life, since your mother died, taking care of people. You've taken care of everyone from your father to your brothers to your first husband to Donny. I thought you might like a break."

Thelma stared at him.

"I'd like to take care of you, Thelma."

She didn't know what to say and even if she had, the lump in her throat was so big she didn't think the words would be able to get out around it.

Stanley continued. "We'll work things out, we'll figure out what's best for us."

She still couldn't speak, which was nothing short of miraculous.

"Do you want me to pay the bills, or do you want to pay them?" he asked and added quickly, "Because in the whole scheme of things, I don't care."

"I'd like to pay them," she said. "But I don't have any money."

He rolled his eyes and sighed in frustration. "Will you stop saying that? When are you going to get it through that thick skull of yours? You're my wife, we're married now. Your name is on the checking account with mine. Just take the checkbook and pay the bills. Do what you need to do."

She nodded. It was going to take some time getting used to this version of marriage with Stanley.

"All right, are we okay? You know where the checkbook is, and you can be in charge of the bills."

"Okay, Stanley."

"Is there anything else we need to clear up before I go to work?"

Thelma shook her head. "No, we're all set."

He placed his hands on her arms. "Are we good?"

She nodded quickly. "We're good."

"I've got to get to the restaurant." He leaned in to kiss her cheek like he did every morning, and she tipped her cheek toward him.

As he walked away, he asked, "What's for dinner tonight?" Although he owned a restaurant, he preferred to eat his dinners at home with Thelma and Donny.

Thelma glanced at the stew meat thawing in the sink. She thought for a moment and said, "I was going to make chicken cacciatore tonight."

"Aw, that's great, that's my favorite." He walked out the door, whistling.

She stared at the space he vacated, smiling. When she heard the car pull away, she threw the stew beef back into the freezer and grabbed her coat, heading out the door. She'd have to get to the store to get some chicken and other ingredients.

Chapter Thirty-One

Alice

"Is that your phone, Alice?" Lily called from the kitchen.

Alice dropped her magazine, lifted herself off the sofa, and went in search of her phone. Just as the ringing stopped, she located it in the pocket of her jacket out on the hook in the back hall. She'd left it there after her early morning walk on the beach and had forgotten about it. She glanced at the screen and saw she'd missed a call from Jules.

She pressed the green phone icon to return Jules's call.

"Alice?" Jules answered.

"You called?"

"I did. I have a favor to ask."

"Go ahead," Alice said.

It was Saturday morning, and she and Lily had just finished a leisurely breakfast of scrambled eggs and bacon and sausage. Her day was wide open.

"It's my turn to go to the beach and collect litter, but I've got the flu and wondered if you wouldn't mind switching with me." Jules said. She coughed.

"Not a problem," Alice said. "It's at nine this morning, right?"

"That's right. My partner is Mr. Lime."

"Okay, I'll look for him."

"Just a heads-up, he's kind of slow-moving and whatever you do, don't try to help him as he takes offense."

Alice laughed. "Point taken. Will he have supplies or do I have to get them from somewhere?" She had yet to have her own turn on the beach, but she knew that the senior member of the team carried the litter grabbers and the plastic bags. There was a collection point at the parish hall. Getting involved in the cleanup initiative had made her more aware, and she'd gotten into the habit of watching out for trash on her morning beach walks.

Jules assured her that Mr. Lime would have everything they'd need. They chatted a few more minutes before hanging up. The display on Alice's phone told her she had about half an hour before she needed to meet Mr. Lime at the beach. She did not want to be late. There were a few things to do before she left, and she ran upstairs and brushed her teeth and grabbed a warmer hoodie to protect her against the late-April chill.

As she headed out the front door, she grabbed her phone and her keys and shoved them into her pocket. She popped her head into the dining room, where Lily had set up her craft station and was hard at work creating pieces with beach glass. It had turned into a small cottage industry for her sister, one that she truly enjoyed, and Alice was happy for her.

"Jules asked me to cover for her this morning collecting litter," Alice said.

Lily looked up from her work, glue gun in hand. She was affixing shards of beach glass to a frame. "Okay. What time do you think you might be home?"

Alice shrugged. "I don't think this will take more than an hour, but then I might walk into town to look around."

Lily smiled. "All right. I'll see you later."

Alice hopped off the porch and made her way to the end of the street to the boardwalk that led to the beach. This was the starting point for all the litter-collection teams. She was early, but then she didn't want to keep Mr. Lime waiting. She stood on the boardwalk, waiting for him to show up, her hands in her pockets.

The day was cool but sunny. There was no real heat in the sunshine, but at least it wasn't raining. Cool air blew in off the lake. After a few minutes, she walked up and down the boardwalk, scanning the beach and the street for any signs of Mr. Lime. There were a few people out on the beach. A man jogged past, his German shepherd on a lead at his side. There were quite a few walkers, mostly in pairs, ranging from middle-aged to elderly.

After a while, she spotted the Colonel pulling up and parking his car against the curb. When he got out, he popped open his trunk and started pulling things out. Alice walked toward him when she spotted him holding litter pickers and garbage bags.

"Hello, Alice," the Colonel said.

"Hi, Jack," she said, remembering to use his first name.

The Colonel leaned on his cane and looked around. "I'm supposed to meet Jules."

"Oh! I'm here for Jules today. She called me and said she had the flu and asked me to cover for her," Alice said. "I was waiting for Mr. Lime."

"He called me and asked me to take over. Said his arthritis was acting up," the Colonel said.

"Well, here we are."

"It shouldn't take us long," he said. He handed her a couple of plastic bags, one for trash and one for recyclables, as well as a litter picker.

"Thanks," she said.

They walked side-by-side to the end of the boardwalk.

"We split up and walk the beach in a grid," he instructed. "You go that way" —here, he pointed north—"and I'll go in the opposite direction."

"Should I meet you back here to give you the picker back?"

He shrugged. "If you like, but you don't have to wait for me. It's not necessary."

Alice nodded and with a wave headed off to cover her side of the beach. She looked over her shoulder to see him hobbling off, using his grabber to pick up litter as he went. He was too proud of a man to be pitied, she concluded.

As he'd instructed previously at the very first meeting, Alice viewed her section of the beach in grid form, walking the area in a deliberate manner to cover the entire thing. When she reached the end of the beach, she turned and spotted the Colonel about halfway through his own portion. It was then she realized he'd given her the shorter stretch of the beach. She made her way back toward him, her gaze sweeping the sand as she went in case she'd missed anything. As she covered ground, she worried that the Colonel might be insulted if she joined him to help him finish up. Then she thought that if it were anyone else, she'd be doing the same thing. Her conclusion: she worried too much.

When he spotted her approaching him, his face broke into a smile. "Finished?"

Alice held up her two bags of trash and recyclables. "Almost. I'll help you. That way we can get it all done."

"I appreciate that, Alice," he said.

She ended up walking his grid with him, but he didn't say anything, like suggest they split up.

"Chris Metzger told me you're the director for community events for Hideaway Bay," she said, brushing back an errant strand of hair and tucking it behind her ear. "I had no idea."

"Oh, you know Chris? He seems like a good kid. Yes, I've been doing this job since I retired from the army," he said. "I like it."

"That's important."

"How are you getting on with Ben?"

"We're well-suited to work together," she said. It wasn't her place to say anything about his drinking problem.

And the Colonel must have felt the same, because he changed the topic of conversation. "I heard from Thelma that you're staying in Hideaway Bay long-term."

Alice nodded. "I am. I put my apartment in Chicago on the market, and I'm happy to be back."

Jack Stirling stopped and looked around. His gaze swept the beach and, in the distance, the town. "It's truly a great place. I feel so lucky to have found it."

This brought a smile to her face. It was nice to hear someone say that about her hometown. It compelled her to ask, “How did you discover Hideaway Bay?”

“Simon Bishop,” he said, referring to the writer Lily worked for.

That jogged a memory for Alice. Lily had mentioned this to her in the past.

“He and I met when he was researching for a book—this was when he first started out—and I had just returned from my first tour of duty in Afghanistan. We became friends and he invited me up here. That was almost fifteen years ago.” He paused and looked at her. “It was love at first sight.”

“Do you believe in love at first sight?” she teased.

His gaze circled around her face and with all seriousness, he said, “I do, actually.”

Feeling as if she might have landed herself in a minefield, Alice concentrated on picking up a crushed water bottle with her picker. To defuse the sudden serious turn the conversation had inadvertently taken, she said “How can you be in such a good mood when you’re lugging trash bags around on a Saturday morning?”

“What do you mean? The sun is shining, we’re doing important work here, and I’m in good company.”

They’d reached the end of the south side of the beach and turned and headed back toward the boardwalk. The

Colonel swept his gaze over the area to make sure they hadn't missed anything.

"There's nothing in my life right now to be in a bad mood about."

She liked that answer. They reached the boardwalk and made their way in silence to his car.

"Do you need help taking all that to the parish hall?" Alice asked with a nod toward the garbage bags.

"Nah, I got it," he said, throwing everything into his trunk. He slammed down the lid and looked around.

Alice felt compelled to linger, which she couldn't explain. She wasn't quite ready to leave. They made their way around the car to the driver's-side door.

"Thanks for your help this morning, I appreciate it," he said.

"No problem."

"Enjoy the rest of your day, Alice!" he said with a wave.

Reluctantly, she turned in the direction of home. Over her shoulder, she called out, "I'll see you Tuesday at the parish hall."

"Good stuff. Your salted caramel brownies are the bomb," he replied with a grin.

Alice laughed and made her way home, feeling happy and light.

Chapter Thirty-Two

1978

Thelma

Thelma had never gone on a vacation before, but Stanley insisted. Canada was just across the border, but she'd only gone there two or three times for day trips. There'd been no honeymoon with either her first or second marriage. With Bobby, there'd been no money. And with Stanley, there'd been money, but no time. They were too busy running the Old Red Top to take any time off.

"I've always wanted to go to Vegas," Stanley said as they drove over to the travel agency.

Thelma didn't even care whether they went on vacation or not. Her life was in Hideaway Bay now with

Stanley and Donny and she was . . . well, happy. And as to where they went, she didn't care about that either. If Stanley had his heart set on Vegas, then they'd go to Vegas.

The trip to the travel agent was both eye-opening and exciting. All those colorful brochures with exotic places not only in the US but abroad in Europe. Stanley took a brochure about every cruise. She had to smile at him. He was as excited as a kid on Christmas morning. He pointed things out to her, saying "Look at this, Thelma," or "We should go here, Thelma," or "I bet Donny would love to go here."

In the end, they circled back and decided on Vegas. Stanley had mentioned Walt Disney World in Florida, suggesting they could take Donny with them, but Thelma put her foot down and said, "Maybe next year for Disney. But this year, Vegas." She'd already spoken to Junie, who said that Donny could stay with them while they were gone.

The truth was, Thelma wanted to be alone with Stanley. This was something she'd never admit to him or to Junie and perhaps not even to herself. But they were so rarely alone between the restaurant, where they spent the majority of their time, and home with Donny and his friends, who always seemed to hang around at their house.

When they flew into Las Vegas—the first time Thelma had ever flown—they landed in the middle of the afternoon. Out her airplane window, she thought it looked as if someone had thrown a big, glittering city out into the middle of the desert. Now that they'd arrived, she was nervous. She held her handbag close, the handle looped over the crook of her arm with her elbow bent. They checked in to their room at the Flamingo Hilton, and she couldn't believe the size of it. Two double beds—what a waste! There was no need for more than one. Unlike her first husband, Stanley had never slept on the couch.

They walked the city blocks, marveling at the size of them, looking at all the hotels. They had big plans for their trip. There were shows to see: Stanley had his heart set on Frank Sinatra or Dean Martin or any member of the Rat Pack. Thelma didn't know what she wanted to do; going away on vacation and doing things of leisure seemed so foreign to her. And forget about the casinos. She was hesitant to enter one. It seemed like a colossal waste of time and money to just sit there in front of a machine. But Stanley was itching to get in there too. He wanted to do everything.

On their first full day there, they took a tour bus and spent the day at the Grand Canyon. Thelma had never seen anything so magnificent. She'd bought an Instamatic camera specifically for this trip. Another couple offered to take their picture in front of the Grand Canyon if they'd take theirs. At the last moment, Stanley threw his arm around Thelma as she held her handbag down in front of her. It was a "Stanley moment," as Thelma liked to call them, and it caused her to laugh. When the photos were developed, this shot became one of her favorites: they looked happy, settled, and in love.

On the third day, they sat in the lobby of their hotel after eating breakfast at the buffet. Thelma was stuffed.

"Come on, let's try the slot machines," Stanley said. He stood up, put his hands in his pockets, and gave a nod to the casino in front of them.

Thelma remained on the couch. "Oh, I don't know, Stanley. I'm not much of a gambler." She didn't know if she wanted to waste money on something so frivolous. She'd worked too hard for it. The entrance of the casino beckoned them like the opening to Aladdin's cave. From where she sat, she could see the blinking of the lights and hear the bells and whistles of all the various slot machines.

"Let's give it a try, and if we don't like it, we can go on the tour out to Reno or the Hoover Dam."

He rocked back and forth on his heels.

Thelma sighed. It was hard to refuse him, he was so good to her. Finally, she stood. "All right, let's go meet this one-armed bandit."

Stanley broke into a huge smile, took her by the hand, and led her into the casino. When they stepped through the entrance, Thelma was surprised to see that it was bigger than she anticipated and louder. All kinds of slot machines stretched as far as the eye could see. She followed Stanley up to the cashier's cage, where he traded in some bills for a couple of plastic buckets of quarters. Her eyes widened at all the coins and when Stanley handed a bucket to her, she couldn't believe the weight of it. She didn't know if she wanted to lug that around all day, but then she thought she'd soon be handing it right back over to the casino.

She followed Stanley through rows of machines, and he turned to her and said, "What type of slots do you want to play?"

Thelma shook her head. "I don't know. There are two seats over there."

He nodded. "Let's try our luck."

They took seats together at a row of slot machines called Lucky Sevens. Thelma thought it was appropriate as she and Stanley had been married on the seventh day of the seventh month. Maybe these would prove lucky. They were quarter machines. Stanley threw in some quarters and pulled the arm down. For a few minutes, Thelma watched him, content to do that.

Then he looked at her. "Aren't you going to play?"

"I will." She put a quarter into her machine and pulled the lever. Nothing. After fifteen minutes, she was beginning to put a dent in her bucket of coins. *At this rate, I'll be back in my room before dinner*, she thought sourly.

"Thelm? What are you doing?" Stanley asked.

She stared at him, uncomprehending. "What do you mean?"

"You're only playing one quarter? You gotta play three if you want to win a jackpot," he said.

Thelma blanched. Seventy-five cents a go? That would add up pretty quick. She felt queasy.

Stanley stopped sliding his quarters into the machine and swiveled in his seat to face her. "Thelma, we're on vacation. This is money that we planned to blow this week. This money is earmarked for our good time. It's not like we have to pay the mortgage with it."

She snorted. "Good thing."

"Come on," he coaxed, "we're here to have fun."

Thelma nodded but still didn't move. Stanley reached over and plucked three quarters out of her bucket and inserted them into the coin slot. "Go on, pull the arm," he said.

She did, watching the wheel spin at a dizzying speed. When it stopped, it showed a lemon and one seven and one wild bar. A lemon, Thelma thought sourly.

"Never mind the lemon," Stanley said beside her with a laugh as if reading her mind. "Put your next set in."

For the next fifteen minutes, Thelma put three quarters in at a time.

The bells went off on Stanley's machine, and quarters poured out of the bottom of it into a metal tray.

"Yes!" Stanley said excitedly, scooping up the quarters with both hands and throwing them back into his plastic bucket. It brought his quarters almost level to the top of the bucket.

A half an hour later, Thelma pulled the lever, starting to get more comfortable despite her dwindling pile of quarters, and three sevens appeared in a row on the horizontal line. Immediately, the bells rang loudly, startling her. The lights on the top of her slot machine blinked in rapid succession. She watched the bottom tray, ready to scoop up the waterfall of quarters.

Stanley stared wide-eyed at the window of her slot machine.

"How come no quarters are coming out?" Thelma asked, disappointed.

He swallowed and whispered, "Gosh, Thelma, I think you've won the jackpot."

"What?" she asked. "What do you mean?"

He nodded, pointing to the top of the electric banner. "You've hit three lucky sevens." Before she could ask any more questions, an attendant wheeled a cart up to her and said, "Congratulations on winning your jackpot."

"How much did I win?" Thelma asked.

The attendant looked at the slot machine Thelma had been playing, and said with a smile, "A little over three thousand dollars."

"What?" Thelma asked, incredulous.

Stanley laughed, bent over, and slapped his thigh.

"May I take your picture for the winner's circle?" the attendant asked. She was younger than Thelma with strawberry blond hair. She wore a casino uniform of orange and red and had thinly penciled eyebrows. Thelma was reminded of the flight attendants on the airplane on the flight out.

Thelma nodded and stood next to her slot machine. Stanley stepped out of the frame, but Thelma grabbed his hand and pulled him close to her. "I want my husband in the picture with me."

"That's fine," the attendant said.

After the photo was taken, the attendant unlocked her cart with a key and counted out Thelma's winnings, handing them to her. She turned and handed the bills to Stanley. "I don't want this much money on me, it makes me nervous."

He nodded, pulled out his wallet, and tucked the bills inside before folding it in half and returning it to his back pocket. "When we go up to the room later, I'll put it in the safe."

Thelma didn't want to say that she trusted Stanley with the money more than she trusted the room safe. The two of them stood there for a moment, staring at the winning slot machine.

Stanley leaned in and kissed her on the lips. "You're lucky, babe."

She glanced at him, her expression softening, and she thought to herself, *Yes, I am lucky*.

"Do you want to leave now? Go for lunch?" he asked casually.

Thelma shot him a look. "Not on your life. What will we play next?"

He burst out laughing. "Ha, I thought as much. Didn't take much to get you hooked."

Thelma smiled, looping her arm in Stanley's as they walked off. "No, not much. Only a major jackpot."

They did take Donny to Disney World the following year, but after that week in Vegas, the two of them never went anywhere else for vacation. Every year for the rest of their marriage, they spent a week out in Sin City; it was always something they both looked forward to. Some couples went to Florida or went on cruises, but Thelma and Stanley loved the bright lights and the gambling and the shows that Las Vegas had to offer.

Chapter Thirty-Three

Alice

Alice swept the front porch. It was the first nice weekend they'd had since the beginning of spring. The sun was warm, and there wasn't a cloud in the deep blue sky. She was anxious to get on with summer. It would be her first full summer in Hideaway Bay since before she left for Chicago. Earlier that morning, she'd had good news. Her loft apartment had sold well above the asking price. Lucky for her it was a seller's market, and she couldn't be happier with the outcome. That was her last tie to Chicago.

She attacked the corner of the porch where rotted leaves and debris left over from the winter had accumulated. When the sweeping was done, she removed the black tarps that had covered the furniture, and she'd marched the bags of sand that had held the tarps in place through the winter over to the beach and emptied them. The porch furniture, which had been power-washed earlier, currently sat on the front lawn, soaking up the afternoon rays of the sun. The last thing she did was power-wash the porch.

It didn't take long for the porch to dry as there was a gentle breeze blowing in off the lake. Alice stood on a utility stool, hanging the two wind chimes she'd picked up at the gift shop in town. She stepped down and was admiring her handiwork and enjoying the tinkle of the chimes when she spotted Gram's attorney, Arthur Stodges, walking down the sidewalk and heading in her direction. He turned at the end of the driveway and called out to her with a wave.

Curious, Alice stepped down off the porch and absentmindedly brushed her hair back with her hands.

"Hello, Mr. Stodges," she greeted him.

"Hello, Alice, and please, call me Arthur or Art. Your grandmother did," he said.

He was dressed casually in a polo shirt, khakis, expensive sneakers, and a cardigan.

"Would you like tea? Or can I offer you something else?"

Arthur put his hand up and said, "No, thank you. I apologize for showing up without calling, but I'll only take a minute of your time."

"That's all right," Alice said, dying to know the reason for his visit.

"I'll get straight to the point, Alice."

She waited expectantly. The wind chimes on the porch behind her tinkled softly in the breeze.

"It turns out I should have kept hold of your resume. Alan Hindermarsh is retiring at the end of June," he said, referring to the other partner in his law firm. "And I wanted to offer you a job at the firm as an attorney. There's too much work for one person and to be honest, I'm hoping to retire myself in the next year or two."

Alice's heart rate increased exponentially. This was exactly what she wanted, what she had hoped for. A nice job with a lovely firm in Hideaway Bay. It was like all her dreams coming true at once.

"I am definitely interested," she said. She could barely contain her excitement or her smile.

"I'm glad to hear that. Look, can you come by the office sometime next week? We'll discuss your employment and finalize the details," Arthur said.

Alice nodded. "I'll be there."

"Great, see you next week," he said.

She waved goodbye and returned to work on getting the front porch ready for summer. But now there was a spring in her step, and she hummed an easy tune. Things were looking up. It was going to be a great summer.

“I thought you liked your job at Ben Enright’s office?” Lily said when Alice told her later that evening about the job offer from Stodges and Hindermarsh.

The two of them sat in the living room. It was still a bit chilly in the evenings to sit outside. They’d ordered a pizza, which now sat in its box on the coffee table, the lid open, revealing half a pie consumed. There was a large plastic bottle of Pepsi on the table, half empty. Charlie sat next to Lily, his eyes never leaving the pizza. As it was Friday night, both were tired and had wanted an easy dinner. Lily had managed to figure out how to work Gram’s ancient VCR, and they’d gotten comfortable and chatted while an old black-and-white movie played: *Enchantment* with David Niven and Theresa Wright.

Alice pressed the pause button on the remote. Unlike some, she could not follow a movie and have a side conversation. Lily leaned forward from her chair and took another slice of pizza, the cheese hanging off it in strings she wound around her finger.

“I do like working for Ben. The people I meet are certainly interesting, but I don’t want to be another lawyer’s assistant,” Alice said. “It was fine in the beginning when I first moved back, but I need a bit more.”

"Will you be happy at Stodges and Hindermarsh?" Lily asked.

Alice frowned. "Why wouldn't I be?" She'd thought Lily would be happy for her.

Lily shrugged and chewed thoughtfully for a moment. "Every night when you come home, you tell me about your day."

"And?" Alice asked, her hackles rising.

"Well, it sounded like you enjoyed working at Ben Enright's law office. As you've said, you find the clients—and Ben—interesting."

"I do, but I can't stay there forever."

"I understand," Lily said. "I just want to make certain you're sure about the move."

Immediately, Alice's head was filled with doubt.

"Oh, you're mad now," Lily stated, wincing.

"No, not at all," Alice said tightly.

"I am happy for you," Lily said. "Truly. But is this what you really want?"

"I think I know my own mind now," Alice said. She had to bite back her tongue so she wouldn't say something more acerbic.

Lily wiped her mouth with a napkin. "Of course you do. I spoke out of turn. I'm sorry."

"Forget about it," Alice said. She crossed her hands over her chest and lay back on the sofa. "Can I press play? I thought we were going to watch this movie."

"Yeah, go ahead."

When she arrived at work first thing Monday morning, Alice was still on a high from her visit on Saturday from Arthur Stodges. She was surprised to find Ben already there. And what surprised her even more was the fact that he stood behind his desk and appeared to be straightening up. She thought she might be seeing things.

Ben's drinking binges had been unpredictable. There was no rhyme or reason to when they happened. He could be tooling along and by outward appearances, everything was fine, and then he wouldn't show up for work or, worse, she'd arrive and find him passed out at his desk.

Despite her excitement over her new job with Stodges and Hindermarsh, Alice was hesitant, and doubt niggled at the back of her mind. What would happen to Ben's clients after she left? What would happen to the firm? And what about the likes of Chris Metzger and Avery Winslow—where would they go?

She shoved those thoughts from her mind; pretty soon it wasn't going to be her problem. Before she'd left for work, she had called the office of Stodges and

Hindermarsh to make an appointment to meet with Arthur Stodges later in the week.

She stood in Ben's doorway and rapped on the doorframe. "Good morning."

Ben smiled. He looked paler than usual. He also looked bloated, and there were dark purple circles beneath his eyes. There was a faint whiff of cologne as if he had made an effort, and it was an improvement over the yeasty scent of stale beer.

They never spoke of his drinking problem. Alice knew that both Baddie and the Colonel had spoken to him from time to time, and she figured he didn't need her jumping on the bandwagon as well. Plus, he never brought it up. They usually carried on once he returned, with no mention of his absences. The only hint was her bringing him up to speed with what had happened while he was missing.

"You've done good work on the Avery Winslow case," he said evenly. His voice sounded tired.

"It's been interesting, to say the least," she said truthfully. She'd been educated quickly on copyright law.

"Where are we?" he asked. He held a Bic pen in his hand.

"We're going to court, and he's seeking damages," Alice said.

Ben nodded. "Good for him. Brilliant stroke of luck that he registered his songs with the copyright office."

The background to that had been touching, Alice thought. "A favorite uncle looked out for him."

Ben smiled; it was his first one. But it didn't quite reach his eyes. "He's lucky."

"His uncle may have recognized Avery's talent and was trying to protect him."

Ben nodded. He appeared to hesitate, as if he wanted to say something but did not.

"I'm making tea, would you like some?" Alice asked.

Ben shook his head. "No, thank you, Alice." He sighed, looked up at her and asked, "Would you mind sitting down for a minute?" He collapsed in his chair, leaning to one side and resting against the arm.

"Not at all," Alice said, and she sat down in the chair across from his desk.

"Look, I won't waste your time. I wanted to let you know that I'm going away for a bit," he said.

"You're taking a vacation?" Whatever was troubling him, a vacation might be just the thing. Of course, if it was an excuse to drink, then maybe not. She withheld her judgment.

Ben stared at a point on his desk. "No, it's not a vacation." He looked up and met her eyes. "I'm going into rehab for a month. A place out in Arizona."

"Good for you," she said encouragingly. Now was probably not the time to tell him she was quitting. She didn't want him to not go to rehab. That was what was most important. But her mind raced about her new job. She wondered if she should stay until Ben came back, if only to hold down the fort.

"You may have noticed I have a drinking problem," he said. There was a smile now, a Ben smile, one full of mirth.

Alice tilted her head to one side and matched his tone. "I may have noticed it on more than one occasion."

Ben chuckled. "Anyway, it's time I deal with my demons."

"I think it's a good call," she said. "You've got a lot of people rooting for you, Ben."

"I know that. The Colonel got me a contact with this place. I finally made a phone call last night."

"I'm happy to hear that." Relief swept through Alice. She prayed for her friend, because that's what he was. When he was sober, they got along fabulously.

"I can't thank you enough for keeping the practice afloat while I was . . . um . . . unavailable," Ben started.

"I was glad I could help. And besides, it allowed me to do the job I love doing."

"That's what I wanted to ask you."

"I'm not sure what you mean."

"If you'd consider coming on as a partner. I wouldn't ask you to join as anything less, especially in light of everything you've done. You've covered for me more than once."

"You want me to work here as an attorney? As an equal partner?" she asked, dumbfounded. She thought of all those years she'd chased a partnership in Chicago. Finally, she'd been offered one, and it was for a law office in a low-rent strip mall.

Alice's smile was wide and generous. She didn't even have to think about it. "I'd love to, Ben. I accept."

Chapter Thirty-Four

1980

Thelma

"You feel all right?" Stanley asked for the third time.

Thelma rolled her eyes. "Ask me that again and I swear I won't speak to you for the rest of the day." She was only pregnant; she wasn't an invalid, for crying out loud. But him hovering around all the time and asking if she was all right drove her around the bend. Under the scrutiny of his watchful gaze, she pulled on her maternity shorts.

He threw his hands up. "All right, all right."

She had made the mistake of mentioning earlier that morning that she'd had some abdominal pain. It was tolerable, but she tried to think back to when she was pregnant with Donny and if she'd ever had that feeling before, and nothing came to her. But that didn't mean anything. Her last pregnancy was sixteen years ago.

As she pulled her maternity top over her head, Stanley asked from behind her, "Do you still want to go to Junie's? We could stay home. I'll run over to the restaurant so you don't have to cook."

Thelma slipped her arms into the sleeveless shirt and tugged it down. "No, I'm fine. I want to see Barb and Sue Ann while they're in town." She'd made up her mind. It'd been a while since Barb had been home, and Thelma was eager to see her old friend. Besides, she had a few things for Sue Ann she wanted to give her.

"Maybe we could invite Barb and Sue Ann over here tomorrow," Stanley suggested. He'd migrated to the doorway.

Thelma looked up to the ceiling as if help or relief might be found there. Still, she modulated her response. She couldn't be mad at him, not really, not for the way he fussed over her.

"Stanley, I'm all right. If anything changes, I'll let you know, I promise." She went to her jewelry box and tried on her wedding set again. But the rings were too tight, and she couldn't advance them past her knuckle. The heat and the pregnancy had caused everything to swell. She hated not wearing her wedding rings; she felt naked without them.

"We'll drive, though," he said.

"Okay," she agreed.

Satisfied that he'd gotten his way with one thing, he headed out of the bedroom and down the stairs.

Thelma eventually made her way down to the kitchen. Donny and his friends were sitting around the dining room table, eating. Of course. Thelma spied her big Tupperware bowl.

"That better not be my potato salad, Donny!" she said.

"Aw, Ma, we were hungry," he said.

She leaned over the table, grabbing the bowl. All four boys looked up at her, disappointed when she removed it from the reach of their spoons.

As she carried it back to the kitchen, she overheard the tail end of their conversation.

"Your mom looks like she's going to burst," said one.

"You're going to be seventeen years older than your brother or sister," teased another.

"Shut up!" said Donny.

Thelma knew he was sensitive about the fact that there was going to be a baby in the house. She smiled. When they first told Donny they were expecting a baby, he had stared at her and Stanley before scrunching up his face and declaring, "Gross!"

She stood at the counter, smoothing out the top of the potato salad with a large serving spoon. The boys had eaten the slices of hard-boiled egg she'd laid on top, but there was nothing to be done about that now. She reached for the small tin of paprika and sprinkled it over the salad. It looked like orange snow falling.

She heard Stanley come in through the front door. He stopped at the dining room, and she heard him ask, "Donny, do you need any money?"

Thelma didn't have to hear Donny's response to know it had been affirmative.

Stanley arrived in the kitchen. "Everything's in the car. Is that the potato salad? I was looking for that."

"The boys helped themselves," she muttered. As she placed cling wrap over the bowl, she said over her shoulder to her husband, "You can't ask Donny if he needs money, because he'll always say yes." She'd warned Donny about taking advantage of Stanley's good nature.

Stanley shrugged. "It doesn't bother me."

She handed him the bowl of potato salad. "Come on, let's go. We're already late."

He stepped back and allowed Thelma to go first.

It was to be a simple get-together at Junie's house. Just the three of them, like the old days. Thelma, Junie, and Barb. Barb had flown in from the west coast with

Sue Ann and was going to spend the remainder of her summer in Hideaway Bay.

Thelma pulled herself up the porch steps and waddled through the screen door. From the kitchen at the back of the house came voices and laughter, and she smiled. *Just like the old days*, she thought.

"There she is!" Junie said, standing at the kitchen sink when Thelma entered. "We were just going to send out a search party for you!"

"No need. I'm here." She made for Barb, who wrapped her in a hug. Barb smelled of something floral and, knowing her, something expensive.

"Barb, how are you?" Thelma asked, squeezing harder and lingering in the embrace of her friend.

"I'm well," Barb said, pulling back and holding Thelma by both arms. "But look at you! How much longer have you got?"

"About six weeks. And it can't come fast enough!" She looked around the kitchen. "Where's Sue Ann?"

"Nancy took her down to the beach," Junie told her.

Stanley brought in the potato salad and the hot dogs and the container of Texas hot sauce. He opened up a package wrapped in butcher paper and showed Paul the Italian sausages.

"I'm telling you, we'll fry up some green peppers and onions and we won't know what hit us!"

Paul laughed. “Come on, Stanley, let’s get the grill going. Junie, what time do you want me to put on the burgers?”

“As soon as the grill is ready, Paul,” Junie said.

“Will you sell those at the restaurant though?” Barb asked.

“Oh, they’re already on the menu,” Thelma told her. “The grass doesn’t grow under Stanley’s feet.” She laughed but pulled up short when that abdominal pain she’d experienced earlier gripped her. She placed her hand across her belly.

“Are you all right?” Junie asked.

Thelma caught her breath and nodded. “It’s been so long since I’ve been pregnant that I’ve forgotten what it feels like.” To put her mind on something else, she asked Barb, “How long are you here for?”

“A few weeks, until Labor Day,” Barb said. “Sue Ann doesn’t start kindergarten until the week after, so you’re stuck with us.”

“We’ll have a great time. Will Trevor come for a bit?” Thelma asked, referring to Barb’s third husband.

Barb reddened and pressed her lips together until they disappeared. When she spoke, her voice was soft and low. “No. He’s been sleeping with his secretary, so we’re getting divorced.”

“Oh, Barb, I am so sorry. How are you doing?”

Barb sighed. "I've been married three times. I often think if Jim hadn't been killed, we'd still be together, but it wasn't meant to be. You know, I'm okay with it. Disappointed, of course. But at least I have Sue Ann. And that means everything is going to be fine."

Thelma reached out, took her friend's hand, and reassured her, "You're going to land on your feet, Barb. You always do."

"After dinner, we'll sit on the porch and make plans for what we're going to do for the rest of the summer," Junie suggested. "I made a big pitcher of lemonade."

Thelma peeled the cling wrap off the potato salad as Barb laid out a pan of Texas sheet cake. Junie put mustard and ketchup in yellow and red plastic condiment bottles, bottles that Thelma had taken from the restaurant and given to her. What good was owning a restaurant if you couldn't pass something to your friends every so often. Thelma looked around. There was a tossed salad, hamburger and hot dog rolls, a tray of olives and celery and carrot sticks. There was also a plate of chicken salad. Barb opened a container of coleslaw and put it in a small dish.

Thelma liked it when the three of them were all together. It reminded her of when they were young, walking up and down South Park Avenue. She spun the lazy Susan cabinet until she spotted the paper plates and carried a stack over to the table.

"I wonder if I should run down to the beach and call Nancy and Sue Ann," Junie said.

"I'll do it," Barb said.

A sharp, stabbing pain seized Thelma, her eyes widened, and she gripped the edge of the table and sucked in a lungful of air.

Both Junie and Barb turned toward her, confusion clouding their faces. Immediately, they were at her side.

"Thelma, what is it?"

Another stab of pain sliced across her belly and Thelma panicked. This didn't feel right. Something warm gushed from between her legs. She looked down, expecting to see that her waters had broken—albeit early—but all she saw was bright red blood. Junie and Barb's gaze followed hers and someone whimpered. Junie cried, "Thelma!"

As the blood drained from her and a clamminess broke out over her body, Thelma managed to whisper, "Get Stanley, please."

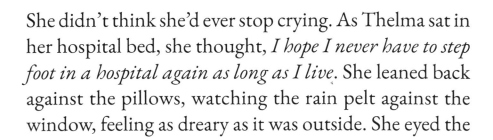

She didn't think she'd ever stop crying. As Thelma sat in her hospital bed, she thought, *I hope I never have to step foot in a hospital again as long as I live*. She leaned back against the pillows, watching the rain pelt against the window, feeling as dreary as it was outside. She eyed the baskets of flowers on the windowsill. She knew people meant well, but how on earth could flowers possibly make her feel better? They didn't and they couldn't.

She hadn't felt this awful since the loss of her mother. Never did she think she'd ever feel that way again, but she'd been wrong. All these years of trying to climb out of that black hole, only to be thrown back into it in what should have been a happy time for her and Stanley.

The door opened quietly, and Stanley slipped in. He looked pale, which made the pockmarks more pronounced on his face.

Oh, Stanley.

On examination, Thelma had often thought their marriage was lopsided. That Stanley had gotten the short end of the stick in taking her on with a kid to boot. She knew she was difficult, not easy to live with. Too loud and too opinionated. But for whatever inexplicable reason, he loved her. Always had. In her wildest dreams, she would never have guessed that Stanley Schumacher would make such a wonderful husband. She bit the inside of her cheek to try to stem the flow of tears that were coming whether she wanted them to or not.

When she'd discovered she was pregnant after years of doing nothing to prevent it, she'd been thrilled. This was the one thing she could do for Stanley, the one thing she could give him after he had done so much for her and Donny. It turned out that Stanley was a great father and more than anything, she wanted him to have a child of his own. He was over the moon, of course. He'd prattle on about their plans for the new baby and how wonderful it was going to be. She'd never seen him so happy. And that's all she wanted, was for Stanley to be happy. But instead, they were going to be burying their newborn, a son who'd only lived a few hours. Stanley had named the baby Thomas. "Tommy," he'd said, his voice quaking.

My God, but life was horrible at times.

Stanley approached the bedside. "Thelma," he whispered.

"I'm here," she said, almost choking on the words for the lump in her throat. She moved her hand toward the edge of the bed and felt nothing but relief when he immediately took hold of it and squeezed it.

"Stanley, I'm so sorry, so sorry," she said, the tears falling freely, the words rushing out, tumbling over one another. Her face contorted in pain.

Stanley climbed onto the bed next to her and took her into his arms. "Shh, why are you sorry?"

"I wanted so much for you to have a child of your own. I wanted to give you a child."

He smoothed back her hair and kissed her forehead. "What are you talking about? You already gave me a child. You gave me Donny."

And that made Thelma cry harder.

Chapter Thirty-Five

Alice

It was funny how things worked out and fell together into place.

The office wasn't the same without Ben, and she missed him. She hadn't heard from him, and she didn't expect to. All she wanted was for him to concentrate on his rehab. It wasn't lost on her that his absence had changed the personality of the place. It seemed almost too quiet. But she'd come to realize the degree to which their small firm served an important purpose.

Since his departure, she'd been busier than ever. She'd notified Arthur Stodges that she wouldn't be taking the job after all, and he'd been disappointed, but Alice knew she belonged here in this law office.

There was only one private office, and that belonged to Ben. She could use it until he returned, but long-term, she wouldn't consistently be able to meet clients out in the reception area; it was too high-traffic and did not lend itself to confidentiality. But she thought she might be able to sort out that problem. The office space next to them in the plaza had emptied, the tenant deciding not to renew his lease. Alice contacted the owner of the strip mall to look at it. It was a much larger space than theirs, and with some renovating, they could easily have two offices for themselves and a reception area. She put a deposit down, realizing if Ben wasn't agreeable, she'd lose it, but it was a risk she was willing to take.

Humming a song to herself, she turned the kettle on for tea. When she turned around, there was a woman standing there.

Alice jumped and placed her hand on her chest. "You startled me."

"I'm sorry, you didn't hear me come in?" the woman questioned and looked over her shoulder at the door.

"No, I'm sorry, I didn't." Alice studied the woman. She was petite—if she was five foot, she was tall. She wore a navy skirt and blazer, and her blouse was white with bright red cherries on it. It looked as if it were vintage. Her dark hair was styled in a neat chignon, and it was capped by a red pillbox hat. She looked as if she'd just stepped out of the early '60s.

"Can I help you?" Alice asked.

"Yes, I was looking for Ben."

"He's away for the month," Alice said. "Can I help you? I'm Ben's partner." She liked the way that sounded when she said it.

When the woman didn't immediately respond, Alice waved her hand and asked her to sit down.

"Would you like tea or coffee?" Alice asked as the kettle began its shrill whistle.

"Tea would be lovely," the woman replied, taking a seat.

"I've got a selection box," Alice said, standing at the filing cabinets and turning off the hot plate.

"Regular is fine."

After she handed the woman a cup of tea, Alice propped her bum on the edge of her desk.

"Are you a client of Ben's?" she asked. She would have remembered the woman if she was.

The woman looked up at her and set the teacup down. There was a red stain of lipstick on the edge of it. Alice noted that it was the same shade of red as the cherries on the woman's blouse.

"I talked to Ben about filing for divorce." She picked up the cup and took a gulp. "After thirty-five years of marriage, I've had enough."

Alice felt sorry for the woman. "I can help you with that."

Deep furrows etched themselves between the woman's finely penciled eyebrows. "Can you?"

Alice stood. "Of course. Why don't you come into my office. I'll take down your particulars and we'll get started on divorce proceedings."

She headed into Ben's office and the woman followed her. Alice indicated to the chair across the desk for the woman to sit, then settled herself behind Ben's desk—her desk for now. "First things first. My name is Alice Monroe."

The woman smiled, and Alice could see how in her youth the woman would once have been considered pretty, where she'd now aged into attractive.

"Lola. Lola Duquesne."

Alice pulled out a manila folder and started a new file.

Chapter Thirty-Six

1992

Thelma

Thelma pulled the one chair in the room up next to the hospital bed. She'd been up early, arriving at the hospital at six-thirty, hoping to see the doctors when they made their morning rounds. She'd talked to Barb on the phone the previous night, and Barb had given her a list of questions to ask, advising her to write her questions down and to bring a small notepad and pen to the hospital with her and to the doctor's appointments. Thelma had thought that was a good idea. She wouldn't have thought of it herself.

They'd been out in Vegas when Stanley had been hit with unrelenting mid-back pain. They'd been in the casino when it happened, causing him to double over. Thelma helped him back to their room and when he hadn't improved by the next day, they got into a rare argument. She insisted he go to the emergency room in Las Vegas, but he had dug his heels in and said he'd only go to a hospital back home. The reason being he didn't want to get "stuck out here." Thelma made the arrangements, changed their flights, and they cut their annual trip short. Stan was still in pain when they landed at the airport, so they had asked Paul to pick them up. He took one look at Stanley and drove them straight to the nearest hospital, where Stanley had been since.

The news had been delivered after a lengthy wait, with Stanley on a gurney behind a curtain as thin as a sheet of paper. It wasn't good. There was a tumor on his pancreas. The doctor had been serious as he delivered the news. Stanley nodded, and Thelma, for the first time in her life, was speechless. It was only when the doctor stepped out of the room that she realized she had a million questions. Stanley was admitted to the floor, and further testing was done to determine the extent of the disease and the treatment protocol it would demand.

He had lost weight. Already lean, it hadn't taken long for him to appear gaunt.

"Who's running the restaurant?" Stanley asked.

"Gus and Trixie," Thelma told him. Both were longtime employees. Between the two of them, they'd take care of the place. She wasn't worried about it. Her main concern right now was Stanley.

"Stanley, have I ever told you that I love you?" she asked, sliding her chair even closer to his bed. She wanted to kick herself for all the missed opportunities to say that to him. Why was she sometimes so pigheaded about things that were important? Especially telling someone how you felt about them. Especially someone who had loved her her whole life. Panic filled her.

He surprised her with a snort, and he burst out laughing. "Jeez, Thelma, I must be at death's door if you're making a declaration of love now after all these years being married."

Despite the gravity of the situation, she laughed too. But she wanted to impress upon him what he meant to her. "But you do know that I love you? That I'm still in love with you."

"Yes. As you know I love you," he said quietly.

"I've known you loved me since the third grade," she said proudly. A love to last a lifetime indeed.

"It only took you forever to give me a second glance," he said with a smile.

"Well, I was busy raising my brothers, and then I got sidetracked—"

Stanley put up his hand and teased, "Excuses, excuses."

She leaned forward on the bed and held out her hand, and he placed his hand in hers. They wound their fingers together.

"But you do know how much I love you, right?" she persisted, a sense of urgency filling her. Although they weren't the type of couple to say it often, she had to make sure that no matter what happened, no matter the outcome, that Stanley knew he was truly loved. That it hadn't been one-sided.

"You are the love of my life," she whispered. No kidding now. She let her eyes fill with tears, and she didn't care who saw them.

But Stanley couldn't help himself. He regarded her, raised his eyebrows, and said, "Really? I thought Bobby was the love of your life."

"Stanley Schumacher, if you weren't so sick, I'd punch you right in the face!"

He laughed again, coughed, and caught his side, looking up at the ceiling with a deep frown etched in his forehead as if it hurt to laugh. "That's my girl."

It felt wrong to be so happy in the face of a grave situation, but Thelma realized she was going to squeeze out whatever joy she and Stanley had left together whenever she could.

"Have you heard from Donny?" he asked.

"He's thinking of coming home for the weekend," she said.

Stanley shook his head. "No, Thelma, I don't want that. I'm going to be stuck in the hospital, and he should be enjoying his new job and his wife and family."

Donny had married and settled in Ohio, not too far but far enough. There were two grandchildren, Maria and Jules, who they didn't see enough of.

Stanley leaned forward, trying to catch his breath. Thelma jumped up, patting him on the back. She didn't want to hit him too hard, because that's where his pain had been. After a few seconds, it subsided, and she slowly sat back down.

She was about to say something when the doctor entered the room. Thelma tried to glean from his face whether the news he'd deliver would be good or bad. But his expression remained neutral. Her heart rate twitched and picked up.

The doctor made small talk with Stanley.

"This is my bride, Thelma," Stanley introduced her. "Have you ever been to Hideaway Bay, doctor?"

The doctor nodded. "I have. It's a beautiful town."

"We own the Old Red Top restaurant," Stanley said proudly. "Best Texas hots around."

Thelma beamed, thinking how he'd turned nothing into something.

"I'll keep that in mind," the doctor said and slowly, his smile evaporated, replaced by a somber expression.

Thelma steeled herself. She leaned forward in her chair as if by getting closer, she'd be able to hear better, to understand better.

The words became lost as the doctor discussed all the tests performed, words that meant nothing. The only words that jumped out at her were "the disease has spread," and he listed the organs: the liver, the stomach, and the lower lung.

Thelma tried to reconcile the fact that Stan had cancer in all these places in his body with how he would survive it.

Stanley was quiet in his bed, his hands folded on top of the white sheet. He showed no emotion, appearing to digest everything the doctor said.

Finally, unable to take it anymore, Thelma asked, "What kind of treatment will he need? Radiation? Surgery? Chemotherapy?"

The doctor hesitated until finally, with great solemnity, he said, "Mr. Schumacher, I don't think you're a candidate at this point for treatment."

"Oh," was all Stanley said, pushing his glasses up on his nose. He leaned back against his pillows and appeared thoughtful.

So maybe conventional treatment wasn't in the cards. "What about experimental treatment? There must be some kind of clinical trial he'd qualify for," Thelma pressed. Barb had put that idea into her head, and Thelma was glad of it.

"Time is a problem," the doctor responded quietly.

Thelma didn't know what to say. So many things crowded her mind and vied for position. Finally, she blurted, "But if he doesn't get treatment, he'll die!"

When the doctor didn't respond, Thelma's gaze swung over to Stanley. In his eyes, she saw the resignation to his fate. Her heart hammered in her chest. This couldn't possibly be happening. Not to him. Not to her. Not to *them*.

"No," she whispered, but it died on her lips.

"How much time do I have?" Stanley asked. His eyes locked on the doctor; he couldn't look at Thelma.

The doctor shrugged. "It's hard to tell."

"Well, try," Stanley insisted.

The doctor sighed. "Two to three months, six months tops."

Stanley nodded but Thelma wanted to scream and shout *no*. She looked at Stanley and studied him. Granted, he had lost weight and looked a bit pale, but he certainly did not look like a man whose life was winding down.

"But he's not even fifty," she protested.

"I am sorry," the doctor said helplessly. He spoke to them for a few more minutes before he left them. Thelma stood there in a state of shock.

As soon as they were alone, Stanley said, "It's going to be okay, Thelm."

She rounded on him. "How can you say that? It's not going to be okay; it's never going to be okay again." She was ashamed of her outburst, especially at him. It wasn't his fault he was sick. But she didn't know what to do. She didn't know how to fix this. Or where to even start.

He patted the space beside him on the hospital bed. "Come on." He scooched over even though it caused him pain, grimacing as he did so.

Carefully, Thelma climbed onto the bed and sat next to him. He was unable to throw his arm around her shoulder, so they held hands, their arms entwined over their adjoining thighs.

"I thought we'd have more time," she croaked.

Stanley squeezed her hand. "We've had a lot of time, Thelma."

She lowered her head and squeezed her eyes shut. All those wasted years. All those years lost when she should have been with him. She wanted to kick herself. If only she could go back and do it all over again.

"Come on, don't do that," he said softly beside her. He nudged her gently with his elbow.

"Do what?"

He laughed. "I know you better than anyone. And right now, you're thinking we wasted too much time getting together."

She managed a laugh. It was true; no one knew her better than Stanley. "Well, not we but me." A sob burst forth. She was horrified—she didn't want to upset him. She clamped her hand over her mouth.

"You weren't ready," he said. "But in the end, you came around."

She nodded as sobs wracked her body.

"We've been lucky," he said quietly. "Not too many people have had what we had."

She nodded some more and pulled a tissue out of her pocket to wipe her eyes.

"Now, listen to me," he said. "I need you to do me one favor. Just one."

"Anything."

"Get me out of here. Let me live what's left of my life with you at home. We have enough money to hire a nurse." He picked up her hand and kissed it. His eyes welled up, and his bottom lip quivered. "Please, Thelma, don't let me die in here. Not in the hospital."

"I'll get you out of here, you can count on it," she said firmly. If she had to carry him out on her back, she'd do it. No one was going to stand in the way of her bringing Stanley home. Now, armed with an important task, she began to feel slightly better.

“I want to see a few more sunrises on Hideaway Bay,” he said quietly.

Chapter Thirty-Seven

Alice

"I thought you knew," Thelma said. "Everyone knows. He's leaving tomorrow."

Alice stood on the pavement outside Thelma's house. She'd been out for a walk when Thelma had waved her over. The older woman had just told her that the Colonel was leaving Hideaway Bay.

Alice blinked and swallowed. "No, I'd heard nothing. He didn't say . . ."

Thelma frowned. "I'm surprised, I thought you two were friendly with one another."

"We are . . . or I thought we were," Alice said, matching Thelma's frown. She saw the Colonel regularly between dropping off baked goods for his veterans' group and helping with the different community projects. Their friendship had grown. It had been easy.

"This is what I heard," Thelma told her.

"Where's he going?" she asked. So many questions tumbled in front of her that she didn't know which one to ask first.

"California."

Alice sighed. How had she not picked up on that? He'd given her the impression that Hideaway Bay was home for him, that he'd never leave. Why hadn't he said anything to her? She'd thought they were friends. Why did it seem that everyone in Hideaway Bay knew the Colonel was leaving but she did not?

"Why is he leaving?"

Thelma shrugged. "An opportunity he couldn't pass up. Golden opportunities don't come around that often and maybe he believes, as I do, that you need to grab life with both hands." She leaned against her white picket fence, studying Alice's face.

"Will there be a going-away party?"

Thelma shook her head. "No, he wouldn't think that was necessary."

All of this news left Alice unsettled and unsure.

As she walked on, Alice examined her feelings. She'd grown to love everything about her life in Hideaway Bay. Everything from working at Ben Enright's law office to living with Lily and Charlie to donating her baked goods to the various community groups. And a piece of that puzzle was Jack Stirling. He'd slotted so easily into her life. Why hadn't he told her? Was he still mad because she hadn't gone to dinner with him?

Alice arrived at the Colonel's house over on Sandstone Lane. Neat pots of tulips and hyacinths were set on the steps of the wide-planked porch. She rang the bell and peered through the screen door. The interior door stood open, and a suitcase sat waiting in the entryway.

Before she could snoop further to see how he lived, Jack appeared in the doorway.

"Alice, this is a surprise." He stepped out to join her on the porch.

It occurred to her that she didn't know what to say. No thought had been given to how she should present herself. He was going to think there was something wrong with her and possibly be very glad she hadn't accepted his dinner invitation. Just when she'd realized she would like very much to go out to dinner with him.

"Thelma said you were leaving." Alice started with that.

He nodded. "I am, I have an early flight in the morning. Can I help you?"

Sighing, Alice brushed her hand across her forehead, pushing her hair back. “I don’t want you to leave.”

He didn’t say anything at first. He turned his head slightly and frowned as if trying to process this information. Finally, he repeated, “You don’t want me to leave.”

“No, I’ve been thinking about this for a while. You asked me out to dinner, and I said no because I was afraid that maybe there was too much of an age difference between us—I don’t think that now, by the way—and now you’re leaving and you’d said Hideaway Bay was home for you, and I hope you aren’t leaving because I wouldn’t go out with you. I’ve given it a lot of thought since that morning I met you in the olive oil shop. I’ve gotten to know you better, and I would like to go out to dinner with you. A lot of dinners. And, well, Thelma said opportunities don’t come around that often. She said you need to grab life with both hands.”

The Colonel threw his head back and burst out laughing. “You’ve given me a lot to unpack here, Alice.”

She frowned, twisting her hands together. “I suppose I have.”

He put his hands in his pockets. He smiled, and Alice thought that was a good sign, but on the other hand she wondered if she should step off his porch and head home. Maybe run home. Fast.

"First," he said, "Thelma says a lot of things."

Alice sighed and agreed. "That's Thelma. She calls it like she sees it."

"Second, I'm going out to California—"

"That's what she said," she interrupted. "Why so far away?"

"Because I'm going for my nephew's wedding. I'll be back next week."

"You're coming back?" Alice said, mortified. Her cheeks went hot, and there was a queasy feeling in her stomach. How had she gotten that wrong? An image of Thelma popped into her mind, and she grimaced. Had the older woman set her up? Thelma was probably at her house right now, laughing her bum off.

She began to shake. Her hands flew up to her mouth, and she took a step back. "I'm sorry," she said. She tried to ignore the hot sting of tears of humiliation.

"Alice." He said her name so softly it was like a knife cutting through warm butter.

She leaned forward, her hair hanging in her face. "I am so sorry."

"Why are you sorry?" he asked. He stepped closer, and Alice's eyes focused on his shoes. They were nice shoes, she decided. An image of them parked next to hers in the hallway filled her head.

His finger pushed back the curtain of her hair and lifted her chin until she had no choice but to look at him. There was warmth and kindness in his eyes.

"Why are you embarrassed?" he asked.

"Because I've made a fool of myself," she said.

Jack shook his head. "On the contrary. This has turned into one of the nicest moments of my life."

"It has?"

"It's not often a beautiful, intelligent, kind-hearted woman lands on your porch and tells you she wants to go to a lot of dinners with you," he said. There was mirth in his smile, and some of the tension in Alice's body seeped out of her. Her posture relaxed.

"So there's no statute of limitations on that dinner invitation?" she asked.

"No, not at all. It's good forever."

"I like the sound of that."

"Me too. When I get home, we'll go somewhere nice."

"I'd like that very much," she said truthfully.

Quickly and unabashedly, she stepped forward, stood on tiptoe, and planted a kiss on his cheek. Before he could respond, she turned, her dress swirling around her, and trotted off the porch. When she reached the sidewalk, she stopped, turned, and waved goodbye to him.

Chapter Thirty-Eight

1992

Thelma

The rain slammed against the roof. Thunder rumbled, and within seconds there was a bright flash of lightning. Thelma didn't notice any of these things. She sat on the edge of the hospital bed in the middle of her living room, holding Stanley's hand. It was still warm. She glanced at the clock. It was a little after three in the morning. She was glad she was alone. She could cry unashamedly.

Stanley looked peaceful. It was the most relaxed he'd looked in a long time. No longer in pain. No longer suffering. She was grateful for that. She looked down at his hand in hers, determined to memorize every detail of it. She knew she should call the doctor. She should probably call Junie and Barb as well. But for now, she wanted to be alone with him.

There was only one small light on. The coffee table was littered with all sorts of medications and the supplies needed to take care of a dying man.

The tears poured out of her. Thelma was no crier, but she couldn't stop. In the course of her whole life, no one had ever loved her the way Stanley Schumacher had: completely, intensely, and without condition.

Eventually, reluctantly, she laid his hand down on the bed and straightened the bedsheet out around him. She took the brush from the end table and brushed his hair. Thunder still rolled through the area. She smiled, thinking *What a night to go, Stanley*. Tears filled her eyes again, and she knelt on the bed, leaned over, kissed his forehead, and whispered, "Goodbye, my love."

With a great weariness, she made her way up the staircase and knocked on the door of Donny's bedroom. After a second, she popped her head in and whispered Donny's name. Her son leaned up on his elbows. He had flown in a couple of days ago as Stanley had begun to sink into unconsciousness.

"Everything all right, Mom?"

"It's time to come downstairs."

"Okay," he said, flinging the sheet back and swinging his legs out of the bed.

She walked along to the bedroom she had once shared with Stanley and sat on the edge of the bed. She picked up the handset of the rotary phone and dialed Junie's number.

It was answered on the second ring.

"Hello?" It was Junie, and she sounded groggy.

"Junie? Stan is gone." Thelma's voice broke on the last word, and a sob escaped her. To say it out loud made it real, made it feel like a punch to the gut.

"We'll be right over."

When she made her way back downstairs, Donny was sitting on the edge of the bed, holding Stan's hand. There were tears in his eyes.

"He was such a good father to me," he said quietly.

She nodded. He was. Stanley had had enough love for all of them. Anger appeared as she thought of moving forward in life without him. How was that possible? What would the world look like without Stanley? What would her life look like without Stanley? She shuddered.

"Who am I going to turn to for advice?" Donny asked.

Although Donny lived out of state with his wife, Annette, and their children, he called every Sunday evening, spending more time on the phone with Stanley than Thelma as Stanley gave him advice about anything from investing his money to what kind of motor oil to use in his car. Donny was right. Stanley had been a good father.

Donny stood up and hugged his mother. “What are we going to do without him?”

Thelma shook her head, the tears falling again. “I don’t know. I just don’t know.”

There was a knock on the aluminum screen door, and it creaked open as Junie and Paul entered.

“Oh, Thelma, I’m so sorry,” Junie said, rushing to her and pulling her into her embrace.

Her best friend was warm, just out of her bed, and she smelled like soap. Thelma buried her head against Junie’s shoulder and cried. Quickly, she pulled away and wiped her eyes, embarrassed.

Paul hugged her and patted her back.

She led Junie and Paul to the hospital bed where Stanley rested. They said a quick prayer at Stanley’s bedside.

Thelma sank down into the easy chair, having no energy to stand. “You know, Stanley Schumacher was the only man in my life who loved me for me,” Thelma said with a shaky laugh.

Junie reached out and took Thelma’s hand. Her eyes glistened with tears. “There was never anyone else for him but you.”

Thelma laughed. “Right back to the third grade.”

Donny reached over and rubbed his mom’s shoulder. “He was a great man.”

"He was," Paul piped in. "He overcame a lot of obstacles to accomplish a lot."

"I don't think anyone in Hideaway Bay will ever be able to eat a Texas hot without thinking about Stanley," Junie said.

"He did a lot for the community," Paul added.

"He did a lot for everyone," Thelma said. She kept looking over at Stanley to see if it was actually true. What would become of her now?

The rain continued, as did the thunder and lightning.

"Did you call the doctor?" Junie asked.

Thelma shook her head. "No, I wanted a little bit more time with him."

Junie nodded in understanding. "I'll make some coffee. And you can call the doctor when you think you're ready."

Thelma didn't know if she'd ever be ready to make that phone call.

Chapter Thirty-Nine

Present Day

Thelma

It had been a year since Junie died, and Thelma still had a hollow ache in her heart over missing her friend. She'd catch herself once in a while thinking how she must tell Junie who she'd run into. It had been like that for a long time after Stan had died too, always wanting to share something with them and then remembering they were gone.

She found herself walking the beach one morning. Although she liked the beach, she didn't love it the way Junie had. What Thelma loved was the town of Hideaway Bay, and she preferred to walk along the streets and around the blocks that shot off of Star Shine

Drive. She liked to see people, many of whom at one point or another had come into the Old Red Top when Stanley was alive and they'd had the restaurant. She supposed she should sell the old place and let someone else take it over. Donny was right; it was prime real estate in Hideaway Bay with its beach location. Time to move on and let someone else make a go of it. But letting go, that was always the hard part.

Earlier that morning, she'd found an old Polaroid picture in her nightstand drawer. It was taken shortly after she married Stanley. Right before the flash went off, Stanley had thrown his arm around her, pulled her close, and kissed the side of her face. She had playfully tried to push him away. But she was laughing, and her face was full of joy. She remembered that moment. It was like it was yesterday and it was like it was a hundred years ago.

She would never stop missing him. Every morning when she woke up, she told herself she was one day closer to seeing him again. To being with him again. Whether there was a heaven or not, she did not know, but Stanley Schumacher had too much energy and joy for life to have let death conquer him. No, she knew he was still out there somewhere.

She put her hands in the pockets of her fleece jacket. There was a crisp breeze blowing in off the lake, and she thought back to last May when Junie had died. That

May had been exceptionally warm and sunny, and this one cold and rainy. *Can't have it all*, she thought.

Sadness cloaked her. Everyone she'd loved and known the longest was gone, leaving her as the last sentinel for their generation of friends. Junie and Paul were gone, and Barb had been gone for a long time. It tired her sometimes to think that she was the only repository left of all their shared memories. At times, that was a burden. There was no one to reminisce with anymore. Donny and his girls, Maria and Jules, had heard the stories a hundred times, but they hadn't been there, not in the way that Stanley, Junie, or Barb had been.

Now that Donny was retired and gone to Arizona, she missed him terribly. For a long time before Stanley came along, it had been just the two of them and then in the immediate aftermath of Stanley's death, it had been just the two of them again until he was joined by Annette, Maria and Jules. But as much as she longed for Donny to stay in Hideaway Bay after his own retirement, her desire for him to be happy trumped that. She'd given him her blessing in his move to Arizona. She understood probably better than anyone.

She'd followed her own heart out to Hideaway Bay and had ended up with a life she loved in a town she loved. And it was all down to Barb and then Junie. If it weren't for Barb's family having that cottage, she and Junie might never have ended up out here.

The air was too crisp, and she wanted to get home and warm up. She thought she might make some coffee in the stovetop percolator and let the smell of it remind her of Stanley.

As she stepped onto the boardwalk and headed in the direction of home, she couldn't help but smile. How lucky she had been.

What a life!

Chapter Forty

Alice

May

There was a boom of thunder, quickly followed by a flash of lightning. The house on Star Shine drive shook and Alice jumped, hitting her toe on the table leg. Grimacing, she reached down and massaged it.

"What did you do, stub your toe?" Lily asked from where she stood at the dishwasher.

There was another boom and flash, and the lights flickered.

Lily loaded the rest of the dishes and looked up as the lights flickered again. "I think I'll wait to turn the dishwasher on."

"Good idea," Alice said. She sat in her chair at the table.

They had a lovely agreement between them: they took turns in the kitchen. If one cooked, the other did the cleanup. It was a nice, simple arrangement. That night, Alice had made chili using a recipe of Gram's she'd found tucked between the pages of one of her recipe books. It had tasted like she remembered it.

"I think I'm going to sit out on the porch and watch the storm," Lily said.

"Is it safe?" Alice asked as thunder rumbled in the distance.

Lily cocked her ear. "It sounds like it's moving away. Come on, grab your tea and we'll go sit outside."

They parked themselves on the porch. The air was electric, and the sky was black. Across the street, the lake was dark and turbulent, crashing with a mighty roar onto the beach. The beach was empty.

"I can't believe what a difference in the weather last May to this May," Lily noted, sipping her tea.

Charlie didn't like storms and so remained inside, wrapped in his thunder blanket.

Gram's one-year anniversary was coming up in a few days. Alice couldn't believe it had already been a year.

"Are you happy with your decision?" Lily asked, curling her legs up under her on the two-seater.

"About staying with Ben and not joining Stodges and Hindermarsh?" Alice asked. With a nod, she said, "I am. This is where I belong. I like our clientele, they're everyday folks."

"You sound satisfied with your decision."

"I am."

"And you already have an assistant!"

"It's like it's meant to be." Alice smiled. It turned out that Lola Duquesne had gone to secretarial school before her marriage and although she hadn't worked outside the home in over twenty-five years, she was a fast learner. And she was organized. She'd casually mentioned during one of their meetings that she was in search of a job.

Alice and Lily were holding their breath about the decision the three of them had to make regarding Gram's house. Both of them agreed that they didn't want to sell it. If Isabelle still wanted to sell—and they couldn't see her changing her mind as she'd been gone for the whole year—then Alice was going to propose buying her out of her share of the house.

How she wished Isabelle had been able to come home for Gram's anniversary. They'd spoken to her the previous week, and she'd said she wasn't coming. That had been a huge disappointment. It had been wonderful reconnecting with Lily, and she was pretty sure Lily felt the same way.

Alice pulled her fleece closer around her, envying Lily the scarf she wore around her neck. "If your neck is warm, you're warm," Lily had once said. Alice didn't know if this was true or not, but Lily appeared cozy unlike Alice, who was beginning to shiver.

They were talking about nothing in particular, and although the lightning and thunder had moved off in the distance, suggesting that the storm had indeed passed, the rain continued to splash down, accumulating in the gutters and causing them to overflow.

"I suppose we should hire someone to get those gutters cleaned," Lily said, peering up under the roofline.

Alice followed her gaze and saw a surge of water pouring out from one side of the gutter. "Ugh, I guess so."

She was about to add something when an unfamiliar car pulled up and parked in front of the house. Alice and Lily both frowned, looking at the car.

"Who's—" Lily started as a figure emerged from the vehicle.

Alice bounced up from her chair and smiled. "Oh my God, it's Isabelle!"

She and Lily ignored the onslaught of rain and dashed off the porch to greet their older sister, who ran toward them, a magazine held above her head. Isabelle laughed, rainwater sluicing off the magazine. Lily and Alice were drenched, their hair hanging in hanks around their faces.

The three of them embraced on the sidewalk until finally, Isabelle pulled them along with her to the porch. "Come on, let's get out of the rain."

Lily spoke first. "Isabelle, what are you doing here?"

"Did you know she was coming?" Alice asked.

Lily shook her head.

"I thought I'd surprise you," Isabelle said, smiling. "I wanted to come home for Gram's anniversary."

Isabelle looked well, her body long and lean and her dark, heavy hair pulled up into a messy bun. A pair of large gold hoop earrings hung from her ears. World traveling had always agreed with Isabelle.

"Come in and we'll make you some coffee," Alice said, remembering her sister preferred it over tea.

"That would be marvelous," Isabelle said with an exaggerated sigh.

The three of them went into the house, shaking off the rain. Charlie, excited at seeing Isabelle, forgot all about his fright over the thunderstorm and came running toward her, jumping on her and sending her reeling back.

She laughed. "Brace yourself. Hello, Clumsy! How are you?"

The dog whined, his tail wagging so quickly it was a blur. When he slobbered all over her face, Isabelle laughed again and said, "I missed you too, bud."

"Get down, Charlie," Lily scolded. "We should get out of these wet clothes." Her T-shirt and sweater were soaked, clinging to her.

"My suitcase is in the car, I'll get it later," Isabelle said, waving her hand with a flourish.

"Give me your keys, I'll get it," Alice said, holding out her hand.

Isabelle hesitated, then relented and put the car keys in Alice's hand. This time, Alice took her raincoat off the stand by the door and headed out to Isabelle's car more prepared. She clicked the key fob, the trunk popped open, and she tugged out the one piece of Isabelle's luggage and carried it into the house.

Lily had disappeared upstairs, and Alice said she'd carry up Isabelle's suitcase. She was so happy the three of them were all together again. Isabelle followed her upstairs, removing her coat.

"It's good to be back," Isabelle said.

Alice left her to get changed, saying, "We'll meet you back downstairs in five."

Isabelle nodded.

Alice flew down the stairs, pulled the coffeepot off the coffee maker, and went about making a fresh pot.

Lily joined her and said with a laugh, "I guess it's a good thing you've been doing a lot of baking."

"Baking is always good," Alice said with a laugh.

As Alice made the coffee, Lily took down a platter and placed a variety of baked goods on it, setting it in the middle of the table. She set three floral dessert plates next to it, along with several napkins and teacups.

Isabelle joined them. "I'm glad to see you're still baking, Alice, then I know all is right with the world."

Alice nodded, putting the sugar bowl and creamer on the table.

Once the coffee was ready and the kettle had whistled for tea, they each prepared their beverages and took a plate, loading it with baked goods.

"Will we stay inside or eat out on the porch?" Lily asked.

"We can go out, we're all dressed warmly," Isabelle said with a shrug. "I don't mind."

Isabelle led the way, carrying her cup of coffee in one hand and a plate of desserts in the other. She looked over her shoulder and said, "Come on, Clumsy, tell me everything you know."

The dog, realizing he was being called, happily raced past Lily and Alice, knocking into Alice and causing her tea to spill over the side of her cup. She ignored it, thinking she'd wipe it up later.

After they got situated in their chairs on the porch, Alice took a quick sip of her tea, relishing the warmth as the rain had turned the air cooler.

"We weren't expecting you, Isabelle," Lily said.

"How long are you staying?" Alice asked. They hadn't seen their older sister since last year when she left shortly after Gram's funeral. But unlike other times in the past, this time the three of them kept in touch regularly. Alice appreciated this new shift in her relationship with her sisters.

Isabelle leaned back in her seat, holding her coffee cup in one hand and balancing her dessert plate on the arm of the chair with the other.

"I don't know," Isabelle said with a shrug. "You know me, I never make long-term plans."

She laughed, broke off a piece of banana bread from her slice and popped it into her mouth. "So, tell me all the news in Hideaway Bay."

Alice laughed. She sipped her hot tea, and her smile was wide and bright. A quick glance over at Lily and she could tell she felt the same way. For now, the three of them were together again. She was happy.

Hideaway Bay, when you sign up for my newsletter at www.michelebrouder.com

If you enjoyed this book, can you do me a favor and leave a review? Many thanks.

Also By Michele Brouder

Hideaway Bay Series

Coming Home to Hideaway Bay

Meet Me at Sunrise

Moonlight and Promises

When We Were Young

Escape to Ireland Series

A Match Made in Ireland

Her Fake Irish
Husband

Her Irish
Inheritance

A Match for the
Matchmaker

Home, Sweet Irish
Home

An Irish Christmas

The Escape to Ireland series is also available in Large Print

The Happy Holidays Series

A Whyte Christmas

This Christmas

A Wish for Christmas

One Kiss for Christmas

A Wedding for Christmas

Printed in Great Britain
by Amazon

38262852R10227